KILLER
IN THE WOODS

A ROBERT VANCE NOVEL

RICK VAN ETTEN

PROUD POINT
-PRESS-

DES MOINES, IOWA

Published by
Proud Point Press
Des Moines, IA

Cover Design by Eric Labacz
www.labaczdesign.com

For JJB, RWC, SDC, RAC, LGG & SAG, JDL, KRM, DAM, LJM, KDN & RAN, FSP, JES, NRS, RRS, TRS, MJT and TJW.
You all knew I'd have to come clean eventually.

VANCE'S RULES FOR CONTRACT KILLINGS

1. No personal involvement...i.e., there must be no personal feelings whatsoever attached, as this would cloud judgment.

2. No collateral damage. Absolutely unacceptable; must remain true to purpose—righting a wrong, stopping a bully, etc. Eliminating bystanders/witnesses not permitted. Ditto letting an innocent person take the fall.

3. Never keep a handgun after it's been used.

4. No politicians (regardless of how much they might deserve it); too well protected; too much public scrutiny and investigation.

5. No organized crime members. Flat-out too dangerous, and too much risk of touching off a gangland war that might result in innocents being killed.

PROLOGUE

The whitetail buck was a magnificent animal, a five-year-old in full prime with a symmetrical 12-point rack, the main beams nearly as thick as a man's wrist. He weighed 270 pounds and his splayed hoofprints measured five inches in length. He was tawny gray with a snowy flag and throat patch, antlers polished to gleaming ivory, and a glistening black muzzle sensitive enough to pick up the scent of man from more than a mile distant if the wind was in the right direction.

He moved cautiously along a trail on a hardwood ridge in west-central Illinois, that part of the state known as "the land between the rivers," those being the Illinois and the Mississippi. Good genetics, mineral-rich soil and an abundant food source from the surrounding croplands had all contributed to the buck's superior size and rack, as had a higher-than-average intelligence that had kept him alive throughout the hunting seasons of the previous four years. The buck had already bred six does within his range and had driven off several smaller rivals this autumn, ensuring not only the perpetuation of his genes but also the continued vigor of the entire species.

It was just before dawn on the second day of the state's annual first firearm deer season (the second would be held three weeks later) and the buck had survived the previous day's frenzy with relative ease. Orange-clad hunters had arrived before daylight, parking along the blacktop highways and gravel country roads, slamming the doors of their pickups and SUVs and noisily (to the buck's ultra-acute sense of hearing) hurrying through the woods to their stands, elevated platforms erected some 10 to 20 feet up against trees near the edges of fields, along trails or overlooking the creek bottom.

It had been a simple matter for the buck to retreat ahead of the hunters as he heard them entering the woods. Keeping downwind of them as much as possible and relying on his hearing and sense of smell to warn him of any danger that might lie ahead, he had quietly slipped into a dense thicket of multiflora on the creek bottom and had lain there motionless throughout the daylight hours. This strategy had served him well in the past and it did so again.

He heard numerous gunshots over the course of the day, especially during the first two hours as younger deer were killed on their way from nighttime feeding areas to daytime bedding locations in the woods. By noon the gunfire had tapered off to the occasional lone report, and the buck shifted slightly in his bed. But he was too wise to risk venturing forth until after dark; he knew from experience that with the coming of sundown the woods would empty of hunters and only then would it be safe to move.

Now, on the second morning of the season, the buck was hurrying to return to his lair in the multiflora thicket. He had fed during the night in a cornfield at the top of the ridge and he paused briefly at the creek, drinking deeply, before continuing along the trail that ran parallel to the creek. Another minute of quiet walking would see him safely hidden within the multiflora.

He didn't know he was being watched.

A full two hours earlier a man had entered the woods and quietly climbed into a tree stand he had erected several weeks before. The stand was just 40 yards from the trail on which the buck was now walking, and the man had selected its location based on the abundance of tracks he'd seen along the trail during his pre-season scouting.

The man, whose name was Frank Reynolds, was dressed in the requisite orange cap and vest and he carried a 12-gauge Remington 870 pump shotgun fitted with a rifled slug barrel. It was the same gun he had used for more than 20 years—Illinois did not permit the use of high-powered rifles for deer—and it bore the marks of those years of service. The bluing on much of the receiver was worn to a silvery sheen and the stock carried numerous scratches. Though he easily could have afforded a newer and more expensive firearm, Frank Reynolds preferred the well-worn Remington. He called it his Buckstopper.

He had loaded the gun as soon as he had settled himself on the tree stand's seat, 12 feet above the ground, and buckled his safety harness. At that time the buck was still a half mile away feeding in a field of standing corn and hadn't heard the distinctive sound of the pump gun being racked to bring the first shell into its chamber.

Now, with legal shooting time only two minutes away and pre-dawn light just beginning to penetrate the dark woods, the man quietly sucked in a breath as he studied the buck below him. The wind was in his favor and the buck hadn't scented him. The man tried to count the buck's antler tines but there was not yet enough light for him to do so. Still, the man could tell from the size of the buck's rack showing whitely in the faint light, and his enormous body, that this was definitely a trophy animal.

He could scarcely believe his good fortune. Though he was an accomplished hunter who had taken many fine bucks on this same land over the years, he had missed hunting the previous morning as he had spent it driving downstate from his home in Evanston, one of Chicago's wealthier suburbs. A business commitment had kept him late the prior evening, and while he had hated missing the opening day of deer season, the meeting had taken precedence.

He had arrived in Macomb, county seat of McDonough County and home of Western Illinois University, shortly before noon yesterday and had eaten lunch at a restaurant near the university campus. He had graduated from WIU twenty-four years earlier so the trip was something of a homecoming for him; he hunted deer every year in neighboring Schuyler County on land owned by a farmer whose acquaintance he had first made when he was still an undergraduate.

After lunch he had driven around the town square and then out East Jackson to the Farm King store, where he stopped and bought two boxes of Winchester Supreme Elite XP3 sabot shotgun slugs. He'd laughed to himself as he made the purchase; the slugs came five to a box and he had brought four full boxes with him from home. That made a total of thirty slugs and he knew he would be unlikely to fire more than two or three at most. He was a superb marksman and usually killed his deer with one shot, only rarely needing a follow-up.

Still, he had felt good about transacting a little business in the community. *Just boosting the local economy,* he'd told himself.

When he left Farm King he returned to his vehicle, crossed East Jackson to the Hampton Inn and checked in. He used one of the wheeled carts from the lobby to move his luggage and gear to his room on the second floor. His shotgun, broken down and cased, he left in the trunk space of his SUV, a midnight blue Cadillac Escalade equipped with an extra alarm and security system.

He had spent the rest of the afternoon reading and napping. He briefly considered donning his hunting clothes and driving out to the farm to get in at least a couple of hours of hunting before sundown but he decided against it. He was tired from his five-hour drive and he preferred to make a fresh start in the morning. He also wanted to avoid contaminating the area with his scent as much as possible and didn't want to risk spooking any deer that might be feeding near his tree stand in the late afternoon.

Deer hunting was, after all, at least partially a battle of wits, and he wanted to give himself every advantage. He was an attorney—he had taken his law degree from Northwestern—and besides golf, deer hunting every fall was his only passion.

That, and rough sex.

The latter was something he indulged with extreme care. His corporate law practice was highly successful—he would be considered wealthy by most people's standards—and he prided himself on iron self-control. He thought those politicians and other public figures who got themselves embroiled in scandals because of their sexual escapades were the ultimate fools; the notion of posting anything intimate online, for example, or exchanging emails or texts with a sexual partner was beyond ridiculous, he believed, and those who did so deserved the crashing downfall and humiliation they so often suffered.

He had always been exceptionally discreet in these matters, partly because he was by nature a highly private person who always played things close to the vest and partly because he simply had the good sense to realize any revelations concerning his sexual practices could have long-reaching and destructive repercussions. Plus, he had already had one extremely close call.

He was married to an attractive woman three years older than himself. Denise was a tall, slim blonde, a graduate of Northwestern's Medill School of Journalism who wrote freelance articles for travel magazines. They were childless—Denise was unable to conceive and neither she nor Frank were interested in adopting—and when work permitted he accompanied her on her research-gathering trips, both at home and abroad. They traveled well together.

Denise was an enthusiastic sexual partner but somewhat unimaginative and rather traditional in her lovemaking. Frank, on the other hand, considered himself more "adventurous" and open to experimentation. In the past few years he'd become increasingly more dominant in the bedroom and when he sensed Denise was growing a bit uncomfortable with his forcefulness, he had begun seeking other partners.

They had proven almost surprisingly easy to come by. At forty-six Frank still had a full head of dark hair, just beginning to gray at the temples, and he kept himself fit with golf, regular trips to an athletic club and careful attention to his diet. His law practice brought him into contact with a variety of attractive professional women, some married, some not; and many of whom were not averse to an affair with a married man.

His practice also provided him with the standard "working late" excuse that, if not overused, seemed to satisfy Denise. If she suspected anything, she never said so. At forty-nine, she was acutely aware of their age difference and the fact that she would soon turn fifty. She was not inclined to rock the boat.

The one rule Frank steadfastly adhered to was avoiding any liaisons with co-workers. That, he knew, could be a fast track to disaster, and no matter how vivacious a female colleague might be, he never succumbed to the temptation.

Until Mandi Collins began clerking at the firm.

Mandi was twenty-four years old with short-cropped auburn hair, green eyes and a light dusting of freckles across her nose and cheeks. She wore a tiny diamond stud in one nostril and had a palm tree tattoo on her nape, and a mature, witty confidence that made her fun to talk to. After she'd worked at the firm only a few weeks—and she and Frank had had a few chance encounters around the office and exchanged several bantering remarks—Frank found himself going out of his way to bump into her.

He knew even as he was doing this that he was on very dangerous ground. As a senior partner in the firm he had little reason to interact with one of the clerks but there was something about Mandi that he found irresistible. That she should captivate him to this degree he found both disturbing and wryly amusing. He also began to suspect that Mandi was playing him, projecting an unspoken challenge and almost daring him to make a move.

When he did, she first responded with a humorous remark about being pretty sure it was not a good idea to date the boss. Frank immediately felt foolish for having suggested they meet for a drink but before he could stammer an apology she had laughed and agreed to his offer. They met at a bar two blocks from the office after work that evening and that was the beginning of what, for Frank, was some of the most exciting sex he'd ever had in his life.

Mandi proved to be every bit as creative and confident in bed as she was in the office, and her energy level was so high she frequently left Frank gasping for breath. They met for their first few rendezvous at one of the downtown hotels but soon began going to her apartment instead, believing it afforded them more privacy and less chance of running into any coworkers or other acquaintances.

Frank was relieved to discover that Mandi fully appreciated the need for discretion—again, a mark of maturity beyond her years—and he had no trouble convincing her of the need to practice absolute restraint in the office, even going out of their way to keep any contact to a minimum.

Then after several months the accident happened.

It *was* an accident, Frank had managed to convince himself. They'd been experimenting with erotic asphyxiation—Mandi had been a willing participant, although initially she'd needed quite a bit of persuading—and had been using the belt from a white terrycloth bathrobe they'd liberated during one of their hotel trysts. It wasn't the first time they'd tried asphyxiophilia but this time Frank had tightened the belt a little too much and kept it tight a little too long.

It was a misjudgment and an accident, nothing more, Frank told himself.

That had been eighteen months ago. The matter had been resolved fairly quickly, thank God, with Mandi's death ruled a suicide by the ME. And while Frank knew there had been a few suspicious looks cast his way in the office for several weeks after her death—apparently their attempts to keep things under wraps hadn't been quite as successful as he'd thought—he'd kept his chin up and concentrated on conducting business as usual. Eventually the unease had dissipated among his co-workers—not that any of them had any real evidence of wrongdoing anyway—and things had returned to normal.

Denise had never questioned the official version of the story.

Now a year and a half had passed since Mandi's death and he was more than 200 miles away, deep in the woods with a trophy buck standing nearly broadside in the trail beneath his tree stand. *I've earned this,* he told himself, the same mantra he always invoked when he was about to take a deer. Let his more politically correct colleagues in the Windy City scoff at his annual hunting excursions; this was something he knew he *had* to do.

He eased off the shotgun's well-lubricated safety and quietly lifted the gun to his shoulder. He was above the buck's line of sight and the deer didn't detect the motion. He settled the shotgun's sights on a spot just behind the buck's right shoulder and midway between the buck's spine and the line of its belly. It was growing lighter and Frank was sure it was now legal shooting time. He tightened his finger on the trigger and again congratulated himself on his good fortune.

With his cheek pressed firmly against the worn stock of the Remington, he concentrated on the spot just behind the buck's right shoulder. He exhaled slightly and continued squeezing the trigger.

At the report the buck instinctively flinched then sprang straight away toward the creek, covering nearly 20 feet in his first bound. His next leap took him across the creek and he crashed through the multiflora thicket toward which he had been heading but he did not slow despite the thick, tangled branches and wicked thorns. Clearing the thicket, he raced up the opposite timbered ridge, snorting loudly and carrying his flag high and flared, an unmistakable danger signal to any other deer in the area. He had not been hit.

Frank Reynolds had not been so lucky.

A 12-gauge sabot slug—coincidentally, the same Winchester XP3 brand as those he had loaded into his Remington 870 some two hours earlier—traveling at 1,700 feet per second and carrying nearly 3,000 foot-pounds of energy, entered his body just below his left armpit and blasted all the way through his chest, exiting just above his right nipple after destroying his heart.

Reynolds slumped in his tree stand, his safety harness preventing him from toppling out and falling to the ground. He dropped his gun but it fell across his lap and lay there unfired, balanced somewhat precariously.

Another man emerged from the still-dark woods and walked carefully up to the tree. He gazed upward at the still form of Reynolds for a moment, noting the shotgun hanging rather crazily across Reynolds' lap. Then he broke the breech of his Ruger Red Label over/under and caught the bottom fired shell as it ejected. He dropped the shell into a pocket, closed the breech and leaned the gun against a nearby tree.

He returned to Reynolds' tree and very carefully climbed the ladder to the tree stand. Reynolds' eyes were open and his mouth hung slack; death had been instantaneous. The other man noted that the Remington's safety was off and with a gloved fingertip he returned it to the safe position. He climbed down the ladder and retrieved his gun, then turned and walked off through the woods toward his own vehicle parked on a deserted farm lane a mile away.

Like Frank Reynolds, he wore an orange cap and an orange vest over his hunting coat and Carhartt brush pants. Anyone encountering him in the woods would immediately assume he was one of the thousands of deer hunters afield in Illinois that weekend. It was a variation of the old "hide in plain sight" strategy and the man was counting on it getting him safely out of the vicinity.

He was in luck. He encountered no other hunters on his way to the vehicle, and once there he quickly unloaded and cased his shotgun and stripped off his hunting clothing. He stowed the clothing and gun in the trunk of his SUV, a pewter gray Chevrolet Equinox. He quickly dressed in blue jeans, navy sweatshirt, leather jacket and a khaki bill cap, and slid beneath the wheel.

Full dawn was just breaking as the man drove down the farm lane, pulled out onto the highway and made the half-hour return trip to Macomb, where he had a room at the Best Western on East Jackson, only a few hundred yards from the Hampton Inn where Frank Reynolds had spent his last night.

He returned to his room, stripped down and took a long shower. Then he dressed again in the same clothes he'd just worn, went downstairs to the lobby and took advantage of the hotel's complimentary breakfast buffet.

After eating he carried a disposable cup of coffee back to

his room and sipped at it as he packed his single bag and shaving kit. He picked up his John Sandford paperback from the nightstand and dropped it into his briefcase and snapped it closed. He did a quick survey of the room to make sure he hadn't overlooked anything—unlikely, as he was traveling light—then he dumped the rest of the coffee into the bathroom sink, rinsed it down and tossed the cup into the wastebasket.

He checked out of the hotel and loaded his luggage into the cargo space of the Equinox. He pulled out of the parking lot onto East Jackson and drove west toward the town square. He would pick up Highway 67 just off the square and take 67 north to Highway 34, where he would then head west, crossing the Mississippi River into Burlington, Iowa, and continuing on 34 for another couple hours before turning north again, eventually returning to his home in Des Moines.

En route, he would make one stop for gas at the Casey's in New London, Iowa. While his tank was filling he would drop a Hardee's bag into the trash receptacle next to the gas pump.

Inside the bag, in addition to a couple of used napkins and an empty sandwich box, was the shotgun shell he'd fired earlier that morning.

PART 1: EDITORIAL LICENSE

Be regular and orderly in your life so you may be violent and original in your work.

-Gustave Flaubert

CHAPTER 1

The money is good, but that's not why I do it.

Kill people, I mean. That's what I do, and I'm very good at it. And yes, the compensation is usually more than adequate.

But don't start jumping to conclusions. I'm not a spook. I'm not some ex-Agency, ultra-ultra-deep-cover, government-trained assassin who got my start in the military and, having discovered a unique talent, couldn't let it go. Nor was I ever encouraged by my "Uncle" to put my special skills to use for the common good, in which capacity I might still have the occasional brush-up with colleagues who might or might not be among the so-called good guys and might or might not be people I should trust.

No. I don't play at espionage. I don't call secret phone numbers and get my orders from people who use lots of acronyms and won't allow their names to be spoken aloud on an open line, and I don't have hidden files tucked away somewhere that I can use as leverage if I find myself running afoul of a power player. I never served in the military, and the extent of my contact with the government consists of filing my income taxes every year, renewing the registration on my SUV and voting in the occasional election. The few times I've been called for jury duty I've managed to get myself excused.

Sounds pretty dull, doesn't it? You're right; it is. And that's by design.

If you saw me on the street or in a restaurant or a shopping mall or an airport—and there's a reasonable chance you *have* seen me in some of those places—you'd most likely give me no more than a passing glance. There's quite a bit about me that's just plain average—size, looks, clothing. I wear glasses, and my hair is getting thin on top.

I dress comfortably and rather conservatively. I recently became eligible for Social Security—I'm old enough to have served in Vietnam, but I was in college at the time and my number in the draft lottery was high enough to keep me there.

I don't go out of my way to attract attention, but neither do I live an introverted, reclusive life. I'm not married, but I date casually, and I occasionally get invited to parties and cookouts and can hold my own in a conversation on a variety of subjects. People usually laugh at my jokes, and I keep myself reasonably well informed about most current events. I read extensively, and my house is full of books.

I also have a Browning gun vault full of shotguns, but those are primarily related to my regular job—I'm the editor of an outdoor sporting magazine, a "hook and bullet rag," as such publications are irreverently referred to within the publishing industry. I'm a bird hunter by avocation, and a six-year-old German wirehaired pointer named Preacher—for Clint Eastwood's grizzled character in the movie *Pale Rider*—shares my home.

Sometimes I use one of my shotguns for something besides upland game or waterfowl. That's a safe enough practice, as I'll explain later. When a shotgun is too large for the job at hand—when it's necessary to get up close and personal to the target, in other words—I'll occasionally use a handgun. But I never keep these after the job is finished. That's Rule Number 3.

I travel a good bit for my job—I get quite a few invitations from advertisers throughout the hunting season, and by taking advantage of these invitations I've hunted in many locations and at many top-drawer facilities around the world. Sometimes—not frequently, but once in a while—my two jobs overlap. The advertiser picks up the tab for my hunt (in exchange for some editorial ink), and by staying an extra day or two—usually on the pretext of visiting an old childhood friend or a seldom-seen relative and always at my own expense—I manage to take care of the other assignment while I'm at it. It doesn't happen that way very often, but it's convenient when it does.

OK, so if I really don't do it for the money, why *do* I do it? Simple.

There are two things I can't abide in this world—a bully, and injustice.

The two often go hand in hand, and when I encounter either, I bristle. When someone else has a problem with either, he or she will sometimes seek me out to make the situation right.

Over the years, I've become very good at this. And that's my real motivation—the feeling of satisfaction that comes from having done a job well, righted a wrong, balanced the scales or eliminated an oppressive threat.

It's my way of leaving the world a little better place than I found it.

ON A FRIDAY MORNING in late November I drove to the branch post office a few blocks from my house. I have two boxes there, one for magazine-related materials and the other for personal use. I need the magazine box because I work out of my home and I prefer not to give out my home address to anyone sending a submission to the magazine. That could lead to contributors—and readers—dropping by unannounced, and that's an invasion of privacy I can definitely do without.

The second P.O. box also helps me safeguard my privacy. It's one of several I have throughout the metro area and through which I conduct my other business—the boxes to which checks are sent for services rendered, and the ones to which occasional inquiries are sent, asking about hiring me for those services. More shortly on how this system works.

On that November morning I was expecting to find a check in the second box. The previous Saturday I'd completed an assignment in Illinois during the state's firearm deer season, and allowing for the time my client would need to confirm this and then send the check, I was reasonably confident it would be there, and it was, made payable to my innocuous-sounding LLC, a copy-editing and proofreading business.

I also checked the magazine box and found three articles from regular contributors, plus a couple of letters to the editor. No one submits actual manuscripts anymore; almost everyone emails me their stories. But the majority of them submit the photos to accompany their articles—and sometimes a copy of the article itself—on CDs, at my stipulation. They could have sent me their photos by email as well, or used an online file-sharing program, but I prefer not having to download their photos—too time-consuming, for one thing—or keep them filed on my computer.

I'll admit I'm something of a dinosaur in these matters. Publishing's digital revolution is moving at breakneck speed and lately I've been thinking it's time to step down and let someone else take over as editor of my magazine, *American Wingshot*.

Magazines printed on paper are now called "dead tree pubs" by those wags in the industry who maintain consumers will soon be reading everything on their iBooks and their Kindles; and in fact, Trimedia, the corporation that owns *American Wingshot* and a dozen other shooting and outdoor titles, recently began offering all of our magazines in digital formats in addition to the traditional paper versions.

I don't believe the transition to an all-digital universe is going to happen quite as quickly as some are predicting but I can't deny the changes are occurring at an almost blinding pace. I've lost track of the number of design and editing programs I've had to learn over the years just to keep current in my job…when I first got into magazine work the writers were still submitting typewritten manuscripts that we sent out to have typeset, and the pages of the magazine were stripped together by hand. Now, of course, everything is done electronically.

Still, retirement is something that doesn't come easily to a lot of folks, and I suppose I'm among them. But while I'm hesitant to take that step, neither do I want to make the mistake made by too many professional athletes, namely, staying one season too long.

The latter is a concern for me in my other line of work, as well. As I already mentioned, I'm not a youngster; and while I've kept myself in reasonably good shape—living with a large, high-energy sporting dog pretty much dictates that a sedentary lifestyle is not an option—there's no denying that I'm neither as strong nor as quick as I once was. Needless to say, that could have fatal consequences for someone besides my intended target...namely, yours truly.

But enough navel-gazing. After leaving the post office that Friday morning I drove to my bank to deposit the check into my LLC account and while sitting in the drive-up lane waiting for my receipt, I thought about what I'd done to earn it.

CHAPTER 2

The job had been fairly easy, all things considered. My client was the brother of a girl named Mandi Collins who had worked as a clerk at a prominent Chicago law firm. She was twenty-four years old and, according to her brother James, she had died during an episode of kinky sex with one of the firm's senior partners, Frank Reynolds, some eighteen months earlier.

She had been found dead in her apartment, an apparent victim of autoerotic asphyxiation. Her death had been ruled a suicide but her brother was convinced that the attorney had actually strangled her and then hung her in the closet (her brother's rather ironic phrasing, not mine) to cover his own ass.

James, by the way, was the one who had found her. He was four years older, and in the tradition of big brothers everywhere he had always kept a protective eye on his kid sister. They were close and had keys to each other's apartments and when she hadn't answered her phone or text messages for several days and missed a standing Friday lunch date with him, he'd gone to her place and let himself in.

Their parents were too distraught over Mandi's death to delve into the matter but her brother had pursued it with pit bull determination. He already knew, because his sister had confided in him, that she was having an affair with the attorney. James had taken this information to the Chicago police but they quickly dismissed it. The girl's death had all the signs of being a straight-forward, accidental suicide and there was no indication of foul play, or even anything to indicate anyone else had been in the apartment when she had died.

Frustrated but determined to see justice done, James Collins had eventually located me.

That's not especially easy to do, but the fact that it is difficult is one of the ways by which I can evaluate the—ahem—sincerity of a prospective client. If said client manages to make it to the first contact stage—and again, I don't make this easy—that tells me that he or she is truly, perhaps even desperately, interested in retaining my services.

The whole exercise involves a circuitous route that begins with responding to a fairly innocent-sounding online ad that hints at what I do. The client is then taken through several "blinds" that lead to some rather convoluted email exchanges. Only after successfully passing through this series of baffles will the client be given one of my P.O. box numbers (not the one reserved for magazine correspondence) with the simple instructions to send me, via snail mail, a phone number.

Why snail mail to a P.O. box? Because, like 'em or not, the U.S. Postal Service is still a lot safer in many ways than any kind of online correspondence. Even before all the revelations about NSA's data gathering on American citizens, it was fairly well known that anything you put online—*anything*—is fair game for anyone. In simplest terms, once you post it or email it, it's out there in cyberspace forever, which means there's a strong likelihood that someone can find it again if they try hard enough.

Also, even if deleting messages completely protected the sender and the recipient, a lot of people are just plain sloppy housekeepers when it comes to keeping their inboxes and "sent messages" file clean. Some folks go for weeks or months without deleting anything, which means—again—the messages are just sitting there waiting to be found.

So when the client and I reach the stage that I'm ready to make actual contact, I provide a P.O. box number and ask for a phone number. I call them on a disposable cell phone—yes, a "burner"; I buy them at various retail stores around the city and throughout the state—and if they ask my name I tell them to call me something like John, or Bill, or Steve. That's for their convenience only, and of course it leads nowhere.

That's how it had worked with James Collins, and I told him to call me Tom.

As clients go, he was almost too good to be true. First of all, he'd done his homework. When I called him and he described the circumstances of his sister's death, it was obvious he'd spent lots of time dotting all the i's and crossing all the t's. He had detailed answers for all the questions I asked, and by the time we finished our first conversation I too was pretty well convinced that Mandi had been killed by her boss.

Whether her death was intentional or accidental I wasn't so sure. But what was certain was the fact that after a cursory investigation Frank Reynolds had walked away from the whole situation free and clear. Correction: he really hadn't had to walk anywhere because he'd never been considered a suspect in the first place. With Mandi's death ruled a suicide and the cops unwilling to probe more deeply into the matter, Frank Reynolds was going to get away with either murder or manslaughter, take your pick.

James Collins wasn't willing to let it go at that.

"I know in my gut he killed her," he said during our first phone conversation. "I know what that probably sounds like but I'm not just some bereaved family member wallowing in denial. There are too many things that point to Frank Reynolds' involvement."

"Such as?"

"OK, this is probably gonna sound a little weird coming from her own brother, but Mandi wouldn't have…*needed* to be doing what she was supposedly doing when she died. She was a good-looking girl—OK, hot—and she never had any trouble finding…partners. In fact, I gave her a hard time about that on a pretty regular basis, always ragging at her to be careful. When she told me she was having an affair with her boss I nearly took her head off."

"Being involved with someone and having a healthy sex life doesn't mean she didn't occasionally…uh, fly solo."

"I realize that but I still don't think she would have taken a chance with the asphyxiation stuff. I mean, she obviously enjoyed sex but she wasn't the kind to keep pushing the envelope looking for bigger and bigger thrills. Especially if it involved something that was potentially life-threatening."

"You're sure that's not just a big brother's biased perception of his little sister?"

"Look, I adored Mandi. I always looked out for her when we were kids, and she and I shared a lot of secrets over the years. We had each other's backs. She probably knew me better than anyone else ever has, including my own girlfriends, and I'd like to think I knew as much about her. I'm telling you; she just wasn't wired that way. That son of a bitch Reynolds killed her."

"The medical examiner and the police said otherwise."

"That's because it was an easy solution. Do you know how many murders there are in Chicago every year?"

"No, I don't. Maybe one a day?" I'm not a crime statistician and that seemed like a reasonable guess.

"Think higher," James Collins replied. "It's over 600 a year. With those kinds of numbers, the cops are run pretty ragged. They're not gonna spend a bunch of time looking into something that appears open and shut."

"All right, but you still haven't told me specifically why you think Reynolds killed her, or even if you have any proof that he was there when she died."

"I'll admit I don't have any proof he was there that night. If I did, I'd have given it to the cops. The only thing that comes close is the fact that her door was locked but the deadbolt wasn't. I have a key to both and when I let myself in I didn't have to unlock the deadbolt."

"So you're saying that when Reynolds left he locked the door but didn't lock the deadbolt because he probably didn't have a key for it."

"Right. And I know for a fact that Mandi was always very careful about locking both, whether she was home or not. You know, single girl in the big city and all that. It was another one of those things I always nagged her about. If she was home alone—and especially if she had been, as you put it, flying solo— I *know* she'd have locked the deadbolt."

I had to admit I couldn't fault his reasoning. "The cops weren't interested in your deadbolt theory?"

"Not really. They were pretty quick to dismiss it as an oversight on Mandi's part. 'Oh, come on, everybody gets forgetful once in a while,' they said."

"What about any kind of forensics?"

"Again, I got the impression they weren't real interested in going that route, spending a lot of time and effort looking for something they'd already made up their minds they weren't going to find. The autopsy didn't turn up anything to show she'd had a partner that evening...actually the word they used was 'inconclusive.' They said there was other DNA present—including my own, which isn't surprising since I'm the one who found her—but aside from ours, they couldn't match what they found to anyone in their system.

"When I asked about fingerprints on the belt, they said they probably wouldn't find anything because the rough texture of thick terrycloth doesn't hold prints worth a damn. I'm guessing a couple of quick wipes with another piece of terrycloth like, say, a washcloth and there wouldn't be anything left that was identifiable. Kinda like brushing the marks off a piece of suede."

"So you think Reynolds wiped down the belt afterwards?"

"That's my guess."

Again, I couldn't fault his reasoning; contrary to what most folks believe because of what they've seen on television, criminals don't go around constantly shedding DNA that makes identification a snap. Also, DNA samples are easily (and frequently) compromised or contaminated, rendering them useless as evidence. Plus, as Collins had already mentioned, the "other" DNA that was found didn't match anyone in the system.

"So it sounds like you were pretty well stonewalled by the cops," I said. "Anything else that points to Reynolds besides the deadbolt?"

"Well, I know for certain that he was really into the whole choking-during-sex thing."

"How do you know that?"

"Because I found someone else he'd tried it with."

CHAPTER 3

That got my attention.

James Collins had definitely done his homework, all right. That is, if what he claimed was true.

"How'd you do that?" I asked.

"I run my own computer consulting business," he said. "In other words, I'm self-employed. I have two partners, both guys I went to school with, and we have three other employees. They were all very supportive after Mandi's death because they knew how close she and I were. So they were willing to cover for me when I said I needed to take some time off."

"And you used that time to do what, exactly?"

"I started stalking Frank Reynolds," he said.

"Stalking him?" That sounded a little far-fetched, even for a protective older brother.

"Right. Of course, I already knew where his office was because Mandi worked there. But the only time I ever met Reynolds face to face was at the visitation before Mandi's funeral. He attended and he shook hands with me and my parents and offered his condolences.

"It was all I could do to keep from throttling him on the spot, the hypocritical bastard, because I was already sure he'd killed her, but I managed to stay cool. If nothing else I didn't want to embarrass my folks—I never told them that Mandi had been having an affair with him—and I didn't want to cause them any more grief than they were already feeling."

"Admirable restraint," I said. "That couldn't have been easy."

"Believe me, it wasn't. But something told me I'd be smart not to confront him. And as it turned out, that *was* the smart move. Apparently I didn't make that much of an impression on him, not enough that he'd recognize me again, anyway."

"You saw him again?"

"Only from a distance. I started hanging around his office at random times, especially late afternoons and early evenings. A few times I caught him leaving for the day and I followed him to a couple of the downtown bars that were within walking distance of his office. I watched him hook up a few times with the same woman."

"Interesting," I said. "But are you sure he never saw you or recognized you?"

"I blend in pretty well," James Collins replied. "I look like any one of a couple million other young professional guys you'd see in Chicago. Besides, he was a lot more interested in this other woman than he was in checking to see if anyone was following him. I think once he knew he was in the clear concerning Mandi's death, that the cops weren't looking into it too closely, he thought he was home free and there was no reason to be concerned."

"How long after her death was it that he started seeing this other woman?"

"A couple months, as far as I know. Like I said, I only did this at random; it wasn't like I staked out his office building every afternoon for weeks. I tried to keep up with my regular job as well, and it was only when I'd catch a free afternoon that I could get over there—say, maybe a couple of times a week at most. And of course, a lot of times I struck out and didn't see him at all."

"OK, so how long did all this go on?'

"Oh, I kept at it for six months or so, long enough to catch him with her a few times. They had this one bar that they seemed to especially like, a place called Nell's."

"You followed them into the bar?"

"I followed *him* into the bar. It was always a busy place, you know, the after-work crowd, and he'd meet her there.

Sometimes she'd be waiting for him; sometimes he'd get there first and have to wait for her. I always made sure I stayed out of his sight."

"So you saw them meet at this bar a few times. What then?"

"They'd have a couple drinks and then they'd leave together. I didn't want to push my luck and to tell you the truth, I wasn't sure what my next move should be. I knew he was married—Mandi had told me that, and I'd given her hell about it—but I knew that just because I'd proved he was a serial adulterer that still didn't get me any closer to proving he'd killed her."

"Right. So what happened next?"

"Then suddenly they weren't meeting any more. I followed him a few more times but he stopped going to Nell's. He'd leave work and head off in a different direction. A couple times I saw him go into a couple of other places and start hitting on other women. I figured that meant that, for whatever reason, he'd broken things off with the one I'd seen him with. Her name, by the way, was Susan Alderson."

"You found that out how?"

"I'll get to that. I realized I was spinning my wheels just following him around, and like I said, watching him hit on other women wasn't getting me any closer to proving he'd killed Mandi. So one afternoon on a hunch I went back to Nell's. Susan Alderson was there by herself, sitting at the bar, and I went up and introduced myself."

I had to hand it to James Collins; he had, as the saying goes, balls like Batman. It was a gutsy move. Or maybe a foolhardy one. But either way, it helped convince me that he was fully committed to seeing Frank Reynolds brought to justice for killing his sister.

"You introduced yourself to this woman who'd been seeing Frank Reynolds," I said. "What happened next?"

"I asked her if I could buy her a drink and she said OK. I sat down next down to her and we started making the usual small talk. I'd already pegged her at about 35, so a little older than me. I kinda sensed she was flattered to have attracted the attention of a younger guy—I'm 28—and I just kinda went with it."

"She was receptive to your advances, in other words."

"You could put it that way. By the end of that first conversation I had her name and her phone number. I told her I'd call her, and I did, a couple days later."

"Don't tell me the two of you became an item." This was starting to sound a little too soap operaish.

"Well, I wouldn't exactly call it that. But yeah, we did get together a few times. She was another attorney, by the way, like Reynolds. And yes, I'll admit we...uh...hooked up."

"You're saying you slept with her."

"Right. I wasn't involved with anyone else at the time and I wanted to see if she could give me anything on Reynolds that might be useful."

I couldn't stifle a laugh. "How in hell did you broach *that* subject?"

"Believe it or not, I didn't have to. She volunteered something. I got lucky, if you'll pardon the pun."

"How so?"

"It was the second time we hooked up. We'd gone back to her place and we'd already started...uh...getting intimate when she suddenly pulled back and said she had to ask me something. She had this really concerned look on her face and she said something like, 'Look, I hope this won't put you off but I've just got to ask—you're not into anything really weird, are you?'

"I asked her what she meant by weird and she said, 'Oh, you know, anything that might be...you know, dangerous.' I said I didn't think so but I asked her what she meant by dangerous. And she said, 'Well, like...choking, or anything like that.' I told her no, I wasn't and then asked her why she asked. I said, do I *look* dangerous, and she said no, I didn't. And then she dropped the bomb."

"I think I can guess."

"You got it. She said another guy she'd been involved with had suggested the choking thing to her several times, promising her it would make the whole experience a lot more intense. She told him no and she said he'd started getting more and more insistent. After a couple more times of this she'd finally broken things off with him and she said she still got chills thinking about it."

"She didn't happen to mention his name?"

"First name only. She said his name was Frank and that he was an attorney."

Well, all right, then. James Collins had indeed, as he'd said, gotten lucky. Sure, it was still all circumstantial, but the stars were definitely lining up. He'd established that Frank Reynolds was into erotic asphyxiation and not hesitant about trying to force the issue if the woman balked. That, plus James' conviction that Mandi would not have been trying it herself, made for a pretty compelling argument.

"What happened between you and Susan Alderson?" I asked.

"We got together a few more times and then agreed to part as friends. I didn't just dump her after I found out what I needed to know, if that's what you're asking. I think she began feeling that the age difference might be a problem and I sort of went along with that, acting like I understood she might be a little embarrassed to be seen with a guy so much younger. I also kinda played up the whole computer geek thing…you know, like that was pretty much my whole life so she'd get the idea we didn't have that much in common."

"Clever."

"Well, I can't deny she was attractive, and I did enjoy those times we got together. Do I feel a little shitty about it, using her like that to get something on Frank Reynolds? Yeah, I suppose so, sure. But again, we parted on friendly terms and breaking things off was mostly her idea, so I don't think any harm was done."

"No, probably not."

"So…where does that leave us? Do you believe now that Frank Reynolds killed my sister?"

"I'll say you've made a pretty convincing case, yes. But based on what you've found out, you could still take this back to the police and ask them to take another look at it. They could talk to Susan Alderson themselves and that might get them a little more motivated."

"I don't want to go that route. I couldn't get them interested the first time around and after all this time has passed, I can't believe they'd suddenly change their minds and decide to investigate Mandi's death after all. And even if they did, then what? They might or might not ever come up with enough to charge Frank Reynolds, and if they did...the guy's an attorney, for Christ's sake. He'd know how to play the system and this could drag out forever."

I had to hand it to James Collins. He'd given this a lot of thought and put a lot of time and energy into running Frank Reynolds to ground. And he was probably right about the futility of trying to get the cops interested at this late date.

"All right then," I said. "You're sure you want to proceed with this and have me get involved?"

"Absolutely. That bastard killed my sister and then just hung her in the closet like a piece of old clothing. I want you to do the same to him. Except I don't care if you put him in a closet afterwards."

CHAPTER 4

"Mr. Vance, is there anything else I can do for you today?" The drive-up teller's voice snapped me out of my reverie just as the carrier containing the receipt for the deposit of my check from James Collins arrived in the kiosk with a loud clunk.

"No, that should do it," I replied, reaching out for the carrier and removing the receipt.

"Then you have a very nice day," the teller said, smiling at me from behind the large tinted window.

"Thanks. You too," I said, replacing the carrier and hitting the automatic window button for the driver's door of my SUV. I pulled on through the drive-up lane and headed for home.

After my first phone conversation with her brother I had gone online and done a quick search for Mandi Collins. I found her obituary in the archives of a Chicago funeral home's website and while there was no specific cause of death listed—her family had obviously chosen to omit those details—everything else matched what James Collins had told me. So far, so good...his story checked out.

I had subsequently spoken to James Collins several more times to nail down the details and finalize a plan to kill Frank Reynolds. Ordinarily, having accepted a job, I do most or all of the legwork myself—it's much safer, I've found, if the client is kept out of the loop and does *not* know the particulars—but James Collins was a resource I'd have been foolish not to utilize.

For one thing, he'd already convinced me of his commitment to see this through, and that he wouldn't be satisfied until Frank Reynolds was dead. Also, he'd shown himself to be fairly resourceful in his own right and willing to take on a certain amount of risk. Getting cozy with Reynolds' latest squeeze was, I thought, a pretty ballsy move, and he'd apparently played that whole scenario very well. Plus, he was right there on Reynolds' home turf, which would save me having to make one or more recon trips to Chicago.

And finally, the fact that he'd sought me out showed good judgment on his part. In the immortal words of Dirty Harry Callahan in *Magnum Force*, "A man's got to know his limitations." James Collins apparently realized that killing Frank Reynolds called for a degree of expertise he lacked, and though he might have been willing to do it himself, he was smart enough to turn that part of the exercise over to someone who would know how to get it done more cleanly and efficiently.

All of which led me to believe that I could trust him.

That might sound a little foolhardy on my part—make that *very* foolhardy—but I've been doing this for a quite a few years now, and I've become very good at spotting the fakes and the faint-of-heart. The bogus ones rarely make it through the first series of email blinds. The others—those people who get cold feet at the last minute and decide they just can't be a party to a killing after all—are summarily discarded.

I have their phone number but they don't have mine—well, except for the number of the disposable from which I called them, and—you guessed it—that phone was indeed quickly disposed of. I change my P.O. boxes often enough that there's very little chance of further contact if they should change their mind a second time and decide they do want to go through with it. That kind of waffling I don't need—if they're that uncertain at the outset, there's a good chance they'll be hit by a major attack of the guilts later, after I've completed the assignment—so having bailed on me once, they don't get a second chance.

I wasn't worried about that happening with James Collins.

It was during our second conversation that I discovered just how invaluable he might be. "I'm going to need more details about Reynolds' personal life," I said. "Daily schedule, where he lives, how much time he spends in the office, how often he's in court if he's a litigator, how often he and his wife go out, that sort of thing."

"Already working on all of that," James replied.

"You are?" I said. I'll admit I was a little surprised, although maybe I shouldn't have been considering how much time and effort he'd already invested.

"Yep. I'm already tapping into his daily work schedule and I can even give you the names of the clients he's meeting with this week. I can also give you quite a bit of his wife's schedule as well."

"What? How are you getting all of that information? Please tell me you haven't hired a private investigator." The last thing I needed was an outsider who was in any way privy to our plans.

"Nope, didn't have to."

"What, then?"

"Well, I told you I run my own computer consulting business. Let's just say that through my business I've come to know some...uh, geeks who are very good at *probing* for things."

"You're tight with some hackers, in other words."

He laughed. "Hacking is such an ugly word," he said, and I laughed myself. Among sporting dog people like me, hacking first refers not to invading someone else's computer, but to overhandling a dog in the field...i.e., constantly blasting the whistle or shouting commands that the dog generally ignores. Hacking is an ugly word among dog trainers and bird hunters also.

But I didn't bother explaining this to James Collins. Instead, I said, "Are you sure these are people you can trust?"

He laughed again. "You want to think about what you just asked me?"

I did, and the answer was obvious. What they were doing was undoubtedly illegal so they were probably bound by some sort of mutual understanding that if one of them went down, they'd all go down, unavoidably. Call it honor among paranoiacs.

"All right," I said. "I think it's risky but I'll admit you might be able to shortcut things for me."

"Well, if it makes you feel any better, the two guys I'm working with don't know your name, or even that we've been in touch or what we've talked about, and they never will. But they did know Mandi, and they know what happened to her."

"Meaning?"

"Meaning even though I'm paying these guys for their help, they'd probably both do it for nothing. They want to see Frank Reynolds go down almost as badly as I do."

So with the help of James Collins and his two hacker buddies, I put together a plan, and like I've already said, it turned out to be much easier than expected. I can't begin to tell you how they managed to do it—even if they'd described the process to me (which they didn't), I doubt if I could accurately recount it here—but within just a few days they were reading almost all of the email traffic in and out of Reynolds' entire office, both business and personal of all the employees, plus all of their interoffice correspondence.

They also tapped directly into several of the employees' computers, including Reynolds' own. The most valuable of these turned out not to be Reynolds' but the computer of his personal secretary, who—cue the bells signaling the grand prize winner—kept his appointment book, scheduled all of his meetings and—another big win here—made all of his travel arrangements.

That last, plus an archived *Chicago Tribune* article they discovered with a quick online search, was what led me to decide that Frank Reynolds would die from an accident while deer hunting downstate rather than being killed during a home invasion or a mugging in Chicago.

The *Trib* article was titled "Prominent Attorney Shoots Wall-Hanger" and it had appeared some three years earlier in the paper's Sunday sports section. Frank Reynolds had shot a whitetail buck that scored high enough to make it into the Boone & Crockett record book, and the paper had done a surprisingly positive write-up...surprising because it didn't include any of the anti-hunting, anti-gun sentiment that pervades so much of the mainstream media these days.

The story had characterized Reynolds as a hard-working and well-known Chicago attorney who was also a passionate deer hunter who never missed a season and almost always took a trophy buck. Reynolds was quoted extensively in the article and he even mentioned the name of the farmer—Patrick Wallace—on whose land he hunted every year. It was in Schuyler County, about five hours southwest of Chicago, an area known for producing large bucks.

From that point on, it was almost a cakewalk.

By monitoring the secretary's computer and her emails to Reynolds, we found out when she made his reservations at the Hampton Inn in Macomb for a weekend in mid-October a few weeks before deer season. I was certain this was for a pre-season scouting trip as Reynolds had mentioned in the *Trib* article that he usually hunted from a tree stand and I was guessing he probably planned to hang one while he was there.

It took a little scrambling—I have a regular job, remember, and it's one that comes complete with deadlines—but I managed to get myself to Macomb that same weekend. We knew Reynolds was driving down to Macomb from Chicago on Friday and I did the same from my home in Des Moines.

I stayed at the Best Western that night, which was next door to the Hampton where Reynolds was staying, and it was easy enough to follow Reynolds (at a discreet distance, of course) as he left town on Saturday morning and drove out to Patrick Wallace's farm. James Collins had provided me with an aerial map of the entire area so I was already reasonably familiar with the topography.

I guessed Frank Reynolds would first go to Patrick Wallace's farm to renew acquaintance—that's what I do every year with those farmers on whose land I have permission to hunt—and sure enough, that's exactly what he did. I was watching through binoculars from alongside the road a quarter mile away (my SUV parked behind a copse of trees) as they stood on the front porch of the farmhouse and visited for 15 or 20 minutes, then Reynolds returned to his Escalade, which he'd parked off to one side of the farmer's lane, and opened the hatchback.

He was wearing jeans and hunting boots and a hooded sweatshirt and cap...dressed for an October day in the woods, in other words, and not looking like an attorney. He removed a lightweight portable tree stand from the Escalade and headed off past the farmer's barn and outbuildings and into the woods, carrying the stand's platform in one hand and its two-piece ladder over his opposite shoulder. By entering the woods a couple hundred yards from where Reynolds had entered, and walking a parallel course—and by doing no small amount of dodging and ducking behind trees—I was able to avoid being seen but still keep him in sight most of the time.

He eventually made it down to a creek bottom and started following a main deer trail. He was in no big hurry, apparently, and he seemed to have an idea of where he was going. My guess was that he was heading back to a spot where he'd previously taken a good buck—maybe the Boone & Crockett qualifier— or somewhere close to that spot, anyway.

It took him nearly two hours to settle on a location and when he did it was along the main deer trail he'd been following, which ran roughly parallel to the creek. He propped the tree stand's ladder against a tree about 40 yards from the trail and stepped back to make a survey of the area, checking for clear shooting lanes. Satisfied, he returned to the tree and began assembling the two pieces of the stand's ladder.

I stood behind a large oak some 50 yards away and watched him. Reynolds appeared to be about my size, six feet tall and maybe ten pounds heavier. He seemed to know what he was doing, as it only took him a few minutes to get his stand positioned and bolted into place against the tree. When he finished he stepped back, gave the ladder one last tug to make sure it was set solidly, then turned and headed back the way he had come.

I waited 15 minutes to make sure he'd left the area. Then I

walked down to the stand myself and, standing just beneath it, withdrew my Garmin GPS unit from my pocket and keyed it to record the coordinates of the location.

That would make it a lot easier to find this spot again, especially in the pre-dawn darkness, when I returned in a few weeks for deer season.

CHAPTER 5

When I got home after making my run to the post office and the bank, the first thing I did was let Preacher out into the back yard to pee. She—yes, Preacher is a female; surely you're aware of the increasing number of women entering the clergy, aren't you?—did her business then trotted around the perimeter of the fenced yard, checking for signs of squirrels and other dangerous invaders. I stood on the deck and watched her for a couple minutes before going back inside to sit down at the computer and start on some editing.

The rest of the Frank Reynolds assignment had fallen into place without a hitch. The deer hunting angle was one with which I was especially pleased, as it went a long way toward helping me adhere to Rule Number 2, which is, "No collateral damage allowed." When I first began taking these assignments, I vowed I would never kill anyone other than the intended target...that is, I would never kill a bystander or a witness or anyone else just to keep from being apprehended. Rather, I'd take the fall.

Sound a little too idealistic? Yeah, I suppose it does. But remember, I do what I do not for the money but to make things right. Killing someone else who just happens to be there—a victim of circumstance or bad timing—isn't justifiable in my book. And I'll admit, so far I've been lucky...it's not a split-second decision I've ever had to make. I hope I never have to.

Shooting Frank Reynolds during deer season in the woods on private land before daylight almost guaranteed that no one else would witness what happened. It was still a gamble, sure, but a small one, and there's always going to be *some* risk involved. Plus, there's also a danger of overthinking these things. While I'm a firm believer in trying to anticipate and plan for contingencies, long ago I learned the wisdom of the old rule of KISS, which means, of course, "Keep it simple, stupid."

For example, early on I briefly considered applying for a non-resident deer permit for Schuyler County, something that would have covered me if by chance I were spotted and stopped by a game warden on my way into or out of the woods. Because of Illinois' growing reputation for producing trophy bucks, more and more out-of-state deer hunters were traveling to the Land of Lincoln to do their hunting. With my driver's license showing I was an Iowa resident, a non-resident permit would easily explain my presence in the woods that morning.

Could I have carried false identification? Yeah, that always sounds good in theory, and I have used it occasionally—it's not that difficult to find a supplier, either on the internet or by word of mouth. (I also know where to buy a handgun off the books, but that's a story for a little later.) But in keeping with my practice of maintaining as low a profile as possible and sticking to the rule of KISS, I opted not to bother this time. The more people who have a hand in helping you do something illegal, the more chances there are that somebody will let something slip.

As far as applying for a non-resident deer permit to explain why I was in the woods that morning, that would create one more paper trail. I had no doubt that Frank Reynolds' death would be thoroughly investigated, no matter how accidental it appeared. And while I didn't know if the Schuyler County sheriff's office or the Illinois DOC would go to the length of checking out every single deer hunter to whom a permit had been issued for Schuyler County, I thought it was smarter to keep my name off that roster altogether. I decided to roll the dice and bet that I wouldn't be spotted during my brief time in the woods.

The odds were in my favor. Many hunters would take their deer on opening day and the fact that Frank Reynolds wasn't going to be on his stand until the second morning of the season—another tidbit we gleaned by monitoring his appointment calendar and travel schedule on his secretary's computer—meant I could expect fewer hunters in the woods and less chance of an encounter.

Also, I was planning to get to the location of Frank Reynolds' tree stand much earlier than he would, even if it meant going out there in the middle of the night. (I was in position by 3:30 that morning, about an hour before he arrived himself.) I hoped to have everything wrapped up and be out of the woods and on my way back to Macomb by sunrise. And, in fact, that's exactly how it had gone down.

There's another old saying to the effect that Fate favors the prepared individual, and that certainly seemed to hold true that morning. I caught a real break with the arrival of the huge 12-point buck that came up the trail just as it was growing light enough for me to have a clear sight picture on Frank Reynolds. Reynolds was so totally dialed in on the big buck—he was just preparing to shoot, in fact—that he couldn't have been thinking of anything else when I killed him. The buck had provided the ultimate distraction.

At the range from which I shot Reynolds—I was less than 30 yards away, partly hidden by a tree—I was sure the slug would pass through his body, and a quick look afterwards confirmed that it had. I doubted that it would ever be found but even if it was, there was no chance it would ever be matched ballistically to any firearm—that's the beauty of shooting a slug through an unrifled shotgun barrel like those of my Ruger.

After confirming Reynolds' death I made a quick hike back to my SUV, parked on a deserted farm lane about a mile away. The night before I'd considered boosting some license plates off a vehicle in Macomb so my Iowa plates wouldn't attract any attention but again decided that was just one more needless complication. The likelihood of my vehicle being spotted where I parked it that morning was pretty remote and I was planning to be back on the highway, where my out-of-state plates wouldn't get a second look, long before anyone would discover

Reynolds' body and raise an alarm.

I changed out of my hunter's clothing when I got back to the vehicle—no need to perpetuate the masquerade any longer than necessary—and was on my way back to Macomb just as dawn was breaking. The rest of my morning and my trip home were uneventful, and I was back in Des Moines by early afternoon. I'd discarded the empty shotgun shell when I'd stopped for gas and by now it would be buried in a landfill somewhere in eastern Iowa.

I was betting that Frank Reynolds' death would ultimately be ruled an accident. The trajectory of the shot would be troublesome for investigators, as it would be obvious that he had been shot from a low angle at fairly close range. But I was still confident that for lack of any real suspects the authorities would eventually be forced to conclude he had been killed by a stray shot fired by a hunter whose identity they could never hope to conclusively determine.

In just about every sense, this would make Reynolds' death—to borrow a term he himself might have used—a clean kill.

Man, was I ever wrong about this.

CHAPTER 6

I left Preacher on squirrel patrol in the back yard and went inside to start some editing. Working from home as I do, I spend most of my day sitting at a computer reading and revising copy, screening photos and answering emails. My associate editor and art director are located in one of Trimedia's production offices in another state.

As I've already mentioned, all magazine pre-press work is now done electronically so when Trimedia purchased *American Wingshot* from its previous Des Moines-based owner a few years ago, the new owners said I didn't have to relocate. They wanted me to stay on as editor and to sweeten the deal they set me up with a company computer in the spare bedroom I was already using as a home office.

The arrangement—it's called telecommuting and it is becoming increasingly common throughout the publishing industry—has proved very workable. Three or four times a year I make a trip to the production office for planning meetings and the rest of the time my staff and I handle all correspondence by phone and email.

It's an ideal situation. Early every morning, weather permitting, I take Preacher for a long run at a public lake about ten miles west of Des Moines. (That is, she runs; I amble.) The lake is surrounded by several hundred acres of woods laced with hiking trails and we usually have the place to ourselves that early in the day, only occasionally encountering another dog walker, jogger or, in winter, a cross-country skier, all of whom Preacher greets effusively. With her wagging tail and whiskered face she charms almost everyone immediately.

We're usually back home by eight o'clock or a little after and I'm online by 8:30. I work until lunchtime, break for a half hour or so, then get back at it until late afternoon. It is, I'll readily admit, about as comfortable a work arrangement as anyone could hope for, and one which, as I said earlier, I'm reluctant to give up, the attraction of retirement notwithstanding.

This being late November, I was currently working on the early spring issue of the magazine, which always includes a six-page spread of puppy photos submitted by readers. Sporting dog articles make up a large part of our editorial content—yes, I'm one of those elitists who believes if you can't hunt birds with a dog, you shouldn't hunt them at all—and the puppy photo spread is one of the most popular features we run all year.

We usually only have space for about forty pictures, so there are several hundred that don't make the cut. In the past few years we've begun posting these on the magazine's website and that seems to partially appease the readers who submitted the runner-up photos, although there's no question that seeing a picture of their pride-and-joy published in the magazine is the ultimate prize.

Because we strive for as much variety as possible, submitting a photo of a puppy from one of the lesser-known sporting breeds increases the likelihood of its being chosen; for example, if someone sends in a good picture of a Bracco Italiano or a Clumber spaniel or a small Munsterlander, it stands a much better chance of being printed than, say, one of several dozen black Labrador submissions.

Of course, everyone thinks his or her puppy is the cutest in the world, regardless of breed, and I occasionally receive nasty follow-up emails from folks whose photos weren't chosen, questioning not only my editorial qualifications but also my parentage and my sanity…is it any wonder I occasionally feel the urge to take on the type of moonlighting job I've described?

I spent about an hour going through the latest batch of puppy photos, selecting five or six and rejecting the rest.

Despite the submission guidelines we publish every year some readers still sent us photos that looked like they were taken with an old Kodak Instamatic—remember those?—not understanding that these don't come close to providing the quality and resolution needed for magazine reproduction. And yes, it's almost a given that these same folks who can't follow the submission instructions are also the ones most likely to complain if we don't run their photo.

After looking at all the puppy pictures I cared to for a while—even a lifelong dog lover like myself can start feeling a little jaded after so many cute furry faces—I opened a story on canine nutrition by Tony Paulsen, one of my top writers. Tony's copy was always clean and tight and required minimal editing, usually nothing more than adding or subtracting a comma or two. An editor's ideal contributor, in other words, the kind who makes my life easier.

Tony had quoted nutritionists from several of the major dog food companies (coincidentally, all of whom advertised in my magazine) and he'd put together a comprehensive piece on feeding sporting dogs. It was informative and the quotes were colorful; apparently his sources knew how to speak in sound bytes. It was the kind of good, solid editorial I like to run, which is one of the reasons I usually respond with a "yes" to Tony's queries.

This particular article also addressed one of my major ongoing pet peeves—namely, the tendency of many bird hunters to skimp when it comes to feeding their dogs. One of those myths that refuses to die says that all dog foods are pretty much the same and there's no reason to pay for premium food when most dogs can "get by" on the bargain brand stuff you buy at Walmart or the grocery store. "You're just paying for their advertising," is the argument Joe Cheapskate usually offers to justify his refusal to buy a high-quality product from one of the major, nationally known dog food companies.

Numerous studies have shown the fallacy of this thinking, and it seems like it would be obvious that you shouldn't expect any athlete—which is what a sporting dog is, in every sense—

to deliver peak performance on a diet of junk food, but that doesn't stop lots of hunters from feeding their dogs food that is primarily waste grain, slaughterhouse by-products and cheap fillers.

Tony's feature included plenty of information to support the concept that you should feed your dog the highest quality food you can afford to buy and that this is no place to be looking for ways to cut corners or save a buck. Whether it would change any reader's thinking on the matter was anyone's guess, but we were giving it our best shot, and it was a message I liked to revisit on a fairly frequent basis.

When I finished editing Tony's piece—a quick exercise as it didn't require much work, as I've already mentioned—I saved it with an ".rev" added to the document name, indicating that it had been revised and was ready for layout. I then emailed it to the associate editor and the art director with a brief message informing them that the photos for the article (which Tony had also supplied) would be on the magazine's ftp site. Steve, the art director, would retrieve them from there while Joe, the associate editor, took another look at the copy, checking for anything I might have missed and perhaps tightening up the wording a bit more.

After sending off Tony's copy I glanced at my watch and saw it was 11:30, close enough to lunchtime for me to question whether I should start working on another story. I told myself to stop procrastinating and get to it.

Bad decision. Forty-five minutes later I was only halfway through an article on spring snow goose hunting written by a contributor I used only occasionally, usually no more than once or twice a year. His writing was mediocre and required quite a bit of work to get it into shape for publication; his saving grace was that he always supplied outstanding photographs to accompany his stories.

That was the case this time as well. The field shots of his Labrador in action were terrific but his copy was too long, too flowery and full of grammar errors. By the time I'd finished cleaning it up and editing it into something acceptable and sent it on to Joe and Steve, I felt like I'd earned not only my lunch but the rest of the afternoon off.

And why not, I thought. It was Friday and a perfect late fall day, we still had a couple weeks to go before we started releasing this issue's files to the printer, and hunting birds was considered part of my job description.

I'd be foolish not to make the most of it.

CHAPTER 7

I ate a quick sandwich and a handful of corn chips, chased it all down with a can of ginger ale and changed into my hunting clothes. I sent an email to Joe and Steve telling them I was playing hooky for the rest of the afternoon to go out and chase pheasants with Preacher, then I loaded my shotgun and shooting bag into the SUV. I whistled Preacher in from the back yard and opened the tailgate and she jumped in without being told. She never needed encouragement when we were going hunting—she knew that from the clothes I was wearing—or out to the lake for a run.

We headed out of town to some farmland about a half-hour away that I had permission to hunt. I'd talked to the farmer before the season opened, and he'd told me to come out anytime. In addition to raising corn and soybeans he had a good-sized tract in CRP, and I was betting we could take a rooster or two before legal shooting time ended at 4:30 that afternoon. We hadn't hunted here yet this season and I hoped the farmer, Roland Patterson, hadn't allowed too many others to do so. Yeah, I'm selfish that way.

After stopping at the farmhouse and talking briefly with Patterson's wife—she told me Roland had gone into town to pick up a new chain for his chainsaw, and also confirmed that no one else had hunted their land recently—I parked in the access lane to the CRP field. I slipped on my hunting vest, uncased my shotgun, and opened the tailgate. Preacher jumped down and stood expectantly while I dropped two shells into the breech of my Ruger—yes, the same gun I'd used for the Frank

Reynolds assignment, and no, I wasn't at all bothered by the association—and closed the action. "All right," I told her. "Hunt 'em up."

She coursed into the field and fell into a nice quartering pattern about 50 to 60 yards ahead of me. We covered maybe 200 yards when she began getting birdy, her docked tail a blur and her pace becoming even more animated. "Easy," I called to her, hoping to head off a wild flush, and at the sound of my voice a hen pheasant lifted out of the cover about 20 yards ahead of her.

My mistake. My word of caution had spooked the hen; I should have trusted Preacher to handle the bird without any admonition from me. But Preacher did slow her pace a bit and continue quartering, and in another few moments she locked up on point.

"All right," I breathed quietly to myself, moving up on Preacher with my gun at the ready. When I was within 10 yards of the dog a rooster broke cover, cackling and presenting a going away shot. I mounted the Ruger, centered the rooster's white neck ring and fired. The bird came down almost without a flutter and Preacher broke her point to make the retrieve.

Bird dog purists might take me to task for allowing Preacher to break at the bird's fall rather than remaining steady and waiting for me to give her the command to fetch, but I'm not quite that much of a stickler for letter-perfect performance. Pheasants are notoriously tough birds and hard to kill, and one that hits the ground wounded can be gone in a microsecond, leading a dog on a far-from-merry chase. Allowing the dog to break point on its own and get to the fall a little faster can sometimes make the difference between a recovered bird and one that gets away to provide a meal for a fox or coyote when it later succumbs to its wounds.

But I had killed this rooster cleanly and Preacher had no problem locating it in the tall grass and retrieving it to hand. I patted her and told her what a good girl she was, then stood for a moment and smoothed the rooster's feathers before slipping it into the game bag of my hunting vest. I opened the Ruger's action and caught the fired shell as it ejected and dropped it into another pocket. I don't leave litter in the field if I can help it, and that includes fired shells.

I reloaded and gave Preacher the go-ahead. We hunted on out through the CRP field and moved two more hens—one of which Preacher pointed, the other I flushed myself—before she located another rooster some 45 minutes after we took the first one.

It took two shots to bring this one down; I clipped some feathers with the first shot before dropping it with the second. The bird fell into a volunteer patch of sunflowers and I heard Preacher breaking stalks as she made the retrieve. She emerged from the sunflower patch with the bird held firmly between her whiskered jaws and trotted back to me with tail wagging and amber eyes glowing.

Watching her bring in the rooster, I once again couldn't help thinking the same thought I'd had many, many times over the years—namely, that anyone who keeps a sporting dog only for a pet and denies that dog its heritage by not allowing it to participate in the sport it was bred for is doing something that borders on criminal.

Like I said earlier, I'm an elitist about this stuff.

CHAPTER 8

The following Wednesday the smug satisfaction I'd been feeling over the completion of the Frank Reynolds assignment went right out the window.

I made another run to the post office that morning and checked both boxes. I found the usual assortment of magazine-related material in the magazine's P.O. box, and a letter from James Collins in the other.

This was an immediate red flag. As a rule, once they've sent me the check for my fee, clients never contact me again. I prefer that—insist on it, actually—and I suspect that in most cases the clients prefer it as well, wanting to wash their hands of our transaction as quickly as possible. Living with killing someone—even when it's someone who deserved to die, and even if they've paid someone else to do the actual killing—is something most people find at least a little difficult to do.

But wrestling with their conscience is their business. I don't give refunds, nor do I offer words of consolation or reassurance to anyone suffering after-the-fact regrets. As I mentioned earlier, my screening process pretty much eliminates the faint-of-heart anyway, so I don't worry about my clients confessing to anyone…and by extension, implicating me.

Even if they do suffer some guilt pangs, their instinct for self-preservation is usually all-powerful and will override those feelings. They *will* eventually find a way to make peace with what they've done, because it's true that time heals almost all wounds, even if the wounds are those of conscience and self-inflicted.

Also, as someone once noted, self-forgiveness is typically a very easy trait to acquire…especially when you can remind yourself that you're not the one who actually pulled the trigger.

None of this seemed likely in James Collins' case, however. If I'd read him right—and I was confident I had—he wasn't the sort to have dedicated himself to avenging his sister's murder and then have qualms about the rightness or wrongness of it after the deed was done. His commitment to the entire exercise, as evidenced by his months of tracking Frank Reynolds and compiling enough evidence to convince me to take the assignment, plus his willingness to pay the fee I quoted him—$10,000—told me that he was solid and would be able to live with what we had done.

I was reminding myself of this as I tore open his envelope. I could have waited until I got home but I'll admit my curiosity got the best of me. Best-case scenario, he was just sending me a follow-up thank you, although he'd already included a sticky note to that effect when he'd sent me his check. So I couldn't help wondering why he was contacting me again, unless it was to send me a copy of Frank Reynolds' obituary, which would have undoubtedly run in the *Chicago Tribune* the previous week.

It was not a thank you note. Nor was it an obituary, although it was a newspaper clipping from the *Trib*. Affixed to the clipping was another sticky note with a handwritten message that read, "I know I'm probably breaking the rules by contacting you again but I thought you should see this. Do we have a problem? J.C."

I peeled off the note to read the clipping. It was dated three days earlier. The headline read: "Deer Hunter Arrested in Attorney's Death."

Shit.

I gave the story a quick read. It stated that Carlyle Wilson, 32, of Rushville, Illinois, had been arrested and charged with manslaughter in the death of prominent Chicago attorney Frank Reynolds. According to the story, Wilson was the hunter who had discovered Reynolds' body, and he had immediately reported it. He led a team of Schuyler County Sheriff's police to the scene and explained that he'd been attempting to track a deer he'd shot at and missed earlier that morning when he had come upon Reynolds slumped in his tree stand.

So far, so good. Although Wilson's gun had been fired, the police had no reason to doubt his story about missing a deer or suspect that Wilson had fired the shot that killed Reynolds. His promptness in reporting what he'd found and his willingness to lead them right to Reynolds' body were points in his favor.

Then Charlie Flanagan entered the picture.

Charlie Flanagan, also 32 and also of Rushville, had come forward to say that the night after Wilson had found Reynolds' body, he and Wilson had been drinking at the Rushville Tap and Wilson had confided to him that he had accidentally shot Reynolds. Flanagan claimed Wilson broke down at that point, saying that he didn't know if he could live with himself, knowing he had killed another man, even though it was an accident.

Flanagan waited until Monday morning to report Wilson's confession, presumably out of a sense of civic duty. Wilson was arrested later that day, although he denied making the confession Flanagan claimed to have heard. Wilson was charged with manslaughter and was now being held in the Schuyler County jail without bail.

Shit.

I re-read the clipping twice, and it raised several questions. My first instinct was to discredit Charlie Flanagan's account, if only because I knew with absolute certainty who had really killed Frank Reynolds. But knowing that as I did, I then had to ask why Charlie Flanagan would fabricate Wilson's confession and turn him in, especially if the two were at least drinking buddies.

There could be a hundred answers to that question, and most of them would probably involve some petty grudge, the kind that flourishes in small towns...hell, in towns large or small, for that matter. Maybe Carlyle Wilson had somehow wronged Charlie Flanagan in the past, or Flanagan at least believed he had done so. Pinning Reynolds' death on Wilson would more than even the score.

But—trying to give Flanagan the benefit of the doubt for a moment—I also had to wonder about Wilson's alleged confession. Had he really confessed as Flanagan claimed, maybe as a result of too many beers and the mistaken belief that the shot he'd fired earlier at a deer had accidentally struck and killed Frank Reynolds?

It seemed unlikely. There was no mention in the newspaper story of Wilson's location when he shot at the deer (and perhaps the police hadn't bothered to ascertain this), but if Wilson was a reasonably competent hunter, he had to be aware of where his shot had gone…at least approximately, even though he missed the deer.

Shooting at a deer standing on the ground, Wilson wouldn't have been firing at an upward angle from close range (as I had when I killed Reynolds) and because Reynolds had been sitting in a tree stand, the only other possibility of Wilson hitting him accidentally would have occurred if Wilson had been up on one of the adjacent ridges, firing downhill.

Of course, I had the advantage of knowing that wasn't what had happened. But if Wilson had been uphill from Reynolds, taken a shot at a deer below him, perhaps through some trees or screening brush, then gone downhill to follow up on the deer he'd missed and found Reynolds, was it conceivable Wilson might have concluded his shot had struck Reynolds?

Again, I couldn't make it fit. It called for too much coincidence. Wilson had to know the direction and basic trajectory of the shot he'd taken at the deer, and he would have been able to determine immediately that the trajectory didn't match up with where he'd been when he shot in relation to where he found Reynolds' body. Unless, that is, his shot at the deer *had* been in the same—almost exact—direction as where he found Reynolds.

No. Too much coincidence. Nor did I believe Wilson would have jumped to the conclusion that his shot at the deer might have ricocheted and struck Reynolds. According to the newspaper story, Wilson had told the police he discovered Reynolds' body when he'd been attempting to *track* the deer he'd missed. That suggested he had come some distance and had not fired the shot at the deer anywhere close to where he found Reynolds.

So back to the first conclusion I'd reached, which was that Charlie Flanagan was lying when he claimed Wilson had confessed to killing Frank Reynolds. When they'd come to arrest him, Wilson had denied making this confession but apparently the police chose to believe Charlie Flanagan.

At that point they also must have erroneously concluded that Wilson's account of shooting at a deer was false, and that he had accidentally shot Reynolds from nearby, as indicated by the upward angle of the shot, something that would have been easily determined by any reasonably competent medical examiner. Apparently they believed that Wilson had simply pulled the trigger unintentionally—maybe he'd stumbled?—as he'd been passing close to where Reynolds was sitting in his tree stand.

It wasn't rock solid. For it to have happened that way, Wilson would have had to have been walking along with the safety off and his finger on the trigger—something no responsible hunter would have done. Even if Wilson had been following the deer he'd shot at and was anticipating having another shot if he jumped the deer a second time, it was unlikely he'd have been walking with the safety off...or at least, I was inclined to give him the benefit of the doubt on this.

Obviously, the police weren't similarly inclined. Following the old "think horses, not zebras" line of rationale, they were going with the simplest and most likely explanation, which was that Wilson accidentally shot Reynolds, reported it but attempted to hide the fact that he was the shooter, then later, under the influence of several beers, confessed to his buddy Charlie Flanagan what he'd done.

And who could blame them for accepting all of this at face value? It made a nice neat package, even if, again, it wasn't rock solid. Wilson had been charged with manslaughter in accordance with the supposed accidental nature of the shooting. Murder would have been a tough sell to a jury, as it would require the establishment of some sort of motive. Since it would quickly become obvious Wilson hadn't known Reynolds and had no reason to kill him, that wouldn't have flown.

Still, a charge of manslaughter was bad enough. If convicted, Wilson would be doing some hard time. And that meant I was going to have to intervene. Rule Number 2—no collateral damage—demanded that I do so. I couldn't let Wilson go down for a crime I'd committed.

I was somehow going to have to figure out a way to get him exonerated and at the same time—I hoped—keep myself in the clear.

Shit.

I already said that, didn't I?

CHAPTER 9

I waited until the next day to call James Collins.

I was hoping for some sort of inspiration or magical solution (no, I can't bring myself to say "magic bullet" here) that would show me how to get Carlyle Wilson off the hook without revealing anything about my own involvement in Frank Reynolds' death.

Of course, no such solution presented itself.

I spent quite a bit of time turning the whole matter upside down and inside out and I kept coming back to the same conclusion. For some reason Charlie Flanagan had lied when he told the police Carlyle Wilson had confessed to killing Frank Reynolds.

The newspaper clipping James Collins sent me hadn't exactly been loaded with details, so I had very little to go on besides my own inferences. But somehow my gut told me that Charlie Flanagan was the bad guy here; that Carlyle Wilson was a stand-up citizen who'd had the misfortune of being the one to find Frank Reynolds' body and, by an unlucky coincidence, was carrying a recently fired shotgun when he'd done so.

Wilson hadn't hesitated to report what he'd found and had led the police right back to Reynolds. At that point it probably hadn't even occurred to him that he might be considered a suspect.

Well. No good deed goes unpunished.

I also couldn't help reflecting on how badly I'd miscalculated a few things myself. After shooting Reynolds I'd walked out of the woods that morning feeling almost jauntily confident that his death would ultimately be ruled an accident—the result of a stray shot—and no one would ever be charged.

I knew his body would eventually be discovered but I hadn't considered the possibility that the person who found him would almost immediately become the primary suspect. Truth is, I'd pretty much assumed Reynolds' body might not be found for several days, say after he failed to return home that weekend and his wife contacted authorities and initiated a search. If it had gone down like that, all of the other deer hunters in the area would have long since been gone from the woods and my stray shot scenario might have played out as I hoped.

No such luck.

I went online and did a bit of searching for more information but I didn't turn up much. There was a story about Wilson's arrest posted on the *Peoria Journal-Star's* website but it was basically just a replay of the story James Collins had sent me from the *Chicago Tribune*. I didn't learn anything I hadn't already known.

Then I did a search on Rushville, Illinois, and came up with a few semi-interesting tidbits. Rushville was the county seat of Schuyler County, with a population of a little less than 3,200. Translation: It was a small town in which I'd likely be noticed almost immediately if I showed up and started poking around or asking questions about any of its residents.

One of Rushville's most notable citizens had been a Dr. Russell Dohner, who had charged only $5 (originally $2) for home and office visits for over 60 years until his retirement in 2013. When I read this I couldn't help wondering if he'd ever treated Carlisle Wilson or Charlie Flanagan.

Also, the *Rushville Times* was the town's newspaper, published once a week on Wednesday. The paper didn't have a website so there was no immediate way to check for any stories it might have run on Carlyle Wilson's arrest, although I had to assume there would be something, as this would be big news in such a small community.

For the moment, I'd hit a dead end.

That, plus the feeling that I should at least acknowledge

receiving his note, led me to call James Collins. I still had his phone number and I called him on a new burner at 10:30 Thursday morning. Remembering the question he'd posed on his sticky note—and that I'd told him to call me Tom—when he answered I invoked Tom Hanks' classic line from Apollo 13: "Houston, we have a problem."

He gave a quick laugh and said, "I see you got the clipping."

"Yes, I did. Thanks for sending it, and no, I don't mean that sarcastically."

"I thought you'd want to know."

"Well, I can't say it's good news, but yes, I appreciate you letting me know. I'm going to have to do something about it, although I haven't figured out what."

"You're not going to let this Wilson guy take his chances at trial?"

"No, I can't do that. There's too much chance he'll be convicted. That's...unacceptable."

He gave another short laugh. "A hit man with a code of honor...I love it."

My turn to laugh. "I realize that sounds a little paradoxical," I said, "but it is what it is. Carlyle Wilson didn't do anything except happen to be in the right place at the wrong time, or the wrong place at the right time, or however the hell that expression goes."

"Right," James Collins said. "And for what it's worth, I kind of expected you might feel that way. In fact, that's the way I feel myself. You wouldn't have been there if it wasn't for me. And I don't feel good about this other guy taking the fall for what we did."

What we did. I liked that. James Collins wasn't trying to diminish his role in this in any way. Once again, my instincts about him appeared to be accurate. Right now it was nice to know that I'd been correct about something, at least.

"I'd like to find out more about these two guys, Wilson and Charlie Flanagan," I said. "For starters, I'd like to know if they were friends, just casual drinking buddies, or if there was any known animosity between them. That clip you sent me said Flanagan claimed Wilson had confessed to killing Reynolds while the two of them were drinking at some local watering hole. That suggests they were on friendly terms, but then why would Flanagan have turned Wilson in?"

"I wondered about that too," James Collins said. "If your best friend tells you he's killed somebody, you probably don't turn around the next morning and rat him out...at least most people wouldn't. I wouldn't, anyway. I might try to talk him into turning himself in, but I wouldn't go behind his back and give him up myself."

"Right," I said. "So the obvious answer is that they weren't really all that good of friends. Friendly enough to sit and have a beer together, maybe, but nothing more. So maybe Flanagan thought about it overnight and by the next morning decided he should tell the police what he knew. But I still have a problem with that whole scenario."

"What's that?"

"I don't believe Wilson really confessed to Flanagan. He denied it when he was arrested, and I think Flanagan was lying. I also think the story Wilson told was true about shooting at a deer and missing, then finding Reynolds' body when he was trying to track the deer. The whole confession thing makes no sense unless Wilson somehow convinced himself that he'd accidentally shot Reynolds. And unless he'd happened to shoot at a deer that was standing exactly in line with where he found Reynolds' body, which was pretty unlikely, he'd have to know he didn't shoot him."

"So you're saying you think Flanagan made up the whole bit about Wilson's confession?"

"Yes. I don't know why he'd have done that, but that's my gut feeling. Wilson was completely up front about contacting the police and telling them what he'd found and then leading them to the scene. I don't think he had any idea that he might be implicating himself by doing that. He knew he hadn't killed Reynolds, and my guess is, he was totally taken by surprise when he heard that he'd supposedly confessed and then was arrested."

"So the question is, why did Flanagan make up the story about Wilson confessing and then turn him in?"

"That's what I need to find out. But I'm kind of at a loss as to how to go about it. I did a quick search on the town, Rushville, and it's a very small place. Anybody who's a stranger is going to be spotted almost immediately, especially if he starts asking questions about the townspeople. And even more so if the people he's asking about were involved in a recent crime."

"Kevin and Mark and I might be able to do a little digging and see if we can come up with something."

"I was kind of hoping you'd say that," I said. Kevin and Mark—I'd never learned their last names—were the two hackers who had provided much of the information I'd used to build the plan for taking out Frank Reynolds. "But are you sure you want to involve them again, or for that matter, that you want to involve yourself?"

"I don't feel like I have much choice. Like I said, you wouldn't have been there if it weren't for me, and I don't want to see an innocent bystander go to prison for something I…uh…caused to happen."

"OK," I said. "Let's start with any background you can get on those two guys, Wilson and Flanagan. If we go with the assumption that Flanagan made up the story about Wilson confessing to him, that suggests Flanagan had a grudge against Wilson, some reason for wanting to burn him. We need to find out what that reason was."

"On it," Collins said. "Can I call you back at this number when I have something?"

"Sure," I said. "I'll hang onto this phone for at least another few days." I realized even as I said this I was breaking another one of my rules for protecting my privacy but I figured at this point James Collins was in this almost as deeply as I was and I could trust him as much as I trusted anyone. "In the meantime, I want to ask you one more thing."

"Shoot," he said, and we both laughed uneasily at his bad

pun.

"I'm just curious…how did you initially find out that I'd completed the assignment on Frank Reynolds?"

"Easy. His wife got a call that Saturday evening from the Schuyler County Sheriff informing her of her husband's death, plus we didn't quit monitoring her email or the stuff coming out of his office until just a few days ago. There was an absolute shitstorm when he didn't come home from deer hunting that weekend. Calls and messages from the office to her, asking where he was, plus some stuff from her to her sister saying something terrible had happened to Frank, etc. That's when I cut your check and stuck it in the mail."

"All right," I said. "I wondered if there'd been something in the *Trib* that you might have seen."

"There was, but I already knew by then that Reynolds was dead. It was a short piece saying that his body had been found by another deer hunter, and it named Carlyle Wilson, but that was about all…well, the usual stuff about his death being under investigation. But that was before Wilson's arrest."

"OK," I said. "Now we have to figure out a way to clear Wilson…and I'd prefer we do that without revealing who really killed Frank Reynolds." James Collins laughed. "And there's one more thing—we need to do this as quickly as possible. I don't know how long it will be before Wilson goes to trial, but I'm guessing not long. He's not sitting in Chicago where there's a huge backlog of cases. Best case scenario, we find out a way to clear him before the trial gets underway."

"Got it," Collins said. "I'll get back to you as soon as have, something."

CHAPTER 10

After we hung up I sat for a few minutes and replayed our conversation in my mind. That's something I often do, not only with clients but almost everyone with whom I've just talked. I've occasionally been accused of overanalyzing things and the people doing the accusing are probably onto something. But I can't help it; it's my way of making sure—or at least *trying* to make sure—I haven't missed anything critical.

Of course this exercise can quickly turn into a major self-inflicted mind-fuck as well, especially if I let myself get caught up in the "Here's what I *should* have said" game. That can lead to dreaming up various scenarios that will never transpire because the opportunity has already passed, but sometimes those lines of thought are unavoidable.

As I reviewed my conversation with James Collins just now, he still impressed me as a stand-up guy and someone I could trust to come through with the needed information on Carlisle Wilson and Charlie Flanagan, assuming he and his hacker buddies could turn up anything useful. I realized I'd probably need to give them at least a couple days to do this.

In the meantime, I could work with what I knew, which wasn't much. But I could put it down on paper to help organize my thoughts, anyway, and maybe looking at it in writing would trigger some additional ideas. I pulled out a yellow legal pad and went to work.

I started out by listing the facts as I knew them. Number one on the list was, of course, that Carlyle Wilson didn't kill Frank Reynolds. Number two was that Wilson's confession was almost certainly fabricated by Charlie Flanagan. Number three was that the alleged confession was what led to Wilson's arrest, i.e., the police believed Flanagan's story and acted upon it. Number four—I was jotting these down as they occurred to me, somewhat at random—was that the police had no real physical evidence of Wilson's supposed involvement except for his fired shotgun. No slug or empty shell had been recovered, nor would there be.

Or would they? I was certain that the slug that killed Frank Reynolds—the one I'd fired from my Ruger—would never be found in the woods, and I knew the empty shell would never be found, either, because I'd disposed of it. But what had Wilson done with the empty shell *he'd* fired at the deer?

I wondered if he'd ejected it from his gun and left it lying in the woods, or if—like me—he'd caught it and pocketed it. If he'd done the latter, would he still have it, maybe in the pocket of his hunting vest or coat? And if he did, could it somehow be used to clear him?

Unfortunately, I couldn't see how. Without the slug, the empty shell was a dead end. Having it in his possession would only confirm that Wilson had fired a shot that morning, which he'd already admitted. If anything, that strengthened the case against him.

On the other hand, if he'd ejected the shell and left it lying where it fell, and that location was some distance from where Frank Reynolds had been shot, could that be used in his defense? If someone were to find the shell, tie it to Wilson's gun—a ballistics technician could probably do this, based on the firing pin's imprint on the primer—and point out that where the shell had been found was nowhere near Frank Reynolds' body, wouldn't that at least bolster Wilson's claim that he'd shot at a deer?

It was a stretch, but I wondered if it was worth pursuing and how to go about pursuing it. It would require finding out from Wilson, somehow, where he'd been when he fired at the deer, then finding that spot in the woods and scouring it thoroughly to find his discarded shell. That is, *if* he'd discarded it.

The more I thought about this scenario, the more implausible it seemed. I didn't know if Wilson had been on a tree stand when he shot at the deer or if he'd been still-hunting through the woods, but if it was the latter, the chances of finding the exact spot he'd been when he shot at a deer—and then finding the shell if he'd discarded it—were almost totally nil.

Wilson would have to be able to pinpoint exactly where he'd been in such a way that I could return to that spot to look for the shell. It was your classic needle-in-a-haystack search and I'd stand about as much chance of finding the shell as I would of scoring a date with Sandra Bullock the following weekend.

The whole task of finding the shell would be much easier if he'd been on a tree stand. The stand wouldn't be that difficult to find, assuming it was still in place and hadn't been dismantled, and a shell ejected from the stand should be somewhere on the ground beneath it, probably no more than a few yards away. But again, I'd have to somehow ask Wilson at least a few questions to first determine if he'd been hunting from a stand and if so, where it was, and finally, if he'd ejected the shell and left it lying in the woods.

And assuming he provided that information, and that I found the location and the shell, what would I have? An empty shell that matched the firing pin on Wilson's gun, maybe proving his claim that he'd shot at a deer that morning, but nothing more.

A prosecuting attorney could argue that Wilson fired a second time and it was the second shot that killed Frank Reynolds. Finding an empty shell near a tree stand in the woods would do nothing to clear him, to say nothing of the risk I'd be taking myself by trying to find the shell and then somehow getting it entered into evidence.

I scratched the idea of contacting Wilson and trying to find his spent shell. The potential payoff—minimal, at best—wasn't worth the risk. Which left me back at square one, trying to find out why Charlie Flanagan had set up Wilson to take the fall for

Frank Reynolds' death.

And that wasn't going to be easy. Having to work from long distance and not make contact with either Wilson or Flanagan—or, for that matter, any other Rushville residents—certainly complicated things. My best hope was that Kevin and Mark could turn up something that would explain why Charlie Flanagan had, as James Collins had put it, ratted out Carlyle Wilson...not only ratted him out, but most likely fabricated the whole confession.

I wondered if it had anything to do with a woman. Or an old rivalry. Or a grudge carried over from childhood. Or...I quickly realized there was little sense in speculating along these lines. It could be any one of a thousand reasons and quite possibly it was something I couldn't even imagine.

I pushed aside the legal pad on which I'd been doodling. I needed to do something to free up my mind and stop clawing at intangibles. I was in no mood to edit magazine copy—and I knew my mind would wander if I tried to do so, almost guaranteeing I'd make a sloppy job of it—so I decided to clean my shotgun.

While I keep my guns in a locked vault upstairs, I clean them in the basement on a workbench I've equipped for that purpose. I retrieved the Ruger from the vault in my den and headed downstairs. As I passed through the kitchen, I glanced into the living room where Preacher was sprawled asleep on the sofa.

"Wanna come downstairs with me?" I asked and she opened an eye and favored me with an expression that clearly said, "Get real!" I was used to this sort of response and wasn't offended. "Suit yourself," I said, moving on downstairs.

I spread some old newspapers on the workbench, then removed the Ruger's forearm and barrels and laid the pieces out side by side. I pulled a bore snake out of its box and unscrewed the lid from a bottle of Hoppe's No. 9, enjoying the scent as always.

I dipped the end of the bore snake in the Hoppe's, then dropped the snake's weighted cord through the bottom barrel from the breech end. I grabbed the weight and pulled the snake through, noting the accumulated fouling on the snake as it emerged from the muzzle end of the barrel.

I'd wiped down the Ruger with a silicone cloth after my last outing with Preacher but I hadn't broken down the gun and cleaned the barrels—yes, shame on me—and I had to make two more passes with the bore snake before the inside of the bottom barrel was gleaming. When it was, I repeated the procedure with the top barrel.

The dirtiest part of the job completed, I set the barrels aside and picked up the stock. I carefully wiped out the gun's action with a dry rag, removing a few more bits of fouling and chaff, then wiped the action again with a silicone cloth.

That done, I eased the barrels back into place and closed the action. I wiped the barrels thoroughly with the silicone cloth, leaving them covered with a slight film, then I snapped the forearm back on and wiped the latch on its underside as well. I finished with a final polishing wipe of the trigger, trigger guard and receiver, and the cleaning was completed.

As I'd worked I'd made a conscious effort not to think about the whole Frank Reynolds/Carlyle Wilson/Charlie Flanagan situation. I'd concentrated on the task of cleaning the Ruger, something which always left me in an appreciative mood. The gun had been with me a long time and yes, it had been used to take a lot of lives, some of them human.

In simplest terms, it had served me well.

I'm usually not one to develop much sentiment toward an inanimate object but I couldn't deny that over the years the Ruger had become, as the old western gunfighters used to say of their favorite revolvers, almost an extension of myself. It fit me well and I shot it well and of all the guns I owned, it was far and away my favorite.

There was a certain amount of irony attached to that favoritism, however, predicated on how I'd originally come to own the Ruger. It had been an anniversary present from my wife.

Our sixth anniversary, to be exact. The year before we'd

struck a deal. We weren't exactly well-heeled at the time, but my wife wanted diamond earrings for our fifth anniversary and she got them…but with the caveat that the following year it would be my turn for a pricey gift—specifically, a shotgun of my choosing.

I did a lot of shopping and comparing and finally settled on the Ruger Red Label. It was a well-built, American-made gun and comparably priced to what I'd paid for her earrings, and I especially liked its sleek lines, which gave it a more streamlined look than many of the other over-and-unders then on the market.

Because I was primarily a pheasant hunter, I chose the gun in 12 gauge rather than a lighter 20, and because I have rather long arms, I opted for 28-inch barrels instead of 26. This was in the mid-1980s, just a year or two before Ruger introduced interchangeable choke tubes in their shotguns. I held out for one with improved and modified chokes rather than the more common configuration of modified and full.

I took delivery of the gun a few days before our sixth anniversary, which, coincidentally, was also just a few days before the opening of pheasant season. I shot the heck out of the gun that first year and had been doing so ever since.

Unfortunately, my wife and I were not destined for such a long-term relationship. We were divorced four years later, shortly after our tenth anniversary—we were separated for the final year of our marriage—and that was more than twenty years ago. I hadn't spoken to her for at least the last fifteen.

But I was still shooting the Ruger. It's pretty obvious, isn't it, which love affair lasted longer?

CHAPTER 11

I was returning the Ruger to its place in the gun vault when a curious idea hit me. Maybe thinking about how I'd acquired the shotgun—a gift from a woman to whom I was no longer married and with whom I no longer had any contact—was the trigger. Something about the final resolution of that situation— my marriage was long over but I still had the gun and I used it regularly—suggested a different perspective regarding Carlyle Wilson and Charlie Flanagan.

I *knew* Carlyle Wilson hadn't killed Frank Reynolds. I *didn't* know why Charlie Flanagan said he had. But maybe at this point I didn't *need* to know Charlie Flanagan's motive. I could formulate a game plan without that piece of information.

When my wife and I separated during the final year of our marriage, it was with the intention of giving ourselves some time apart to clear our thinking, stop antagonizing each other on a daily basis and attempt to rebuild what had been lost in our relationship—all the usual reasons couples cite for a so-called "trial separation," in other words.

I knew from the outset it was a lost cause.

I knew that despite our best efforts—and in fairness, we *did* make a real try at reconciling, including several months of counseling—we weren't going to make it. Call that pessimistic, fatalistic, whatever; somewhere deep down I knew our marriage was over. And indeed, at the end of a year's time, it was. It ultimately became a matter of our both realizing and admitting this and then moving ahead with the divorce, which, in hindsight, was inevitable.

In a similar way, I realized now that I needed to push past the "why" and start concentrating on the "how." What I'd been looking for so far was some justification for the course of action I'd known all along I was probably going to have to take. That's why I had James Collins and his hacker buddies digging into the backgrounds of Wilson and Flanagan, hoping to come up with an explanation for Flanagan's frame job.

The answer to this problem—seeing Carlyle Wilson cleared of the charges against him for the death of Frank Reynolds—was a fairly simple one, actually. Without Wilson's alleged confession, the police had nothing but circumstantial evidence against him, and not much of that. So the obvious solution was to get rid of the confession.

That meant either somehow getting Charlie Flanagan to retract his story—admit that he'd fabricated the confession, in other words—or eliminating him so he couldn't testify in court.

The latter course would probably be the easier of the two.

Of course, I could always sit back and hope that Wilson's attorney would be sharp enough to poke holes in Flanagan's story and trip him up on the witness stand. If Wilson's attorney could show there was at least some doubt regarding the veracity of Flanagan's account, that might be enough to sway the jury, especially if the attorney could also point to some bad blood between the two.

The newspaper clipping had mentioned that, according to Flanagan, Wilson had "broken down" after making his confession. This had taken place in a bar, so I had to suppose there were other people around—customers and at least one bartender. In a town the size of Rushville it wouldn't be difficult to locate some of those people and perhaps they could testify that they hadn't seen Wilson showing signs of him appearing distraught…again, this would weaken Flanagan's claim of Wilson's confession.

But would that be enough to see Wilson exonerated? I had no real confidence that it would. The police had believed Flanagan's story and there was a good chance the jury would also. Juries were notoriously unpredictable in their thinking…and notoriously unreliable in being able to separate fact from preconceived notions and prejudices. I was more than willing to give Wilson the benefit of the doubt and believe he'd never confessed as Flanagan claimed because, of course, I was privy to information no one else had in the matter…well, no one except James Collins.

But was knowing—or believing, anyway—that Flanagan had deliberately framed Wilson sufficient reason to kill him?

That was the dilemma I'd really been struggling with. I'd probably known after reading the newspaper clipping the first time that this was where things were headed, and that's why I'd been searching for some justification. I didn't want to kill Flanagan on nothing more than a hunch.

I also had to consider the possibility that killing Flanagan might make things worse for Wilson. Flanagan would be the key witness in Wilson's trial and his sudden elimination would arouse all kinds of suspicion. I had to assume Wilson had family and friends in the Rushville area and, given the general public's willingness to latch onto any conspiracy theory that comes along, it was a good bet that many people would immediately assume Flanagan's death was caused by someone in Wilson's camp.

So…what if Flanagan disappeared instead of turning up dead?

That would require a little more planning than a simple execution, but it could be done. The beauty of Flanagan disappearing was that it would create yet another mystery…people might assume Wilson's supporters were responsible, but they couldn't be sure. And with no real evidence of what had happened to Flanagan, an equally plausible explanation was that he had simply fled rather than risk being grilled and exposed as a liar on the witness stand.

Just as the public love conspiracy theories, they also love unsolved mysteries…the two go hand-in-hand, actually. Flanagan's disappearance would be the talk of the town, undoubtedly. Rushville residents could wear themselves out speculating about what had happened to him, and they'd enjoy every minute of it.

There were still plenty of variables, however. I didn't know if Flanagan and Wilson had families, but James Collins and his buddies should be able to discover that without too much trouble. If Flanagan had deep roots in the community—had lived there all his life and was happily married with children, say—then his sudden disappearance would seem much less likely and much more indicative of foul play.

I found myself hoping he didn't have those deep roots. I realized I *wanted* him to be the bad guy in this. I'm not a particularly religious sort of person (big surprise, right?) but if my suspicions were correct, then Charlie Flanagan was certainly guilty of violating the Ninth Commandment by bearing false witness against Carlyle Wilson. Which brought me back to the essential question: Was that enough to justify killing him?

I wasn't sure. It would be helpful if we could turn up some major dirt on him that would convince me he was one of those people who, as the expression goes, just needed killing. All the protests of bleeding heart liberals aside, there are plenty of such people out there—people who have irreparably damaged—or destroyed—the lives of others and, simply by their presence, continue to threaten the lives of those around them.

If Charlie Flanagan was one of those people, it would make my job a lot easier.

Or at least, easier to accept.

CHAPTER 12

The next morning, on the way home from our run at the lake, I saw a bobcat.

Bobcats were on the increase in Iowa but they were still something of a rarity and seeing one was definitely noteworthy. While I regularly saw deer as we were driving to and from the lake and on the lake property itself—it was a rare day when I *didn't* see deer, in fact—and even the occasional coyote or flock of wild turkeys, a bobcat sighting was a little out of the ordinary.

For one thing, bobcats are crepuscular—most active at dawn and dusk. So you're not likely to see one out rambling around in the middle of the day. For another, they tend to be secretive, sticking to heavily wooded areas and usually going to great lengths to avoid any human contact. Unlike raccoons and possums, they're probably not going to be found raiding a garbage can in a suburban back yard.

We'd left the lake a few minutes earlier and were driving east on the road that would take us to the four-lane bypass on the south side of Des Moines. I happened to glance over at a wooded creek bottom bordering a field of corn stubble just as the cat was slipping into the woods. I saw its rear end and recognized the short tail, long legs and distinctive cat gait, and then we were past.

I pulled into the driveway of a farmhouse a couple hundred yards up the road and quickly made a U-turn. I returned to the spot opposite where I'd seen the cat and pulled off on the shoulder. I pulled out the pair of Bushnell mini-binoculars I keep in the SUV and spent the next five minutes or so glassing the creek bottom. Preacher, settled in the back of the SUV and probably snoozing after her hour-long run at the lake, was quiet.

I saw no further sign of the cat so finally gave it up. I pulled up to the next crossroad, made another U-turn—thank goodness there were no state troopers prowling in the vicinity—and started back toward home. When I came abreast of the creek bottom again I slowed down for one more scan and that's when things *really* got interesting.

I spotted the cat a second time. It was sitting at the edge of a patch of snow—we'd gotten a couple inches earlier in the week—at the far end of the cornfield. I pulled off again and put the binoculars on the cat and just as I did it crouched down and went into stalk mode.

I watched for a good minute or more as it stalked something, slipping forward a few feet and freezing, then moving forward and freezing again. I heard Preacher whine behind me and realized she'd probably awakened when I stopped the vehicle and had seen the cat and was watching it also. A glance in the rearview mirror confirmed that's what she was doing. I guessed the cat was stalking a field mouse or a bird feeding in the corn stubble.

It finally broke and charged, and I saw the flash of an orange-red tail a few yards ahead of the cat—the cat's quarry was a fox squirrel. The squirrel raced to the tree line at the field edge and ran up a small tree not much larger than a sapling and the bobcat went right up after it. The cat got about halfway up then turned and jumped off, probably because the tree wouldn't support its weight.

It came down in some tall grass on the far side of the tree line. Behind me, Preacher let out a sharp yelp. I wondered if that was meant sympathetically for the cat losing out on a meal or, more likely, if she was hoping for a chance to pursue the cat. In Germany, her breed was originally developed not only to hunt and retrieve upland gamebirds and waterfowl but also to trail and dispatch predators and vermin and I knew she still possessed those instincts.

I watched for another few minutes but the cat didn't show

itself again and I guessed it had probably continued on down the tree line away from the road. I wished it good hunting.

I also wondered if there was a lesson for me in what I'd just observed.

I pondered that question on the rest of the drive home. I knew that predators like bobcats were not prone to making half-hearted stalking efforts just for recreational purposes. When they hunted something they fully intended to convert it into a meal. They couldn't afford to expend energy stalking and chasing prey if there wasn't a reasonable chance of success.

I'd been too far away to see exactly what had happened—whether the squirrel had spotted the cat closing in on it and had then made a mad dash for safety, or if the cat had begun its final charge prematurely and that was what had alarmed the squirrel—but regardless, there might have been a miscalculation on the cat's part that had provided the squirrel with the margin it needed to escape.

Then again, maybe the squirrel just got lucky.

If the cat *had* made a miscalculation, what was it? Had it sensed that the squirrel had noticed it and figured it had better make its charge in a now-or-never effort? Or had it merely jumped the gun while the squirrel was still far enough away to get away safely?

I'd made a few miscalculations myself lately, and I didn't want to make any more of them. I'd do well, I realized, not to jump the gun in the matter of Carlyle Wilson and Charlie Flanagan. I'd also do well not to assume I could get close to Charlie Flanagan and pull off either a disappearance or a kill without running the risk of being noticed.

I'd already figured that any appearance I made in Rushville would probably attract attention I couldn't afford. That seemed to indicate I was going to have to operate from a distance, relying on whatever information James Collins and his buddies Kevin and Mark could come up with about Charlie Flanagan and Carlyle Wilson and then use that information to form a plan to slip in, execute and slip back out, still unnoticed.

On the other hand…

The bobcat had stalked the squirrel at the edge of a field of corn stubble, basically out in the open. Though over a hundred yards away, I'd been able to follow the entire progress of the cat's stalk and while I couldn't see what precipitated its charge, the cat had been visible the entire time, relying on keeping low to the ground and moving forward cautiously only a few feet at a time.

Maybe I could do the same.

What if I showed up in Rushville, using my job—my regular job, that is—as cover? I could let myself be known around town and say I was there to do a little bird hunting for a story I was planning to write for my magazine. A night or two at the Rushville Tap—if I remembered correctly, that was the name of the bar where Charlie Flanagan claimed to have heard Carlyle Wilson's confession—might get me the name of two or three local landowners who would let me hunt their property.

It was a long shot. I didn't know offhand if there were any public hunting areas around Rushville but I did know that most of the land in Illinois—well over 95 percent—was privately owned. I also knew that landowners—farmers and everyone else—were increasingly reluctant to allow strangers to hunt on their property.

Part of that was due to liability concerns; part of it was due to the increasing trend to lease the hunting rights to those willing to pay a hefty fee. Walking up to an unfamiliar farmhouse door, knocking and receiving permission to hunt was pretty much a thing of the past unless you'd spent some time previously cultivating the landowner and/or agreed to pay for the privilege of hunting his land.

But if I could find a couple of people willing to let me hunt their land, or better yet, locate some public hunting ground in the area, that might give me enough of a cover story to spend a little time in Rushville and the surrounding area. Once again, I'd be hiding in plain sight, relying on my regular job to explain my being there and counting on my credentials as the editor of a national magazine to keep me above suspicion. This ploy had worked for me in the past.

The more I turned it over in my mind, the better I liked it. I'd have to be careful not to start feeling foolishly optimistic— I'd already made enough mistakes along those lines—but if I could discipline myself to proceed cautiously (like the bobcat stalking the squirrel) I could probably pull it off. I'd just have to be careful to not tip my hand, not act precipitously and not leave behind any traces of what I'd done.

That was a lot of "nots." But at this point it seemed like the best way to accomplish what needed to be done—eliminate Charlie Flanagan as the key witness against Carlyle Wilson— in the most expeditious manner. And again, my job would provide the cover I needed—over the years I've told quite a few people that hunting is part of my job description. I've usually said this half-jokingly, but there's actually quite a bit of truth to it.

"How about it?" I said over my shoulder to Preacher. "You up for a trip over to Illinois?"

She whined in response and I took that as a yes.

CHAPTER 13

To borrow a favorite expression of a former colleague: Once in a while you get plain old dumbass lucky.

After seeing the bobcat and deciding to make a run over to Illinois on the pretext of hunting in the Rushville area, I was feeling better about the way things were shaping up. I didn't have any of the details nailed down yet but I had a basic plan, and that was progress. Once you feel the forward momentum start to build it is easier to keep rolling and the pieces generally begin to fall into place.

When we got home I fed Preacher her morning meal—I'm a firm believer in feeding my dog two smaller meals a day, rather than one large one, as a means of reducing the risk of gastric torsion—and then headed back to my office. I logged onto my personal computer and did a search for public hunting areas in Illinois.

There were a number of state-managed public hunting areas throughout Illinois, I discovered, but none were within easy driving distance of Rushville. That was a setback but not an insurmountable one. It just meant I'd have to dig a little deeper—or get lucky with some hunter-friendly landowners—to come up with a reason for being in the area. I did another search, this time typing "Illinois hunting preserves" in the search window.

That's when I hit pay dirt.

Among those preserves that came up was one called Hidden Hollow in Schuyler County. I clicked on Hidden Hollow's website—attractive and professionally done—and started reading. The preserve was owned and managed by a fellow named Mitch Halvorsen and his wife, Amy. Judging from the photos, they were an attractive couple, probably in their early to mid-thirties. Mitch appeared to be tall and lean with a neat brown beard; Amy had a nice smile and wore her blond hair in a short bob.

The preserve consisted of 1,200 acres of mixed croplands—most likely corn, soybeans and sorghum—cover strips and hardwood timber. A handsome log lodge—there were several photos, both interior and exterior—had accommodations for 12 clients. Deer and turkey hunting were offered in season, and there was also a released bird program for upland hunters like myself. Pheasants, chukar and bobwhite quail were the species available.

Best of all, the preserve's mailing address was Rushville.

Bingo.

I checked my magazine's production schedule thumbtacked to the bulletin board above my computer. We weren't due to begin releasing the files of our spring issue to the printer for another two weeks. All of the edited copy and photos were in the pipeline—the associate editor would be making a few final tweaks to the copy and the art director would be working on layouts. Until they began emailing me the layouts for proofing, I had relatively little to do beyond answering daily correspondence, fielding occasional phone calls and maybe—if I really felt ambitious—a little editing on a few stories for the following issue.

In other words, schedule-wise, I was pretty much free to go.

I'd need to clear it with my boss, the publisher, of course. But Bill McKenzie was a hunter himself and usually pretty reasonable about OKing such requests, especially when everything was on schedule with the magazine and there was no danger of missing a deadline. And this was one area in which I was golden.

In putting together my magazine, I've always tried to follow Clint Eastwood's philosophy of movie-making—

namely, you bring your projects in ahead of schedule and under budget. Once you've established a track record for doing this, it will buy you a fair amount of wiggle room with the higher-ups. So I was reasonably confident that when I contacted Bill and told him I was planning to take a couple days off to drive over to Illinois for a bird hunt at a promising-looking preserve, he'd be on board with the idea.

And that's exactly what happened. A five-minute phone call later, I was good to go. The only caveat Bill attached was that while I was there I was to make a pitch to the Halvorsens to consider advertising in the magazine. I told him I'd be happy to do so, knowing this would give further credibility to my whole reason for being in the area. The more legitimate business activity I could attach to my visit, the more solid my cover would be and the less likelihood there was of anyone connecting me with Charlie Flanagan's death or disappearance.

It was starting to come together.

My next call was to the number posted on the Hidden Hollow website. Mitch Halvorsen's wife answered the phone. "Hidden Hollow, this is Amy!" she said in a cheerful voice.

"Hi," I said. "My name's Robert Vance and I'm the editor of *American Wingshot* magazine. I'm going to be over in your area in the next week or two and I was hoping to book a hunt. Do you have any times available?"

"Were you thinking of something on a weekend or sometime during the week?"

"Either/or," I said. "I realize this is awfully short notice but I just caught a break in my production schedule and I've heard some good things about your place and wanted to check it out. It's possible we might want to do a feature on Hidden Hollow in the magazine."

"Oh, that would be wonderful!" Amy said. "We take your magazine and we'd love to have you come over for a hunt. Where are you coming from?"

"I work out of my home in Des Moines, Iowa," I said. "I'm guessing it would take me about five hours to drive over." Actually, there was no guessing involved as I knew almost exactly how long it would take, having been over in that area just a couple weeks earlier. But of course there was no reason to go into any of that with Amy.

"Well, we'd love to have you," she repeated. "We're booked up for the weekend after next as that's our second firearm deer season, but almost any other time would be available. Will it just be you who's coming, or will there be others in your party?"

"Just me…well, I'd like to bring my dog also, if that's permitted." I knew this was a dicey area with some preserve operators, many of whom preferred you leave your own dog at home and use the ones in their kennels. And you couldn't really blame them for feeling that way, as many clients' dogs had little or no training—despite their owners' claims to the contrary— and could wreak havoc on a preserve if they ran wild and were out of control.

But Amy gave me the answer I was hoping for. "Of course you can bring your dog," she said. "We don't allow dogs in the guest rooms of the lodge but we have very nice kennel facilities and if your dog is used to being kenneled, I'm sure he'll be quite comfortable."

"That's good to hear," I said. "My dog is actually a six-year-old female German wirehair and she's used to being kenneled from time to time so I'm sure she'll be fine. And just for the record, she *is* well trained…I'm sure you hear that all the time."

Amy laughed. "Yes, we do, and it's not always true, but if you're the editor of *American Wingshot* I'm willing to give you the benefit of the doubt." I was liking Amy more by the moment. "What is your wirehair's name?"

"Preacher," I replied. "She's named for a character in a Clint Eastwood movie."

"*Pale Rider*!" Amy said. "That's one of my husband's favorites…well, mine too. We've probably watched the DVD a couple hundred times."

"Well, with her whiskers, Preacher looks a lot like Clint in that movie," I said, wondering if Amy had any unmarried sisters.

"I look forward to meeting her!" Amy said. "In fact, I look

forward to meeting both of you…what dates are you thinking of, specifically?"

"What about next weekend?" I said. "Say, arriving on Friday, a week from today, and leaving on Sunday? I'd plan to hunt both Saturday and Sunday, maybe a half-day hunt each day, if something like that's available."

"Yes, I think we can make that work," Amy said. "Now, were you thinking pheasants, quail or chukar? Or maybe a combination package?"

"Let's go with a combo," I said. "Maybe quail and chukar. I've already shot quite a few pheasants in Iowa this year so let's try something a little different." I laughed. "I'll see if I can hit something that's smaller and faster."

Amy laughed in return. "We can do that," she said. She quoted me the price for a daily 12-bird package and I told her that was fine. After receiving Bill's blessing I was planning to expense this hunt anyway.

I gave her a credit card number to confirm my reservation for the following Friday and we concluded our conversation with Amy inviting me to have dinner at the lodge that evening if I got there in time. "Dinner is at 6:30 so you'll want to get here a little earlier to check in and get Preacher taken care of," she said.

I thanked her and hung up wondering if Amy was as cute in person as she'd sounded on the phone. I suspected she was; in the few pictures in which she'd appeared on the website she looked a lot like the actress Amy Carlson, who—before they killed off her character—played Donny Wahlberg's wife on *Blue Bloods*. Was it just a coincidence that they shared the same first name?

I shook my head and reminded myself of the real reason I was heading over to Hidden Hollow. Amy Halvorsen's attractiveness was the last thing I needed to be thinking about right now. I had some preparations to take care of, and I hoped that before next Friday I'd hear from James Collins…specifically, that he and his hacker buddies had turned up something useful about Charlie Flanagan and Carlyle Wilson.

I had to believe they would.

CHAPTER 14

My next call was to a pawnshop on the south side of Des Moines.

"Pawnshop," the proprietor answered, and I recognized his voice.

"A.C.," I said. "It's Rob Vance. Need to stop by this afternoon if you have a few minutes."

"Two o'clock," he said, and I answered, "Fine. See you then." I wasn't surprised to hear the click of him disconnecting almost before I finished speaking. A.C. is a man of few words, none of them frivolous.

He's also my source for untraceable handguns.

I've known A.C. for about ten years. The initials by which I addressed him were actually the first two of four which stood for his nickname, As Cold as They Come. The name on his pawnbroker's license was Gerald Matthews but I'd never heard anyone call him Gerald or Jerry. I *had* occasionally heard him addressed as Cold, which struck me as a nice little play on words, in that A.C. is also the abbreviation for air conditioning.

Either name was an appropriate fit, matching both his personality and the merchandise in which he sometimes dealt. No, I'm not talking about air conditioners.

I still hadn't figured out exactly how I was going to handle things with Charlie Flanagan but I had a feeling I'd have to get fairly close to him at some point, and that meant I was probably going to need a handgun. Whether I used it to kill him or simply to intimidate him—say, as a means to overpower him in the first step toward making him disappear—or ended up not using it at all was an unknown I wouldn't be able to resolve until I got over to Rushville and had a better handle on the situation.

But it was better to have a handgun and not need it than to be without one more than 200 miles from home, and wishing I'd brought one along. I was confident A.C. could provide what I needed…he'd done so quite a few times in the past. I was probably one of his best repeat customers, in fact, because— remember Rule Number 3?—I never kept a handgun after a job was finished.

If A.C. ever wondered about any of that—why I kept coming back or what had happened to the guns he'd sold me previously—he never asked. Nor would he. Ours was a relationship based on an unspoken but completely understood no-questions-asked agreement.

Such agreements are often what makes the world go 'round…at least the world of killers-for-hire like myself.

I had a few hours between now and my appointment with A.C. and I wasn't in the mood to tackle anything magazine-related, so I placed another call. I'd been lucky so far this morning—my plan for taking care of Charlie Flanagan was beginning to come together—so I decided to see if my luck would hold in another area.

"Daryl Nelson," said the pleasant, slightly husky female voice who answered.

"Hi, Daryl," I said. "It's Rob Vance. Just wanted to touch base and see if we're still on for dinner this evening." We'd had an email exchange earlier in the week—shortly before I found out that Carlisle Wilson had been charged with the manslaughter of Frank Reynolds, in fact—and had agreed to meet for dinner tonight.

"We are," she said. "What time were you thinking, and where?"

"How about Skip's on Fleur?" I said. "Maybe seven o'clock?"

"That sounds good," she replied. "I'll just meet you there. See you then."

"See you then," I echoed.

Daryl Nelson was a reporter and op-ed writer for the Des Moines *Register* and her office was in the newspaper's downtown headquarters. A few months earlier I'd read one of her op-ed pieces and had been impressed by her writing. She was witty and articulate and—I couldn't deny this—I'd also been impressed by her thumbnail photo at the top of the column. She was a brunette with the dark eyes and strong jawline of actress Marcia Gay Harden. I guessed her age at somewhere in her early 50s, which put her—at least to my thinking—within suitable dating range.

I was intrigued enough to email her at her office (her address was shown at the end of her column) and compliment her on her work. I mentioned that I too was a writer and an editor and as such, I always appreciated good writing. She'd responded the following day, thanking me for my comments, and that led to an ongoing exchange, albeit one that was decidedly sporadic.

We'd had lunch together a couple times but I sensed a bit of stand-offishness on her part, so I hadn't pushed things. This would be our first dinner date, and I was hoping to advance the relationship at least another step or two.

Hey, just because I kill people doesn't mean I can't have the occasional crush on someone.

I GOT TO THE PAWNSHOP a few minutes before two. I walked through the door and tried to avoid clanging the little cowbell at the top, but as always, I was unsuccessful. A.C. was sitting behind the counter reading a gun magazine and he glanced up as I entered.

"A.C.," I said, and he nodded. As I mentioned, he was a man of few words. I glanced around to make sure there was no one else browsing the used stereo equipment, boom boxes, outdated computers, guitars and amplifiers and other miscellaneous merchandise. I didn't see anyone and I wondered if that was because it was a slow afternoon or if A.C. had made sure there wouldn't be anyone there when I stopped by. Maybe both.

I walked to the counter. The center section supporting the cash register was wooden with a glass display case on either side. The case to my left, the side closest to the door, was filled with wristwatches and pieces of vintage jewelry. The case to my right held maybe a dozen handguns, both semiautos and revolvers.

The gun I'd come to buy, I knew, was not on display in this case.

A.C. closed his magazine and stood up from the tall stool on which he'd been sitting. He was a little shorter than I am, maybe five-ten, and as lean as a whippet. I figured his age at either side of forty. He was wearing stonewashed black jeans, a black Hornady t-shirt and a large diver-style wristwatch on a black nylon band. Curiously—or maybe not—he had no tats.

His black hair was cut short in a military fade and his eyes were almost as black as his hair and his clothing. Looking him in the eye always made me feel a little uneasy, like I was staring into a pair of gun barrels. I doubted there was another person on earth who could match him in a thousand-yard stare.

He dropped the magazine on the countertop, and I was pleased to see it was one of those published by TriMedia. I'm always happy to see my colleagues' work appreciated, and I hoped they felt the same about my rag. He leaned both fists on the counter and said, with the slightest trace of a smile, "So?"

For A.C., this was almost verbose. He usually waited for me to speak first and state my needs, and he seldom used words if a nod would suffice. I guessed he must be feeling good today and I wondered if that meant he'd gotten laid last night. I didn't ask.

I also knew his "So?" was short for "So what can I help you with?" and that he wasn't interested in any chitchat. I came right to the point.

"The usual if you have it," I said, smiling, and he nodded.

"A snake six OK or do you need something smaller?"

"A snake six will be fine," I said.

"Come back tonight at seven."

"Could we make it 6:45?" I asked. He raised his

eyebrows—my request was a little unprecedented—and I added, "I have a dinner date and it's someone I don't want to keep waiting."

Again the slight smile and another nod. "Six-forty-five," he said. "And…five."

"I'll see you then," I said. "Thanks." I turned and left.

For five hundred dollars I'd just bought an ice-cold .357 magnum Colt Python with a six-inch barrel. It was a gun I'd used several times before, and I was sure it was more than enough to intimidate the bejesus out of Charlie Flanagan— and/or kill him deader than the proverbial doornail, if it came to that—no matter how much of a badass he turned to be.

After meeting with A.C. I swung by my bank and withdrew five hundred dollars from the LLC account. When I got home I let Preacher out into the back yard and then settled in at the computer and spent a couple hours working on magazine copy. At a little after 5:00 I saved the last story I'd just finished editing, logged off and headed for the shower.

I dressed in black jeans, a gray t-shirt and a darker gray crew neck sweater. I clipped my black-faced Seiko wristwatch with the stainless steel band onto my wrist and glanced at myself in the bedroom mirror. I wasn't quite as monochromatic as A.C. had appeared earlier, but I was close. I thought about changing sweaters but decided to hell with it…Daryl would either like what she saw, or she wouldn't.

I fed Preacher and a few minutes later—it never takes her long to finish a meal—I let her back outside. I still had a little time to kill before heading back to the pawnshop so I sat down at the kitchen table and glanced over the notes I'd jotted down yesterday on the yellow legal pad. I picked up a pen and added a few lines about my upcoming hunt at Hidden Hollow and doing this raised another question.

I'd told Amy Halvorsen I wanted to hunt quail and chukar rather than pheasants. That suggested I should take a different gun than the Ruger—namely, one a little better suited for the smaller birds. I had a sweet Remington Premier over/under in 20 gauge that would be ideal. Like the Ruger, it fit me well and

I shot it well. And because it was a smaller, lighter gun, it was a dream to carry.

It didn't have—ahem—quite the romantic history that my Ruger did, but I'd bought it a few years earlier after using it on a Georgia plantation quail hunt where it had performed almost magically. I had it on loan from Remington at the time and when I returned from the hunt I contacted them and asked if they'd sell it to me. They were happy to do so.

So the Remington earned a slot in my gun vault next to the Ruger, and I shot it often enough on early-season pheasants and other smaller gamebirds to keep in practice. Because of its lighter weight it was actually faster to mount and swing than the Ruger, even if it lacked some of the latter's knockdown power.

With the Remington and the Colt I was soon going to pick up from A.C., I was confident I had the armament matter covered for my upcoming trip to Illinois.

Now all I needed was some background information on Charlie Flanagan that would confirm he deserved what either firearm could deliver.

CHAPTER 15

Dinner with Daryl Nelson was an absolute hoot.

She was already at Skip's when I arrived. Remember, I'd had to make a stop and conduct a transaction on the way. We both laughed a little self-consciously when we first saw each other—she was wearing a thick-ribbed black turtleneck with charcoal slacks and tall black boots. We couldn't have been more color-coordinated if we'd tried, and I immediately noticed how nicely the black turtleneck complemented her dark hair and eyes.

She looked lovely, and I told her so, although I used the word "great." She laughed and said thanks, giving my forearm a quick squeeze. As native Midwesterners we did not do the silly air-cheek-kissing thing that coastals practice, but I'd be lying if I said I wasn't happy with the arm squeeze.

Any standoffishness I'd thought I detected previously on her part had completely vanished by the time we'd finished our first round of drinks—a margarita for her, a Seven-and-Seven for me—and a half-order of onion rings. By the time our dinners arrived we were both laughing at each other's jokes with the kind of enthusiasm that comes from discovering you actually do have a few things in common and the other person is as bright and articulate as you'd hoped.

Of course, having somewhat similar jobs—day jobs, that is—helped. We traded war stories and I was delighted to learn Daryl was no more enamored with the push toward digital than I was. She also shared my opinion that putting a publication's editorial content on a website where anyone could read it for free—now standard practice throughout the magazine and newspaper industry—constituted cannibalism and was a sure way to hurt print copy sales.

She was no more convinced than I was—which is to say, not at all—that this was an effective way to generate reader interest and thereby boost sales or subscriber numbers. In fact, we agreed that it had the opposite effect—why would anyone bother buying or subscribing to a publication when they knew they could go online and read the contents at no charge?

We both mock-growled at this realization but didn't let it sour an otherwise promising evening. It's hard not to fall into a romantic mood—or at least a convivial one—at Skip's. The restaurant is located at the southwest corner of Fleur Drive and Watrous Avenue and is actually an old converted two-story family home, white on the outside and paneled in dark wood on the inside. You enter through a porch on the north side of the house and come into a room with a three-sided bar and a few tables and booths. Adjoining small rooms—you could almost call them alcoves—provide additional seating. If you had to pick a single word to describe the ambience, that word would most likely be "cozy."

And the food is to die for.

Daryl ordered seared ahi tuna and I had a ribeye steak, medium rare. She'd taken no more than four or five bites of her fish before she offered me a taste, which I accepted. Maybe I read too much into these gestures, but it's my theory that when a woman offers you a bite of her food, especially when it happens early in a relationship, it's almost an act of intimacy. Or at the very least, an indication that she's willing to share something of herself and is not an insufferable germophobe.

Those are very good signs.

I reciprocated by cutting off a good-sized bite of my steak and depositing it on the edge of her plate. She immediately cut the piece in half and popped one of the pieces into her mouth. She did this without a bit of hesitation and no complaints about the steak being too rare...another very good sign.

"Mmm, that's good!" she said, and I nodded.

"So is yours," I replied. I'd just swallowed the bite of tuna.

"I might have to order that myself sometime."

"I don't think you'd be disappointed."

"No, I'm sure I wouldn't."

"So tell me," she said, changing the subject. "Isn't this hunting season?"

"Yes, it is. In fact, I was out just a few days ago."

"What were you out for?"

"Pheasants."

"Did you get any?"

"Yes, it was a good afternoon. We got two nice roosters."

"Cool," she said, smiling, and I didn't detect any sarcasm. At one of our earlier lunches she'd told me that although neither she nor anyone in her family hunted, she wasn't opposed to the idea, especially since I wasn't just trophy hunting and I brought the game home and prepared it for the table.

That's a reasonably common attitude among non-hunters (as opposed to anti-hunters) and one with which I could get along quite nicely. I smiled and said, "Maybe I should invite you over for a pheasant dinner."

"Maybe you should," she said, smiling again.

"Consider it done," I said. "I'm going out of town next weekend but let's plan on it after I get back."

"OK," she said. "Where are you going?"

"Over to Illinois for a hunt at a lodge we're thinking of featuring in the magazine." As I said this my guard came up slightly, not so much because of the other matter associated with this hunt—my real reason for going—but because some non-hunters do have a problem with shooting released birds…i.e., birds that are pen-raised and put out shortly before the hunters take to the field. It was a subject that, for the moment at least, I preferred to sidestep.

"Oh, so kind of a busman's holiday?" she asked.

"I guess you could call it that. Hunting is part of my job description, after all."

"Must be rough!" she said, and I had to laugh.

"Yeah, well, somebody's gotta do it," I said, smiling. "The

bad news is, if the place checks out, I'll have to write the feature when I get back…you know, pound the keyboard, do some actual work."

"Awww, poor baby."

Our server, a tall blonde named Keri, arrived at that moment to ask how we were doing and if we needed anything else. I made an open-palms gesture toward Daryl and she said, "I'm going to need a box to take the rest of mine home…Ivy won't forgive me if I don't bring her a couple bites."

"I'd better have a box also," I said. I still had a few bites of ribeye left that I knew Preacher would enjoy.

"Are either of you thinking of dessert?" Keri asked.

We decided to share a piece of key lime pie. One plate, two forks. And another round of drinks.

As Keri left our table I asked, "I'm guessing Ivy is your cat?"

"Good guess. Whenever I mention Ivy, a lot of people think I'm referring to my grandmother because it's kind of an old-fashioned name. But yes, she's my kitty. I named her Ivy because when I got her as a kitten she loved to hide in a big ivy plant I had on my patio and ambush me when I'd walk by."

"Not poison ivy, I hope."

Daryl laughed. "No, although I call her that sometimes when she's naughty. She's twelve years old and definitely rules the household."

"Well, she wouldn't be a cat if she didn't," I said, falling back on the hoary cats-reign-over-all-they-see cliché. "What kind is she?" Although I considered my knowledge of sporting dog breeds to be almost encyclopedic, I couldn't pretend to say the same of cats. I could maybe identify a Siamese if I got lucky.

"She's a golden tabby," Daryl said. She dug into her large black leather handbag and pulled out her phone. (Another plus, she hadn't kept the phone on the table or checked it during dinner.) "Here, I'll show you."

I laughed. "Time to share pictures of our kids?" I said.

"Sure, why not!"

I dug out my own phone and turned it on. After a quick scroll, Daryl handed hers across to me. I took it and checked out the photo. Ivy was a beautiful cat, striped gray and russet, with striking white cheek patches and large gold-green eyes.

"She's beautiful," I said. "I like those white patches on her face."

"Thanks," Daryl replied. "She's my baby." I did a quick scroll on my own phone and found a picture of Preacher I especially liked. It wasn't a field shot—I didn't know if Daryl could appreciate one of Preacher locked up on point—but one where she was sitting with her head cocked, wearing a quizzical expression. I handed the phone to Daryl. "This is my roommate."

Daryl laughed. "She's adorable! I mean...is she a she?"

"Yes," I said. "Her name's Preacher."

"Preacher? And she's a girl?"

"She's named for a Clint Eastwood character. If you ever saw the movie *Pale Rider*, Clint wore a beard that was about the same color as hers, the mix of gray and brown. When I got her as an eight-week-old pup that was the first thing that popped into my head."

"I like it," Daryl said. "What kind is she?"

"German wirehaired pointer."

"So...you must hunt with her?"

"Yes. She's a heckuva pheasant dog." I hoped that didn't sound too boastful.

"Will she be going with you next week?"

"Yes. She's kinda like my American Express card...I never leave home without her. At least, not for a hunting trip."

Daryl smiled. "How old is she?"

"Six."

"She's a cutie."

"Thanks."

Keri returned with our drinks and the key lime pie. We both dug in.

CHAPTER 16

Daryl offered to split the dinner check with me but I refused on the grounds that I'd invited her. I said she could pick up the tab next time. She agreed and that left me feeling good about the way things were playing out. She'd already accepted my invitation to come over to my place for a pheasant dinner and this further confirmed that there would, in fact, be a next time or times. The evening was ending on a promising note.

Or at least, that was my read on it.

I put down enough cash to cover the bill and a healthy tip for Keri, then helped Daryl into her coat, a long, dark gray wool number that hit her about mid-calf. I shrugged into my own hip-length black leather jacket and we headed out to the parking lot.

I walked her to her car, a medium blue Toyota Corolla that was several years old. "Yeah, I know, the unsexiest car on the road," she said as we arrived at the driver's door. "I really need to trade it but as long as still gets me around..."

"Hey, there's nothing wrong with sticking with something reliable," I said in an attempt to be chivalrous. We'd arrived at that awkward moment of do-we-kiss-goodnight-or-don't-we and I decided to go for it. I pulled her into a hug and she came willingly, face upturned and wearing a half-smile.

I kissed her, holding it for a couple seconds but not wanting to overplay things. She reciprocated and when we broke, she laughed and said, "This was a great evening. Let's do this again soon."

"Absolutely," I said.

"And I'm going to hold you to that pheasant dinner you

promised. I want to meet Preacher."

Did this woman know the right buttons to push, or what?

WHEN I GOT HOME PREACHER lazily hauled her big wiry body off the sofa, did the fore-and-aft stretch thing, then trotted to the kitchen door. I let her outside and headed into the office, carrying the plain brown box I had picked up from A.C. en route to my dinner date with Daryl.

The burner I had been using to communicate with James Collins was lying on the table I use as a desk, next to my personal computer. I set the box down, picked up the phone and turned it on, waited a few seconds for it to power up, and saw I had a text.

It read: "Got some info on CF and CW. Call me. – JC"

CF and CW. Charlie Flanagan and Carlyle Wilson. The message I'd been waiting for.

I glanced at my watch. 9:30. Not too late to call, I decided. I dialed James Collins' number.

It rang four times before going to his voice mail. "Hi, this is James. You know the drill. Leave me a message and I'll get back to you. Thanks."

Well, crap. But I guess I shouldn't have been surprised. It was, after all, Friday night and James was probably doing what millions of young singles do in Chicago at the end of a work week. He was out for the evening and apparently engaged in something he didn't want to interrupt. Having just returned from a very pleasant dinner date of my own, I couldn't begrudge him.

But I also couldn't help feeling some impatience. I wanted to keep things moving and get a plan in place, and any information James and his hacker buddies could provide about Charlie Flanagan and Carlyle Wilson would facilitate the process. Or so I hoped.

I disconnected without leaving a message. When James checked his phone he would see that he'd missed a call, and I knew he would recognize the number of my burner. He'd get back to me, I was sure. Or, if I hadn't heard from him by, say, midday tomorrow, I'd try him again.

Out in the backyard Preacher barked sharply a couple times. Raccoons and possums weren't uncommon in our neighborhood, to say nothing of wandering housecats, but I tried to keep Preacher's barking to a minimum to as to not upset the neighbors.

Carrying the burner, I walked back through the kitchen and stepped onto the deck to shush her. Preacher trotted up through the darkness, whining softly. Something had disturbed her but the fact that she'd stopped barking suggested it had moved on.

The burner in my hand rang.

"Hey," I said.

"Hey," James Collins replied. "You got my message."

"Yes, I did. You've got something on those guys in Rushville?"

"I do. But it's pretty standard stuff so I don't know how helpful it's going to be."

"Anything is more than I have right now, so I'll take whatever you can give me."

"OK. But I'm, uh, kind of in the middle of something right now—out for the evening with some friends, actually—and I don't have it right in front of me. Could we maybe postpone this until tomorrow sometime? I know you're anxious to get something going but I could either give you a call in the morning or even text or email it to you. Like I said, it's pretty basic. We're not talking novel-length bios here."

I had to laugh at that. And yes, although I was eager to get started, I could afford to wait another 12 or 14 hours or so. Even if I got the information tonight, there wasn't much I could do with it immediately, and it wasn't the sort of thing I wanted on my mind when I went to bed.

"Sure," I said. "I'll probably be out myself for a couple hours in the morning; why don't you call me at, say, 11:00." I planned to take Preacher for a short hunt and figured that would give me time to knock down a bird or two for her and get back home.

"Sounds good," James Collins said. "I'll talk to you then."

"Sounds good," I echoed, and disconnected.

I headed back inside and returned to the office. I turned off the burner and dropped it on the table and picked up the box I'd placed there a few minutes earlier. It was an Amazon shipping box, about the size a large hardcover book might ship in, but a little deeper. It was also a lot heavier than most hardcover books.

I opened the top flaps and withdrew the .357 Colt Python that A.C. had placed inside, wrapped in grease paper.

With its satin stainless finish and black grips, it was a beautiful piece of hardware. I'd used its twin—correction, twins—several times before and knew it to be a formidable firearm. Although Colt discontinued the line in 2005, the company had just recently reintroduced the Python in an updated version. I'm no expert on handguns, but I knew by its black grips this was one of the early model "snake guns"—the new model has walnut grips.

Not as punishing to shoot as the larger calibers—yes, I've shot a Smith & Wesson Model 29, the .44 magnum made famous by Clint Eastwood in the Dirty Harry movies, and it's no picnic—the .357 still packed a hell of a wallop, more than adequate for my purpose. A number of prominent gun writers, including several of my colleagues, have called the Colt Python the finest revolver ever made.

I pushed the lever that allowed the cylinder to swing free. I flicked the cylinder with its empty chambers and it spun noiselessly. I snapped the cylinder back into place and gently replaced the revolver in its grease paper bed inside the Amazon box.

It pained me a bit to think that in just a few more days, this gun would quite possibly suffer the same fate as others before it—disassembled quickly and the pieces tossed in different directions off a bridge and into a river, the deeper the better. I knew that if the revolver had come with legitimate provenance, it would have been worth at least three or four times more to a collector than what I'd paid A.C. for it.

But I couldn't let that sway my thinking. Once used, it would have to be disposed of immediately.

Rule Number 3.

CHAPTER 17

Rain thwarted my plans to take Preacher out for a short hunt the next morning.

My itinerary follows a well-established pattern on those mornings when we hunt. I get up, let Preacher outside, start a pot of coffee, get dressed and pull together my gear. By the time I'm done loading the SUV—under Preacher's watchful eye, of course—the coffee has finished brewing and I fill a thermos, load Preacher and head over to Hardee's for breakfast.

I usually have either the biscuits and gravy with a side of hash rounds or the low-carb breakfast bowl, again with a side of hash rounds. Preacher is used to the 15- or 20-minute delay while I'm inside eating, and during hunting season it's usually cool enough that I don't have to worry about leaving her confined in the vehicle and getting overheated.

If it's warm enough to be a concern, I don't stop at Hardee's but opt for doughnuts or a couple of slices of breakfast pizza from Casey's instead—food that can be eaten while driving, in other words. Not exactly the breakfast of champions, but I've never been a cold cereal fan.

But on this Saturday in late November I woke to heavy rain that showed no signs of ending anytime soon. When I was younger I'd have donned rain gear and gone out anyway, but I'm getting picky—OK, lazy—in my old age. I don't enjoy hunting in miserable weather, slogging through wet, heavy cover, and I especially dislike getting my gun soaked, requiring a complete stripping, drying and thorough cleaning and oiling after the hunt.

Or to rationalize it another way, I feel like I've reached the age where I no longer have anything to prove and can afford to stay home when the weather is disagreeable.

So I made an executive decision to hole up for the morning and wait for the call from James Collins. I settled in at the kitchen table with a cup of coffee and Michael Connelly's latest Harry Bosch novel and tried to concentrate on the book rather than my upcoming trip to Illinois and the task that awaited me there.

I didn't have much luck. Connelly is one of my favorite authors but my mind kept wandering. And wondering. I couldn't help speculating about the information James Collins had turned up on Charlie Flanagan and Carlyle Wilson. He'd told me the night before that it didn't amount to a whole lot, so I wasn't overly optimistic. But as I'd told him, anything was more than I had, so I was hopeful there'd be something that I could use to start putting together a plan.

The phone rang at 9:15, an hour and 45 minutes earlier than the time we'd agreed on. I grabbed it in the kitchen, one of the old landline extensions that doesn't have a caller ID window. As I picked it up I realized this couldn't be James Collins, as he didn't have my home number and could only call my burner.

"Hello?"

"Hey, Rob? It's Mike." It was Mike Stevenson, a good friend and hunting buddy. There was a catch in his voice, almost like he was trying to hold back a sob.

"Hey," I said. "What's up?" I knew there was something serious going on.

"Oh, man," he said. "It's Beaver. He died last night."

"What?" I said. Beaver was Mike's chocolate Labrador. "What happened?"

"He fell asleep last night on the living room rug while we were watching TV. When I got up to let him outside before bedtime, he didn't get up. He died in his sleep while we were all right there. He didn't make a sound or do anything, just passed away while he was sleeping. I had no idea there was anything wrong."

"Oh, man, I'm really sorry to hear that. How are Janice and the kids?"

"Torn up. Like me."

"I'm sure. Is there anything I can do?"

"Not really. I've already taken him to the vet to be cremated...in fact, I just got back. I just wanted to let you know what happened."

"I appreciate that. And again, I'm really sorry. Tell Janice and the kids I'm thinking of them. I know how much they loved him."

"I'll tell them. We're all kind of in shock this morning. We keep expecting to see him or hear him, you know, like he'll come walking in from the next room or something."

"That's understandable."

"Yeah, and I imagine that will continue for some time."

"Probably. How old was he?"

"He just turned eleven a few weeks ago. We got him as a pup for Christmas when Jessica was two." Jessica was Mike and Janice's oldest daughter.

"I remember that. He looked like a little brown bear cub."

"That's right." His voice broke and I realized I might have just put my foot in my mouth with my bear cub remark. Mike probably didn't need to be reminded right now of how cute Beaver had been as a puppy.

"Well, again, let me know if there's anything I can do," I said. Thinking, *could I sound any more lame?*

"Thanks. Will do." Mike hung up and I knew he and his family were in for a rough day. A rough several days, in fact. Probably weeks.

Losing a loved dog—and I've lost several over my lifetime—is unquestionably one of life's biggest heartaches. Anyone who would counter this claim with the comment, "But it was just a dog," is deserving of...well, maybe not the kind of retribution I occasionally mete out, but a serious ass-kicking, at the very least.

I walked into the dining room that doubles as my library—the walls are lined with bookshelves—and pulled a volume of

Rudyard Kipling's poetry off the shelf. I checked the table of contents and turned to "The Power of the Dog" on page 594. I re-read the six-stanza poem and found myself nodding along with the sentiment.

In those six stanzas Kipling perfectly captured the feelings of heartbreak that accompany the loss of a devoted canine companion. His final rhetorical question—*So why in Heaven (before we are there)/Should we give our hearts to a dog to tear?*—reminded me of another favorite quotation, this one by Robert Louis Stevenson.

Stevenson wrote, *You think there will not be dogs in heaven? I tell you, they will be there long before any of us.*

Amen, brother.

I REPLACED THE KIPLING BOOK on the shelf and looked at my watch. It was just past 9:30, so I still had almost an hour and a half to kill before James Collins called. I looked out the kitchen window and saw that the rain had slacked off to a slight drizzle.

I didn't have enough time to load up my gear and squeeze in a hunt, even if I was willing to get my gun wet and do the necessary stripping and cleaning afterwards. But I had more than enough time to take Preacher for a ramble out at the lake. I gave her a quick whistle to summon her off the sofa, then I headed down to the basement for my rain gear.

She met me in the kitchen when I came back upstairs. "C'mon, dog," I said. "We need some exercise so I can clear my head." I shrugged into my hooded slicker and grabbed a cap off the rack behind the back door. Preacher stood wagging her tail, ready for whatever adventure I had in mind, regardless of the rain.

Dogs are like that.

CHAPTER 18

I spent most of our time out at the lake reminiscing.

With Preacher ranging through the wet cover ahead of me, I ambled along recalling many happy memories of Mike and Beaver. The four of us—Mike, Beaver, Preacher and I—had hunted together dozens of times. Although the dogs' styles differed when hunting pheasants—Preacher was a pointing dog and Beaver was a flusher—they'd proven surprisingly compatible when hunted in the same cover.

Mike and I had developed a system that worked well for all the players. Preacher was by nature the wider ranging of the two dogs, often hunting a hundred yards or more out in front of the guns. But like all well-trained flushing dogs, Beaver never ventured beyond gun range; he was more meticulous in his search than Preacher was in hers, and with his sturdier build he was inclined to cover less ground anyway.

Or to put it another way, Beaver would thoroughly sift through the cover that Preacher often skirted or breezed past on her way to a distant objective—say, a fence line or shelterbelt. If Beaver put up a rooster in front of either Mike or me, one of us would shoot it and he'd make the retrieve.

If, on the other hand, Preacher pointed a bird at some distance, I'd call "Point!" and Mike would call Beaver to heel. The three of us would advance to where Preacher had the bird pinned and then, depending on which way it flushed, Mike or I would take the shot and I'd send Preacher for the retrieve...that is, if we managed to down the bird.

Worked in this manner, both dogs got their share of bird

encounters and retrieves, and neither seemed inclined toward jealousy. After the first couple seasons, they worked together as smoothly in the uplands as Mike and I did ourselves.

We also hunted waterfowl together, and that was where Beaver really shone. Preacher was an adequate duck dog—German wirehairs were developed as all-purpose hunters and were expected to retrieve from water as well as on land—but she wasn't in Beaver's league when it came to marking long falls, handling diving cripples or taking a line for a lengthy blind retrieve across rough water, where Beaver was truly in his element.

As we did in the uplands, Mike and I endeavored to alternate retrieves between the two dogs as much as was feasible, sending one to make the retrieve while the other dog remained in the blind, honoring. But sometimes we changed up the order depending on where the ducks fell; Beaver was the dog we always sent for the long falls while Preacher got most of the easy ones we dropped close.

All in all, it was about as ideal a partnership, both human and canine, as anyone could hope for. I hadn't loved Beaver like Mike and his family did, of course, but I'd *liked* him as a buddy and hunting companion, and I was going to miss him.

I was pretty sure Preacher would too.

WE MADE A BIG CIRCUIT through a field of switchgrass, following a wide path that the caretakers kept mowed for hikers throughout the spring, summer and fall...that is, I stuck to the path while Preacher quartered through the grass. We saw four deer standing along the edge of a patch of woods, a big-bodied eight-point buck and three does.

Seeing the buck reminded me of Frank Reynolds and the buck he'd been preparing to shoot when I killed him. I glanced at my watch and noted it was 10:20. I called to Preacher and we swung back to the graveled turnout where I'd parked. We loaded up and headed home.

It was 10:45 when I stepped into the kitchen. Preacher had already trotted downstairs to the old cloth sofa in the basement;

this was her lair when she came in wet from the field. She'd already shaken most of the water out of her coat and she would finish rubbing herself dry on the sofa —no amount of scolding would prevent her from doing so—then curl up and nap for an hour or so. Her routine was well established.

I took off my rain slicker and hung it over the back of a kitchen chair. I poured a cup of cold coffee and stuck it in the microwave to reheat. I glanced at the clock again, willing the phone to ring.

It did so at 10:55. James Collins was prompt. I picked up the phone and said hello.

"Hey," he said. "I know I'm a few minutes early but I hope that's OK. I know you want this information so you can...uh...start working on a plan."

"That's fine," I said. "I've been waiting."

"OK. Well, like I said last night, it's pretty basic stuff. I don't know if it's going to be helpful but I'll give you what we got."

"Sounds good. Shoot."

He laughed. I halfway expected him to make some sort of joking remark or a pun, maybe, but he didn't. "All right," he said. "For starters, Carlyle Wilson and Charlie Flanagan both grew up in Rushville and they're the same age, 32. They graduated from Rushville High School—they're called the Rushville Rockets, by the way—in 2005. Neither one of them was an honor student, but they both played football. Flanagan was a tackle and Wilson was a tailback."

I was making notes on my legal pad as James Collins talked. "Hold on a sec," I said. "You're getting ahead of me." I jotted down the positions then said, "OK, go ahead."

"Well, that's all I know about their academic and athletic careers," he said. "It doesn't look like either one of them went to college anywhere, and neither of them served in the military. Wilson now works at the Pella Window factory in Macomb, and Flanagan is—you'll love this—a guard at the men's prison in Mt. Sterling."

I laughed. "So Flanagan is a screw," I said. "Why are we

not surprised."

"Right," James Collins replied. "And that's the only employment we could find any record of for him, so he's apparently worked there for quite some time. Oh, and he was married for three years to a woman named Jolene Mitchell—one of their classmates—but they're divorced. No kids."

"OK," I said. "What about Wilson?"

"Never married, the best we can tell."

"All right," I said. "And they both still live in Rushville?"

"Yes. Macomb, where Wilson works, is about 30 miles away, and Mt. Sterling, where the prison is where Flanagan's a guard, is about 20 miles in the opposite direction."

"What about family?"

"Both of Flanagan's parents are dead. We managed to turn up an old obituary...they were killed in a car accident eight years ago."

"Any siblings?"

"None for Flanagan. He's an only child. Carlyle Wilson has a sister named Heather; she's married and lives in Iowa. Their mother is dead but their father is still living; he lives there in Rushville also."

"His name?" You never knew what tidbit might be useful.

"Benjamin Wilson."

"Got it. Anything else?"

"That's about it. There just isn't a lot online about these guys. Oh yeah, one more thing—Carlyle Wilson has a Facebook page. Charlie Flanagan does not. Wilson's page looks pretty typical—the usual bunch of friends, photos and so on, but I don't know if there's anything there you'd find useful. Sorry we couldn't turn up more."

"No need to apologize," I said. "This is actually pretty good. You've given me some stuff to work with, anyway. If nothing else, this gives me a little better idea of the kind of guys they both are, including the info about their families. That's a big help."

"So what will you do now?" James Collins asked.

I hesitated for a moment before answering. I'm always

reluctant to tell clients too much about my actual plans; the old "loose lips sink ships" saying applies here. But James Collins had so far proven himself to be trustworthy—at least as far as our business transaction was concerned—so giving him a general idea probably wouldn't hurt.

"I'm going to be heading over there in a few days," I said. "While I'm there I'll check out the town, do a little scouting around and see if I can maybe bump into Charlie Flanagan. I'm hoping that will give me a better feel for what's going on and why Flanagan claims Wilson confessed to him. Then it will just be a matter of figuring out how to best rectify the situation."

To his credit, James Collins didn't ask me to elaborate.

CHAPTER 19

After hanging up I sat at the kitchen table sipping lukewarm coffee and reviewing the notes I'd just made.

James Collins had apologized for not coming up with more information on Charlie Flanagan and Carlyle Wilson but as I'd told him, he'd actually provided me with some pretty good stuff...enough to help me form some initial impressions at least, and that was a start.

Offhand, I couldn't see anything helpful or particularly telling about Carlyle Wilson working at the Pella Windows factory in Macomb, except for the somewhat ironic coincidence that the company's headquarters was located in Pella, Iowa, about 40 minutes from my home in Des Moines.

Small world.

But I did find it interesting that Charlie Flanagan was a prison guard. When James Collins relayed that piece of information I'd responded with a gut reaction and referred to Flanagan as a screw—an unflattering nickname, for sure. Still, my reaction notwithstanding, I generally try to avoid stereotyping people sight unseen. Tempting though it was to picture Flanagan as a swaggering, uniformed bully just looking for an excuse to bust some prisoner's head, as yet I had no real reason to characterize him that way.

Or did I?

There was still the matter of him bearing false witness against Wilson...that is, assuming he'd fabricated the whole story about Wilson's confession. So far I had no hard evidence on that matter, either. But my gut told me that Wilson hadn't confessed as Flanagan claimed, and I did have evidence—OK, firsthand knowledge—that Wilson hadn't killed Frank Reynolds.

I took another look at my notes.

The two men had apparently known each other all their lives. They'd both grown up in Rushville, were the same age and had been classmates throughout their school years. They'd both been on their high school football team, the Rushville Rockets.

According to James Collins, Charlie Flanagan had been a tackle, Carlyle Wilson a tailback. That suggested Charlie Flanagan was the bigger of the two, probably a large, powerful guy with a fondness for flattening opponents. Wilson, on the other hand, was probably smaller and quicker.

Significance?

Again, it was tempting to imagine Flanagan as some hulking bully, the kind of guy who might have terrorized his smaller classmates. I let my mind follow that train of thought for a moment.

In his classic work, *Of Wolves and Men*, naturalist Barry Lopez describes the "conversation of death" that occasionally takes place between wolves and caribou in the Arctic. When a pack of wolves encounters a herd of caribou, Lopez notes, the animals exchange looks or stares and these looks often determine the outcome of the encounter. Specifically, whether the wolf pack will attack and possibly kill one or more of the caribou or will simply choose to move on without attacking.

Lopez suggests, and other naturalists have subsequently supported this idea, that in some instances the caribou—or at least certain individuals within the herd—may signal a weakness or willingness to become prey, and this is what triggers an attack by the wolves. Should the caribou not signal this willingness, the wolves—especially if they've recently fed and aren't hungry—may simply decide an attack isn't worth the effort, and bypass the herd and move on.

I've long suspected similar "conversations" take place every day in the hallways and classrooms of our high schools.

The bullies—and yes, every school has them—quickly learn how to scan a herd of classmates and determine who's willing—or at least the most susceptible—to becoming a victim. When they identify that person or persons, they move in for the attack.

I wondered if Charlie Flanagan had been that kind of bullying kid, scanning his classmates for potential victims, and if Carlyle Wilson had been one of those victims. And, more to the point, I wondered if Flanagan was still victimizing Wilson all these years later and the alleged confession was just the latest manifestation.

Of course I also realized all of my speculation along these lines could be wrong. For all I knew, Charlie Flanagan might treat prison inmates with respect and rescue newborn kittens from burning buildings. My gut told me otherwise, but it had been wrong before. I knew I wouldn't be able to fill in any of the blanks until I got to Rushville and did some more digging.

I hoped I could find what I needed when I got there and do so without attracting too much attention in the process.

PART 2: HOMICIDE, JUSTIFIED

An investigation was not simply a matter of historical research...It was an act of faith both in one's own capacities and in the possibility of justice in a world that had made justice subservient to the rule of law.

-John Connolly, *The Wolf in Winter*

CHAPTER 20

The five-hour drive from Des Moines to Rushville gave me the opportunity to spend some quality time with several of my favorite ladies—Belinda Carlisle, Natalie Cole, Diana Krall, Loreena McKennitt, Cher and k.d. lang. And oh yeah, the late Lesley Gore. I have her greatest hits CD and it brings back a lot of fond childhood memories, even if many of the lyrics are awfully corny by contemporary standards.

The drive also gave me plenty of time to contemplate what lay ahead. Beyond checking in and hunting at Hidden Hollow with Preacher, I still didn't have much of a game plan. After talking with James Collins I'd logged onto Facebook—I have a page set up under a fictitious name—and pulled up Carlyle Wilson's page but it hadn't told me much. He had 46 friends, several of whom I assumed were relatives because they shared his last name. The rest were probably buddies, coworkers and former classmates. Charlie Flanagan wasn't among them, which wasn't surprising because he didn't have a Facebook page, according to James Collins.

Wilson's page hadn't been updated for a while; the most recent post had been made five months earlier and showed a photo—an obvious selfie—of Wilson wearing an old Chicago Cubs baseball cap and holding up a good-sized largemouth bass. He'd posted, "Caught this morning at Schuy-Rush," which I assumed was the name of a nearby lake. There were a couple of congratulatory replies from friends, but nothing more.

The most interesting thing about Wilson's page was his profile photo, a close-up of him cheek to cheek with a good looking dark-haired young woman, presumably his girlfriend. They were both smiling at the camera. Wilson had sandy hair cut fairly short and looked like a pleasant sort of guy. He certainly didn't look like a killer.

I did a quick scroll through his friends and found a photo of a woman who looked like the one in his profile photo. Her name was Allie Marshall. I clicked on her page and scrolled through her friends and one name and photo jumped out at me—Amy Halvorsen, who operated Hidden Hollow with her husband Mitch.

I wasn't sure how significant this was, though. Rushville was a small town, so it was likely that many of its residents were friends or at least acquaintances. If Amy Halvorsen and Allie Marshall had been classmates, it wasn't surprising that they were friends on Facebook. I briefly considered calling James Collins back and asking him to do some digging on Allie Marshall but decided against it, figuring I could bird-dog this myself when I got over there.

As I'd told James Collins, I figured I'd spend some time looking around Rushville and trying to get a line on Charlie Flanagan; maybe pay a visit to the Rushville Tap one evening and hope to catch some gossip about Flanagan and Carlyle Wilson. It might be interesting to hear what the locals had to say about the whole matter, especially whether they thought Wilson was guilty.

But I would have to be careful not to tip my hand and betray too much interest. If things played out the way I was expecting, I didn't want anyone associating my visit with Charlie Flanagan's subsequent demise.

Bottom line, I was just going to have to play things by ear and see what developed.

I LEFT DES MOINES at a few minutes after ten on that Friday morning. I'd packed most of my gear, including the 20-gauge Remington Premier and the cold .357, the night before. At the last minute on Friday morning, I decided to take along the Ruger Red Label as a backup gun, as well.

Preacher, of course, needed no special prompting to jump into the cargo space of the SUV and settle on her dog pillow. She'd supervised the stowing of the gear and knew a hunting trip was at hand. I wondered if, once the Halvorsens had met her and succumbed to her charm, they'd allow me to let her sleep in my room at the lodge rather than relegating her to a kennel. This had happened before at other facilities.

Earlier in the week I'd called Mike Stevenson to touch base and see how he and his family were getting along after Beaver's death. Not surprisingly, they were still grieving. I asked Mike if he had plans to get another Lab anytime soon.

"Janice and I have talked about it, and of course the kids are saying they want a puppy for Christmas, but I don't think that's gonna happen," he said. "They're all in school right now and with Janice and me both working full-time, there's no one home during the day and that would make starting a young pup kind of a tough proposition, especially with housebreaking and all. Leaving a puppy alone that long during the day wouldn't be fair to the pup."

"What about a young started dog…say around a year old?"

"That might be a possibility, I guess, but I gotta tell you, right now my heart's just not in it. Beaver's death really knocked the wind out of my sails and I can't quite get my mind around the idea of replacing him. I mean, I know I'll never be able to *replace* him, but…aw, hell, you know what I mean."

"Yeah, I do," I said. "Beaver's gonna be a tough act to follow, and I think you're smart not to rush it."

"That's how I feel right now."

"Well, then you're doing the right thing by waiting."

"Yeah. I know we'll have another Lab eventually, just not right away. But I like your idea of a started dog…that would probably work out best for all of us. And I know the kids will love whatever we end up with, regardless, even if it's not a little pup."

"I'm sure that's true."

"Yeah. Well, who knows; maybe something will turn up and I'll feel more like taking the plunge. If you hear of anything, let me know."

"Will do."

We hung up and I knew this Christmas was going to be bittersweet for Mike and his family. But I couldn't fault Mike's reasoning. Much as his kids might be clamoring for a puppy, the timing just didn't sound right. Young pups require a lot of attention, and as Mike had noted, he and his family weren't in a position just then to provide that attention. It was to his credit that he'd recognized this.

Still, I also knew that any dog that eventually wound up as a member of the Stevenson household was going to be in for a very good life. Mike was the kind of owner all dogs should have—firm but loving, responsible and conscientious. In all the years I'd known Mike and we'd hunted together I'd never known him to do anything abusive to Beaver or any other dog.

I hoped people might say the same about me.

WE ROLLED INTO RUSHVILLE at a little before 3:30 that Friday afternoon. Except for a quick stop at the Casey's in New London, Iowa to fill up and let Preacher pee in the grassy area next to the parking lot, we'd driven straight through. While at the Casey's I'd also taken a few minutes to skarf down a quick pork tenderloin sandwich and use the restroom. Then we hit the road again.

We crossed the Mississippi River at Burlington and picked up Highway 67 at Monmouth, Illinois. We took 67 south through Macomb (where both Frank Reynolds and I had stayed a few weeks earlier), passed through the small town of Industry, and kept heading south to Rushville.

I wanted to get a look at the town before heading out to Hidden Hollow and checking in. We weren't scheduled to hunt until the following day anyway so there was no big rush about getting to Hidden Hollow; I remembered that Amy Halvorsen had invited me to have dinner at the lodge that evening but that wasn't until 6:30. If we got to the lodge an hour or so prior to dinner, that would give me plenty of time to unload the SUV and get Preacher settled in the kennel.

Coming into the town on Highway 67, we passed the Rushville-Industry High School, home of the Rockets. We made a left turn at the intersection of Highway 24—also known as Clinton Street—and headed toward the downtown area. I followed the signs toward the business district, passing the red-brick Sarah D. Culbertson Memorial Hospital, and in another few blocks we came to the town square.

I remembered that Rushville was the county seat of Schuyler County, and it looked like hundreds of other small towns throughout the Midwest. The streets surrounding the square were paved with red brick, and most of the buildings, including the courthouse, were also red brick, with the exception of a tan brick post office. The courthouse was topped with a clock tower that was inscribed 1881. A couple of workmen were stringing Christmas lights on a white gazebo-style pavilion in the park area of the square.

We circled the square, the brick pavement causing the SUV's tires to rumble faintly. Preacher shifted around on her pillow in the cargo area while I checked out the storefronts. There was an Ace Hardware, a Subway sandwich shop, a corner drugstore, a barber shop—a typical assortment of businesses, in other words. There were also several bars, including the Rushville Tap, where Charlie Flanagan claimed to have heard Carlyle Wilson confess to killing Frank Reynolds.

Completing the circuit of the square, I saw the police station and jail located just behind the courthouse and I guessed that was where Carlyle Wilson was being held, unless he had made bail. I wondered if there was any way to find this out.

I glanced at the dashboard clock and saw that it was now ten minutes to four. I still had plenty of time before we needed to check in at Hidden Hollow and I considered stopping in at the Rushville Tap for a quick beer. Maybe, I thought, I could catch some of the gossip I was hoping to hear about Charlie Flanagan and Carlyle Wilson.

I decided against it. I didn't want to show up at Hidden Hollow with beer on my breath and get off on the wrong foot with Amy Halvorsen. As the old saying goes, you only get one chance to make a first impression, and I wanted that impression to be as positive as possible—I needed to appear professionally interested in their operation as if I were evaluating it for coverage in the magazine (which I was) and not just some casual hunter who'd driven over to have a good time and shoot a bunch of birds.

Something also told me it would be a good idea to not let my face be seen around town too much. I was definitely planning to visit the Rushville Tap and maybe a few of the other local businesses as well, but I didn't want to make myself overly recognizable or memorable. If Charlie Flanagan came to a bad end—and I had a strong feeling that's where we were headed—I didn't want townspeople recalling "that magazine guy" who'd been hanging around town for a few days when it happened.

"Low-key," I reminded myself. "You have to keep this visit low-key."

Preacher whined and I glanced in the rearview mirror to see her big bristly head looking over the backseat toward me. "OK," I said to her. "Let's go get checked in and see what the place looks like."

CHAPTER 21

Hidden Hollow was indeed located in a hollow that was hidden from the road.

A large sign with the silhouettes of a flying pheasant and a whitetail buck and the printed legend, "Hidden Hollow Hunt Club, Mitch & Amy Halvorsen, Proprietors," was posted at the entrance to the lane leading back to the lodge. When I turned off the highway a rooster pheasant dashed across the lane in front of our vehicle, causing me to tap the brakes, and for a second I couldn't help wondering if this had been arranged by the Halvorsens as a welcome and a harbinger of good things to come.

It hadn't, of course; an occasional lone rooster skulking next to a road near a shooting preserve—usually a bird left over from a previous hunt or an escapee from the bird pens—is nothing unusual, and seeing this one was, I knew, simply a coincidence. Still, I couldn't deny it lifted my spirits and apparently Preacher's as well. I heard her whine and glanced in the rearview mirror to see her standing and looking out the side window, focused on the spot where the rooster had disappeared in the tall grass alongside the lane.

"Take it easy," I said. "We'll be going after some birds tomorrow. Just be patient." Preacher whined again and I smiled at her eagerness.

The lane wound down through a stand of hardwood timber for a little over a quarter mile before coming out into an open area of a couple acres, dominated by the handsome two-story log lodge I'd seen in the photos on the website. A large red barn sat off to the right, along with a clean, modern-looking kennel building and two equipment sheds. A Yamaha ATV sat parked in front of one of the sheds and I noticed a couple of slatted bird crates, held in place with bungee cords, behind the driver's seat.

Beyond the barn the lane continued off into the woods and I guessed it probably led to the preserve's bird pens, which typically would be located some distance away from the lodge and main area of operation. Keeping the birds at a remote location is standard practice at hunting preserves, as it minimizes human contact so when hunting guests go afield, the birds perform more like their wild counterparts.

A circular driveway branched off the lane and ran up to the lodge's covered front porch, with a graveled parking area just beyond. Three other vehicles, all SUVs, were already parked there. I pulled the Equinox into a space next to a dark blue Ford Expedition, got out and walked up the short flight of steps to the wide porch, upon which sat five or six all-weather lounging chairs. I pushed open the heavy front door and entered the lodge.

A reception desk sat to the left of the entrance and a lounge area, complete with dark brown leather sofas and recliners, a pool table and self-serve bar, was located to the right. The entire room was paneled in knotty pine and several impressive whitetail head mounts adorned the walls. In one corner, close to a fieldstone fireplace, a full-body mount of a coyote leaped at a flushing pheasant.

A huge flat-screen TV was mounted on the wall above the fireplace. On the far side of the room a hallway ran back through the center of the lodge where, presumably, guest rooms and the kitchen and dining area were located. Next to this hallway, a staircase with a polished pole railing led up to additional guest rooms on the second floor.

A tall, attractive woman with shoulder-length dark hair, wearing a long-sleeved khaki shirt with the Hidden Hollow logo above the breast pocket, stood behind the reception desk. The sleeves of the shirt were rolled up to her elbows and she held a pen in her right hand. She smiled at me and said, "Good afternoon."

"Good afternoon," I replied, smiling in return and thinking she looked familiar. "I'm Rob Vance. I believe you have a reservation for me."

"Yes, we do. We've been expecting you. I'm Allie." When she said her name the synapses fired and I recognized her as the woman I'd seen with Carlyle Wilson in the profile photo on his Facebook page.

"Nice to meet you, Allie," I said, hoping to keep any trace of surprise off my face.

"Nice to meet you also. Amy said you were bringing your dog…where is she?"

Props to Amy for remembering Preacher and passing along the information. I said, "I left her outside in my vehicle. I wasn't sure if she'd be allowed in the lodge. But I do need to let her out to stretch her legs. Is there an area where I can do that?"

"Just beyond the parking area in the grass is fine."

"OK, thanks. I saw the kennel building…which run should I put her in?"

"I have her in run number four," Allie said. "There are numbers on the gate to each run. So after you let her stretch her legs you can walk her over to the kennel building, or drive over, and get her settled. There's a water bucket in the run and we also have feed dishes if you need one."

"Thanks, but I brought hers from home," I said.

Allie smiled. "Do you want to take care of her now or shall we go ahead and complete your registration?"

"Let me get Preacher squared away and then I'll come back in," I said. "She's been riding for about three hours without a break so I'm sure she needs to pee."

Allie laughed. "That's fine. I'll see you in a few minutes."

THE KENNELS WERE CLEAN and well-kept, with concrete-floored runs enclosed by chain link panels, and while I'd have preferred to have Preacher stay in my room with me, I was confident she'd be comfortable in her temporary quarters. We'd done this quite a few times before at other facilities and she knew the drill.

I unlatched the gate to run number four and Preacher trotted in. She circled the run a couple times, sniffing at the fencing and the entrance to her sleeping area, which was located inside the building. The runs on either side were empty and I wondered if that meant they were unoccupied or if their occupants were currently in the field.

I confirmed Preacher's water bucket was full and latched the kennel gate. "You be a good girl and I'll be back in a little while to feed you," I told her. She wagged her tail a few times as though to say, "I'll be fine." I turned and headed back over to the lodge.

When I entered, Allie was behind the bar, restocking a tall glass-fronted cooler with longneck bottles of Bud Light. She looked over, smiled and said, "Be with you in a sec."

"No problem," I said, and glanced around the room again. As lodges went, this was one of the nicer ones, well-appointed and comparable to some of the top-drawer facilities I'd hunted at in South Dakota and a few other western states. It gave every indication of being an expensive operation and I wondered if it was profitable.

"This is a very nice place you have here," I said as Allie finished her restocking task and came back to the reception desk.

"Thanks," she said. "We're proud of it. We've been open for about five years. Mitch and Amy put a lot of work into this place to get it going and it's finally starting to pay off."

"Amy is who I talked to when I called to make my reservation."

"Right. She's my sister. I've worked here for about three years now. We're always filled up during deer season but we're also starting to attract more and more bird hunters like yourself. We have two other parties of bird hunters here right now; you'll meet them at dinner tonight."

"Look forward to it," I said. "I think Amy said dinner was at 6:30?" I was still assimilating this latest revelation, that Allie and Amy were sisters.

"That's right." She gestured over her shoulder. "If you just follow that hallway toward the back of the building you'll come to the dining room. You're also welcome to help yourself at the bar before dinner; there's usually an informal happy hour here in the lounge for anyone who's staying here."

"Sounds good," I said. "You said there are two other parties here right now?"

"Yes. A father and son down from Chicago and another group of three guys over from Peoria. They're all out in the field right now; Mitch is guiding the father and son and Matt is guiding the Peoria group." She glanced at the wall clock behind the bar. "They should be finishing up and coming in anytime now."

"I look forward to meeting them," I said. Mr. Congenial.

"They're looking forward to meeting you also."

"Oh?" I said. I tried not to look concerned.

"Amy told them at lunch about you, that you were coming over to possibly write a story about our place for your magazine."

"Well, I hope they're not expecting some kind of celebrity," I said, playing for nonchalance but wishing Amy hadn't been quite so chatty. "I'm about as far removed from that as you can get."

"Oh, I don't think they're expecting a celebrity, necessarily. But they all said they knew your magazine so I think they're just a little curious—you know, to see if you can actually do what you write about." She laughed as she said this last and I smiled. It wasn't the first time I'd encountered this attitude.

"Meaning, can I actually hit anything with a shotgun?" I said.

"I'm sure that's part of it," she said. "That, plus they want to see your dog."

I smiled. "Really? She's not a celebrity, either."

"You might be surprised. When Amy told them about you, one of the Peoria guys nodded and said something like, yeah, he hunts with a big German wirehair. See, they know about you *and* your dog."

"Sheesh," I said, shaking my head. "Our fame precedes us."

AFTER I'D FILLED OUT THE REGISTRATION FORMS, including one for a five-day non-resident Illinois hunting license, Allie showed me to my room. It was on the second floor and had twin beds and a small bathroom with sink, stool and shower stall.

Like the rest of the lodge, the room was paneled in knotty pine. There was no closet, but there were plenty of brass hooks to hang clothes and gear. A flying pheasant mount hung on one wall, opposite a framed Robert Abbett print of an English setter on point. On the nightstand between the two beds stood a small shaded lamp with a base made of upright interwoven deer antlers. Above the nightstand was the room's single window, covered with a curtain that featured—you guessed it—flying gamebirds.

"Very nice," I said, glancing around.

"Thanks," Allie said. "I hope you'll be comfortable. Towels and washcloths are in the cabinet under the sink, along with extra TP, etcetera."

"Thanks," I said. "I'm sure I'll be fine."

"Well, just let us know if there's anything else you need. Otherwise, we'll see you at 6:30 for dinner. Speaking of which, I need to get down to the kitchen and give Amy a hand."

"OK," I said. "Thanks again."

CHAPTER 22

After Allie left to help Amy prepare dinner, I went back downstairs and drove my SUV across the driveway to the kennel building. I stepped inside the building through the door next to the kennel runs and went down the row of runs to number four. Preacher had come in from the outer run and stood wagging her tail, no doubt anticipating being fed.

The kennel runs extended into the building for about eight feet, and in the corner of each was a platform raised a few inches off the floor and surrounded on each side by a six-inch rail. The floor of the platform in Preacher's run was bare wood but a large plastic bin labeled "Cedar Shavings…Help Yourself" stood at the end of the row of kennel runs. A two-gallon–bucket stood next to the bin.

The shavings, I knew, were to be used for bedding in the raised platforms. The platforms in a couple of the other runs were filled with shavings but the rest were bare, like Preacher's. The two with shavings were presumably the kennels where the dogs of the other two hunting parties were housed.

I'd brought an old stuffed dog bed of Preacher's from home so I decided to forego the shavings, but I made a mental note to mention this amenity in the story I wrote for the magazine. Supplying fresh bedding material for guests' dogs was one more indication of a well-run, class operation, and worth noting.

I returned to the SUV and carried the dog bed and Preacher's bin of dog food inside. I dropped the dog bed onto the platform in her run, then dished up her food and placed it in her run as well. Never a finicky eater regardless of her surroundings, she immediately fell to.

I pulled the SUV back across the driveway to the parking space outside the lodge, grabbed my two large duffel bags and an old briefcase and went inside and up to my room. It was a few minutes past five, which gave me plenty of time to unpack and take a shower before I headed back downstairs for the "informal happy hour" Allie said usually took place before dinner.

STANDING UNDER THE WARM SPRAY of water, I pondered the fact that Allie Marshall and Amy Halvorsen were sisters. I wondered if Marshall was their maiden name, and whether any of this had any significance beyond the coincidental. It was easy to succumb to the temptation to go chasing after these wild hares, but I couldn't see how that would help me figure out what to do about Charlie Flanagan.

Based on what I'd seen on Carlyle Wilson's Facebook page, I could reasonably assume that Allie and Carlyle were involved in a romantic relationship. If this were the case, Allie had to be worried about Carlyle's incarceration and his upcoming trial. She hadn't appeared distraught when I'd talked to her, but of course, she wouldn't—welcoming Hidden Hollow clients in a friendly fashion would be a basic job responsibility and she wouldn't let her private fears or problems interfere with doing that.

Still, if the subject of Wilson's trial could be broached, she could undoubtedly provide more insight into the circumstances than I'd been able to glean so far. Only problem was, I couldn't think of a way to accomplish this without tipping my hand. I was ostensibly at Hidden Hollow in my capacity as editor of *American Wingshot* and in that role I wouldn't know anything about Wilson's predicament. Unless someone else raised the subject, I was pretty much stuck on first.

I toweled off, dressed and headed downstairs. Several middle-aged men, presumably the members of the other hunting parties Allie had mentioned, were gathered at the bar. I walked up and said, "Good evening. This looks like a place where a guy might be able to get a beer."

"It is indeed," said a fellow in a checked Columbia shirt. He appeared older than the others in the group. "Help yourself."

I moved around the bar and scanned the rows of longnecks visible through the glass door of the tall cooler. "One of these will work," I said, pulling a Sam Adams Winter Lager from the cooler. I popped the cap with the opener lying on the bar. The fellow in the checked shirt extended his hand to shake.

"Dave Larson," he said, nodding toward a younger man a couple of feet away. "This is my son, Michael." Michael stepped forward to shake hands also.

"Rob Vance," I said, and they both smiled.

"You're the magazine guy," Dave said.

"I'm the magazine guy," I repeated. "Drove over this afternoon from Des Moines."

"We're from Chicago. Came down last night and hunted this morning and this afternoon. This is a great place."

"It looks like it," I agreed. "Is this your first time here?"

"No, we were here last year also. Liked it so much we decided to come back. Nice accommodations, great food, strong-flying birds. The guides bust their tails to get you into plenty of birds, which is great for your dog if you bring one."

"That's good to hear; I did bring my dog. You did also?" I was pretty sure I already knew the answer but there's no better way to get a bird hunter talking than to ask about his dog.

"Yes, we did. He's Michael's dog, actually, a black Lab named Jasper."

"How old?"

Michael answered. "He just turned three. So he's still kinda young, but he's beginning to settle down and put it all together."

"Mike's too modest," Dave said. "Jasper does a fine job. We shot more than a dozen birds this afternoon and he retrieved every one of them. He found most of them and flushed them in range too."

"You can't ask for more than that," I said. "My dog's a German wirehair. But a good buddy of mine had a great Lab, a chocolate named Beaver, and we used to hunt them together. His Lab and my wirehair made a good team."

"Interesting. You didn't have any problems working a

pointing dog and a flushing dog together? Or was your buddy's dog one of those pointing Labs?"

"No, Beaver was a flushing dog, although Mike—that's also my buddy's name—trained him to stop and honor my wirehair when she went on point. It took a few hunts and some adjustment by both dogs but we eventually got it worked out. Basically, his Lab took care of the close birds and Preacher, my wirehair, handled the ones farther out."

"You said your buddy had a great Lab and you used to hunt them together…you don't still do that?"

"No, unfortunately. Beaver died just a few days ago, and needless to say, Mike and his family were really broken up about it."

"Oh, man, that's tough. We've been through it several times too, and you're right; it always tears you up."

Before I could reply, the other three men at the bar approached and introduced themselves. There was another round of handshaking and "So you're the magazine guy" comments, and I tried to sound self-deprecating in my response. As I'd told Allie earlier, I don't regard myself as any kind of celebrity, and I was still hoping to keep my visit to Hidden Hollow and Rushville as low key as possible.

The three men were brothers named Aaron, Wayne and Steven Parks. They had driven over from Peoria that morning, eaten lunch at the lodge and hunted in the afternoon with Steven's German shorthair, a dog named Baron.

"It gets a little confusing sometimes," Steven said. "I'll holler something at Baron, telling him to whoa up or whatever, and if I say his name, Aaron thinks I'm yelling at him."

"That's right," Aaron said. "I'm always asking him why he's telling me to whoa when it's the dog that's supposed to point the birds."

I laughed. "I can see where that might be a problem," I said, nodding at Steven. "If you tell Baron to fetch, does Aaron run out and bring back your bird?"

Aaron snorted. "That'll be the day," he said, and all three brothers laughed.

Allie Marshall appeared in the doorway of the hall leading back toward the dining room and announced that dinner was on the table.

AND WHAT A DINNER IT WAS, served family style, beginning with a mixed salad followed by baked quail stuffed with cornbread dressing, mashed potatoes and gravy, green beans seasoned with crumbled bacon, fresh-baked dinner rolls and apple pie a la mode for dessert—a bird hunter's feast, in other words. We all sat at one large table and passed the serving dishes back and forth, and Allie and Amy—this was the first time I'd seen Amy in person, and she did indeed look like the actress Amy Carlson—hovered and made sure drink glasses were filled and no one lacked for anything.

Not surprisingly, the conversation revolved around bird hunting and gun dogs, and I was asked quite a few questions about Preacher, the magazine and other locations I'd hunted that season. They were a bit surprised when I told them that so far I'd been hunting close to home and this was my first out-of-state hunt for the year. "Somebody has to stay in the office and make sure the magazine gets to the printer on time," I explained.

"Oh, sure, that makes sense," Dave Larson said. "So, are you going to be writing about this place for an upcoming issue?"

"That'll depend on whether I can hit what I shoot at tomorrow," I said, getting a laugh from the group. "But yeah, that's my plan. We like to showcase topnotch facilities, and so far everything I've seen says this place would appeal to our readers."

"I think your readers would definitely enjoy themselves here," Wayne Parks said. "We've been coming here for five years now…it's become a family tradition."

"We need a few more families with that tradition," Amy chimed in, leaning over my shoulder to refill my water glass. She smiled and added, "Does anyone need anything else? We have a fresh pot of coffee brewing that will be ready in another minute or so."

"A cup of coffee would be great," I said, and the Parks

brothers and Mike Larson added their request.

"None for me," Dave Larson said, "or I'll be up all night. I need my sleep if I'm gonna hope to hit anything tomorrow." That got another laugh and someone said, "Time to start rolling out the excuses!"

"Speaking of tomorrow, here's the line-up," Amy said. "Rob, you'll be hunting with Mitch, my husband, in the morning. Dave and Mike, you'll be going out with Allie, and Matt will be taking out you Parks brothers. Breakfast is at 8:00, just like this morning, and you'll head out to the fields at 9:00."

"Sounds good," Mike Larson said, and the rest of us nodded in agreement. I wasn't surprised that Mitch Halvorsen was going to be my guide; no doubt the proprietor wanted me to see his operation in the best possible light and make sure my experience was a positive one. Well, I couldn't blame him; a favorable review in a national magazine would give his business a nice boost.

"We'll switch off after lunch," Amy continued. "We like to rotate guides so everyone gets a chance to know everyone else and enjoy a little more variety. Rob, you said you were only going to hunt for half a day, so Parkses will be with Allie in the afternoon and Larsons with Matt." She laughed and added, "That means I have Mitch to myself for the afternoon and I've already warned him that he's going to be putting up Christmas decorations."

We all laughed. Dave Larson looked at me and said, "Only hunting half a day?"

I nodded. "I'll probably spend the afternoon making notes for the article, shooting pictures around the lodge and the grounds, maybe drive into town to soak up some local color. You never know what might turn out to be useful for a magazine feature." I hoped I sounded convincing.

Apparently I did because Dave nodded and said, "Makes sense."

Amy and Allie began clearing our dinner dishes and the rest of us adjourned to the lounge.

CHAPTER 23

I carried my cup of coffee into the lounge with me. The Parks brothers and Michael Larson headed over to the pool table and started a game of eight ball. Michael partnered with Steven Parks and I heard Wayne Parks call them "the dog team," presumably because Michael and Steven owned the dogs their parties were hunting over.

Dave Larson grabbed a beer from the cooler and joined me at the bar. "Never was much of a pool shooter," he said.

"Me, neither. I can maybe make my shots on a good day, but those aren't too plentiful," I said.

He laughed. "That sounds like me in the bird field lately. Anymore it seems like I couldn't hit water if I capsized a canoe."

I had to laugh at that one. "You said you and your son had a good day today, though."

"We did...well, Michael did, anyway. His Lab really performed well and Michael took most of the shots. I'm fine with that." He hesitated, then continued. "I've pretty much reached the age where I don't need to shoot a lot of birds to call it a good day."

I knew the feeling. Much as I love hunting—and I do love it and always will—I too had begun to notice a certain winding down feeling in recent years. Taking a limit was no longer the necessity it had seemed to be when I was much younger, and nowadays I often found myself deliberately stopping a bird or two short. Critics might accuse me of selfishness in doing this, saying I just wanted to "save some for tomorrow," but I knew better. It was simply a matter of knowing that enough was enough.

"I hear that," I said. "These days I'm more interested in watching my dog work and trying to see that she has a good time rather than concentrating on shooting a bunch of birds. Of course to her way of thinking, shooting a bunch of birds for her to retrieve *is* a good time."

"Yeah, that's true, isn't it? They live for hunting," Larson said. "I love watching Jasper work and being out there with Michael…well, for me that's about as good as it gets. Do you have any kids?"

"No, I don't," I replied, and before the conversation went any further, the front door of the lodge opened and Mitch Halvorsen—I recognized him from the photos on the preserve's website—stepped in. He paused on the mat inside the door and carefully wiped his boots, then looked up and gave us all a smile. "Howdy," he said.

Dave and I nodded and someone at the pool table said "Howdy!" in return. Halvorsen nodded in their direction but approached Larson and me at the bar. He was dressed in blue jeans and the same type of khaki shirt with the Hidden Hollow logo that Allie Marshall had been wearing. He stuck his hand out and said to me, "We haven't met yet. You must be Rob Vance."

"That's me," I said, shaking his hand. "Got in this afternoon."

"Sorry I wasn't here a little earlier to welcome you," he said. "Birds to clean, dogs to tend, about a dozen other things to take care of to get ready for tomorrow's hunts."

"No problem," I said. "Amy and Allie have been taking good care of us."

"I'm glad to hear that. Dinner was OK?"

"Dinner was terrific," I said, and Dave Larson added, "It sure was."

"Glad to hear that. I'm gonna scoot back there in a sec and see if they saved me some. But in the meantime, is there anything you fellows need?"

"Nope, I'm good," Dave Larson said.

"I am too," I said. "Amy said that we'd be going out together in the morning."

"That's right," Halvorsen said with a grin. "I want to see that big wirehair of yours in the field. Did you get her settled in the kennel OK?"

"Yes. That's a nice facility you have over there."

"Thanks. Just let us know if you need anything."

"Will do."

"OK, then. If you'll excuse me, I'm gonna go grab some supper."

Halvorsen headed through the doorway at the back of the lounge and down the hallway toward the dining room and kitchen. He had that sense of urgency about him that characterized a proprietor anxious to make sure his clients were taken care of, and more importantly, having a good time. I imagined that he and Amy, and probably Allie as well, put in some very long hours to keep the Hidden Hollow operation running smoothly.

I drained my coffee cup and stood up from the bar stool. I carried the cup around to the sink behind the bar and rinsed it out. I left it in the sink next to several glasses and turned back to the bar. Dave Larson had just grabbed a handful of peanuts from the bowl on the bar. He grinned sheepishly. "My addiction," he said.

"Less dangerous than some," I said, and he laughed.

"Yeah, I guess so."

"I think I'm gonna take a run into town," I said, hoping he wouldn't ask to come with me. "I was going to wait until tomorrow but I want to check things out, get a feel for the surroundings. It's always nice to be able to include a little local color in a magazine article; it helps round things out." I knew I'd said something similar a little earlier when Larson had asked me why I was only planning to hunt a half day, and I hoped this still sounded believable.

He nodded. "Rushville's a pretty small town, but maybe you'll get lucky and find some of that local color you're looking for," he said, smiling. I wondered if there was some implied double entendre

"Here's hoping," I said, and he laughed.

After going upstairs and grabbing my jacket, gloves and cap from my room, I went back downstairs and out to the parking lot in front of the lodge. The night sky was heavily overcast with no moon or stars visible and I wondered if we were going to get snow. I found myself hoping we would; hunting on fresh snow is one of my favorite activities, partly because it always brings back happy teenage memories of hunting rabbits with my dad, my uncle and my cousins. My cousins are still living but my dad and my uncle aren't, so I can't deny those memories are also somewhat bittersweet.

Of course Preacher and I would be hunting birds tomorrow, not rabbits. Still, a winter morning with the sun shining and a fresh blanket of snow on the ground from the night before is about as ideal as it gets in my book, regardless of our quarry. A snowy background might also provide some better photo opportunities than the otherwise drab December cover, and I reminded myself I'd need to carry my camera in the morning, as well as my shotgun.

I climbed into the Equinox and cranked the ignition. As I did so, I had a sudden thought. I pulled out the burner I'd been using to correspond with James Collins—a hunch had told me to bring it along on this trip, and I'd stashed it in the console—and turned it on. I sent him a quick text message: *Can U get me home addresses for Flanagan and Wilson? Thx.*

I waited a moment to confirm the message had been sent, then I turned off the burner and dropped it into my jacket pocket. I hoped James Collins would see the message and respond sooner rather than later, but this being Friday night, I wasn't overly optimistic. I wished I'd thought to ask him for this information earlier.

Oh well. In the meantime, I could take another look at downtown Rushville, and maybe if I got lucky find out a little more about the whole Carlyle Wilson-Charlie Flanagan situation.

Local color, indeed.

CHAPTER 24

During the 15-minute drive from Hidden Hollow to Rushville I pondered what the hell I was hoping to accomplish.

Well, I knew the answer...sort of. I was planning to visit the Rushville Tap and, if necessary, maybe one or two other bars, where—if I got lucky—I might pick up some scuttlebutt about Carlyle Wilson and Charlie Flanagan. In a town the size of Rushville, one of its residents going on trial for manslaughter was almost certain to be a popular topic of conversation.

Then again, maybe not. The townspeople undoubtedly had their opinions as to what had transpired out there in the woods— that is, whether or not Carlyle Wilson had actually shot Frank Reynolds—but how willing they would be to share those opinions with a total stranger remained to be seen. And offhand, I couldn't think of a good way to broach the subject without arousing suspicion, especially since, as an outsider, I theoretically wouldn't know anything about it.

I was just going to have to keep my eyes and ears open and hope for a break, an opening that would allow me to ask a question or two without betraying too much interest.

Little did I know that Charlie Flanagan himself would soon provide me with the break I needed.

I DROVE HALFWAY AROUND the town square and parked in front of the Rushville Tap. I turned off the engine and sat for a moment, still wondering how to play things. I finally decided just to go inside and order a beer and let myself be known as a client at Hidden Hollow. Maybe a conversation about hunting, if I could get one started, might lead somewhere.

I pushed through the heavy wooden door and stepped inside. The Rushville Tap resembled thousands of other small town watering holes—a bar that ran most of the length of the wall opposite the door, with a dozen or so tables taking up the floor space in between and booths along the front wall and at one end of the room. At the other end stood the requisite pool table, behind which were doors to restrooms. Wall decorations consisted of lighted beer signs, posters for the Chicago Cubs, Chicago Bears and St. Louis Cardinals, and two medium-sized whitetail head mounts.

A couple of large screen TVs were mounted high on the wall at either end of the bar and both were tuned to cable channels showing sports talk shows, one football and one basketball, but the volume was muted on both. Captions at the bottom of the screens made up for the lack of sound, in case anyone was interested in what the hosts were saying.

Three of the tables in the middle of the room were occupied, as were about half of the twenty or so bar stools. About three-fourths of the patrons were men, but there were several couples as well. A typical Friday night crowd, I supposed. I walked up to the bar, pulled out a stool and shrugged out of my jacket. I hung it over the back of the stool and sat down.

Most of the stools to my right were empty. To my left, with two empty stools between us, sat a large guy wearing an insulated camouflage vest over a heavy flannel shirt. He had dark hair cut short and a dark mustache. A draft beer and a shot glass sat in front of him. He glanced my way, frowned slightly, then picked up the shot glass and drained it at a gulp. He followed it with a long pull on his beer.

The bartender approached. He smiled and said, "Evening."

"Evening," I said in return. I nodded toward the taps. "Winter Lager," I said. I was a little surprised it was one of the choices—I would have guessed most of the patrons preferred Anheuser Busch products—but I don't question good fortune when I find it.

The bartender nodded. He drew my beer and set it in front

of me on a cardboard coaster with a picture of a full beer mug and the words, "Two wrongs don't make a right. But two beers just might." I took a sip. The lager was very cold and I nodded in appreciation. "Thanks," I said.

"Do you want to run a tab or pay as you go?" the bartender asked.

"I'll run a tab," I said. I smiled. "I may stay for more than one." Mr. Friendly, trying to break the ice.

"You're welcome to do that," the bartender said. He turned toward the fellow on my left. "How about you, Charlie? Ready for another?"

Charlie. Could I be that lucky?

"Sure," Charlie said.

The bartender moved away and drew another draft beer— Charlie was drinking regular Bud—and set it in front of him. "Another bump also?" he asked.

"Sure," Charlie said again. Mr. Eloquent.

The bartender filled Charlie's shot glass with Jack Daniels and nudged it toward him. Like before, Charlie downed it a single gulp. He made a slight lip-smacking noise, then picked up his beer glass.

I did my best not to watch too closely.

I didn't know this was Charlie Flanagan—I'd never seen a photo of him, and quite possibly there was more than one Charlie in Rushville—but I didn't want to be caught checking him out, regardless. I studied the beer glass in front of me and rotated it between my fingers, watching the tiny bubbles rise to the foam head. As I did this I reviewed what I did know about Flanagan.

He'd played tackle on his high school football team and that probably meant somebody larger than average. Check. He was 32 years old, and the fellow to my left looked to be about that age. Check. His short hair was cut in a style that suggested the military or maybe law enforcement...or by extension, prison guard. Check. And, he was drinking in the same bar where Charlie Flanagan claimed he'd heard Carlyle Wilson confess to killing Frank Reynolds.

No, I didn't know this was Charlie Flanagan. But until I

found out otherwise, I thought it was a pretty good bet. And that meant I needed to be careful.

The bartender was standing in front of me again. "New in town?" he asked.

I nodded. "Staying out at Hidden Hollow, the hunting preserve. I'm here to hunt a couple days, maybe write a story for my magazine." I figured this was as good a chance to get the conversational ball rolling as I was likely to get, my earlier idea for keeping a low profile notwithstanding.

"Really!" said the bartender. "What magazine?"

"*American Wingshot*," I said. "I'm the editor. Rob Vance."

"No kidding! And you say you're here to write a story?"

"Well, I'm here to check the place out, anyway. We like to feature preserves that our readers might want to try out for themselves. Getting a firsthand look is about the best way I know to make sure we're not sending them off to some shoddy operation."

"That makes sense," the bartender said. "I've not been out there myself but I hear it's a nice place. I know Mitch Halvorsen and his wife Amy worked mighty hard to get it up and running."

I thought I heard my neighbor Charlie make a snorting sound but I didn't turn toward him. Neither did the bartender.

"It is a nice place," I said. "At least, what I've seen of it so far. I haven't hunted yet, but the lodge is very nice. I checked in this afternoon. Had a good meal and then decided to come on into town to look around. Always like to get a feel for the surroundings." I stopped short of using the "local color" phrase again.

The bartender laughed. "I'm not sure you're going to find much to write about in Rushville...we're a pretty quiet little town. But you're certainly welcome to check things out, see the sights, such as they are."

I was about to say, "That's my plan" when a fellow back by the pool table hollered, "Hey, Flanagan, c'mon back and shoot a game with us."

The three of us—my neighbor Charlie, the bartender and myself—turned toward the pool table, as did several of the other patrons throughout the room. Two men holding cue sticks stood by the table while a third racked the balls. They obviously needed a fourth to play partners.

Charlie Flanagan—I now had my confirmation—shook his head and said, "Not tonight."

"Aw, c'mon!" said the first man. "We need a fourth guy."

"I said, not tonight," Flanagan repeated, then added in a lower voice, almost a growl, "goddamn it."

I made a point of not looking at him. I stared at the bartender and he returned my look, his eyebrows twitching upward just slightly. A warning?

I smiled and said, "That's my plan, anyway. Look around, maybe include a few details about the town in the story. We always try to give readers a complete picture."

The bartender nodded. "Well, good luck. I hope you enjoy your stay out at Hidden Hollow. I know Mitch and Amy will appreciate any business you can steer their way." He moved away toward the other end of the bar to check on refills.

Beside me I heard Charlie Flanagan slam his beer glass down on the bar. I glanced his way and saw him standing up from his stool. He squared his shoulders and turned toward me. I gave him a slight smile.

He was a big guy, all right. I guessed him at about six-two or –three and maybe 225 pounds. He had some belly overhanging his belt but not a lot and I guessed it was probably hard, not flabby. He looked like he might lift weights or had at one time. I had no problem envisioning him as a prison guard, and a mean-ass one at that.

He didn't return my smile but fixed me with his best thousand-yard stare. He took a step toward me and I couldn't help tensing up. I hoped it wasn't obvious.

He took another step in my direction and then turned toward the door. But as he did so he leaned back slightly and gave me a shoulder bump. Hard.

I couldn't keep from recoiling. He sneered slightly and said, "Watch it, old man."

Then he turned and stalked out the door and into the night.

CHAPTER 25

An old woman walks into a town in the desert Southwest and ties her pack mule to the hitching post. As she stands there brushing some of the dust from her clothes, a young gunslinger steps out of the saloon with a gun in one hand and a bottle of whiskey in the other.

He sees the old woman and laughs. "Hey, old woman!" he yells. "Have you ever danced?"

The old woman looks up at him and says, "No, I never did dance. Never had time for such foolishness."

A crowd gathers as the gunslinger grins and says, "Well, you old hag, you're gonna dance now!" And after taking another swig of whiskey he begins shooting at the old woman's feet.

Not wanting to get her toes blown off, the old woman starts hopping around while the gunslinger blazes away and the crowd roars. When he's fired his last shot, the gunslinger holsters his pistol and, still laughing, turns to head back into the saloon.

That's when the old lady pulls her double-barreled coach gun from its scabbard on the mule's pack saddle. The sharp clicks as she cocks both hammers are clearly audible to everyone present, including the young gunslinger.

He turns around slowly. The crowd holds its breath as the gunslinger takes in the two barrels pointed directly at his chest.

The shotgun never wavers in the old lady's hands as she softly asks, "Son, have you ever kissed a mule's asshole?"

The young man swallows hard and replies, "No, Ma'am...but I've always wanted to."

There are five lessons in this story:

1. Never be arrogant.

2. Never waste all your ammunition.

3. Whiskey makes you think you're smarter, funnier and tougher than you are.

4. You should always be sure who truly has the power; and

5. Don't mess with old people. They didn't get to be old by being stupid.

.

CHAPTER 26

Old man?

OK, I realized that to someone in his early 30s, I probably did look old. And to someone like Charlie Flanagan, I probably didn't look at all intimidating. In other words, I looked like someone he could push around—or at least shoulder-bump—with impunity. He was used to bullying people, apparently, and getting away with it. And obviously the lesson about respecting one's elders had been lost on him.

Still, I couldn't deny that his comment rankled. Bullies always have that effect on me, even if I'm not their specific target.

But I also knew I couldn't afford to let this affect my judgment, and in fact, it was probably to my advantage to shrug it off and pretend a meekness I wasn't feeling. I didn't want to give anyone in the bar the impression that I was thinking about retaliating. Better to play the toothless tiger.

Also—I had to admit this, much as I hated to—I really wasn't a match for Charlie Flanagan physically. When you're north of 60, you tend to think twice about rough-housing…or at least you think twice if you have more than half a brain and don't relish the idea of being pounded into the ground like a tent stake.

But I also knew that, like the shotgun-wielding old lady in one of my favorite jokes, I could eventually even the odds and settle the score. All in good time.

I shook my head and turned back toward my beer. The bartender looked my way and said, "Don't pay any attention to

Charlie. He's always been a hothead and he's been feeling a lot of pressure lately. Best just to stay out of his way."

"What's he been feeling pressured about?" I hoped my question sounded innocuous.

The bartender moved down to stand in front of me with his arms braced against the inside rail of the bar. "He's going to be the star witness in a trial we've got coming up in a few weeks. Big news around here."

"Oh? Trial for what?" Again I hoped I sounded only casually interested.

"It's a manslaughter trial. Another one of our local guys, Carlyle Wilson, got charged with killing a deer hunter a couple weeks ago. A lawyer from Chicago who was hunting up north of here a little ways."

"He killed a deer hunter? Was it an accident?"

"Had to have been...that is, if Carlyle actually shot the guy. Carlyle's a good guy himself and he wouldn't deliberately kill anyone...not even a lawyer." The bartender laughed at his little joke and I smiled in return. "He had the bad luck to be hunting in the same area as the lawyer and he found the body...the guy was up in a tree stand, shot through the heart."

I shook my head again. "Wow." I hoped the bartender would keep talking, and he did.

"Carlyle saw the guy up in the stand, kinda slumped over, and he called to him. Then when the guy didn't answer he walked up for a closer look and that's when he saw that the guy had been shot."

"Did he try to get the guy down off the stand?" That seemed like a reasonable question to ask.

"He climbed partway up and said he could tell the guy was dead. The guy's coat was soaked in blood and Carlyle said he knew he was dead without touching him and there was nothing he could do for him. He said he knew he probably shouldn't touch the guy and he was shook up pretty bad so he climbed back down and drove into town to report it. He said he was almost back to town before he remembered his cell phone and realized he could have called 911 when he was still out there in the woods. Like I said, he was pretty shook up by the whole thing."

"Well, that's understandable," I said. "But I'm confused about something. If he found the guy and the guy was already dead, and he reported it right away, why did he get charged with killing the guy…you said the dead guy was a lawyer?"

"Right, a lawyer from Chicago. Named Reynolds. As for why Carlyle got charged with killing him…well, that's where things get interesting."

"How so?"

"Hold on a minute; I'll be right back." The bartender moved down the bar to refill a couple of drafts for a couple sitting at the opposite end and while he was gone I did a quick mental replay of our conversation so far. I hoped I wasn't overplaying my hand by asking too many questions but the bartender seemed in a talkative mood so I thought I was probably OK.

"Where was I?" the bartender said when he returned. "Oh yeah, why Carlyle got charged for killing the guy. Well, here's what happened. He came in here that same evening after he found the guy. He said he was still pretty shook up. He ordered a beer but instead of sitting here at the bar he took it over to that last booth in the corner"—the bartender pointed past my shoulder and I turned my head to look—"and sat by himself.

"Of course by then everybody in town knew what had happened, that he'd found a dead guy that morning when he was out hunting deer and he'd reported it and gone back out with the sheriff to show them where. I think he went off to sit by himself because he didn't really want to talk about it anymore. He probably would have been smarter to have stayed home and not answered his phone, but who knows; maybe he just didn't want to be by himself."

"He's not married?" I asked, although I already knew the answer.

"No," the bartender said. "He's engaged to a girl named Allie Marshall…in fact you might have met her. She works at her sister's place, that Hidden Hollow hunting preserve where you're staying. She does some of the cooking and cleans the guest rooms but I've heard she also guides out there sometimes."

"Oh, Allie," I said. "Yes, I did meet her. Nice looking girl. Tall, dark hair."

"That's her. Well, anyway, she must have still been working that evening since it was deer season and the lodge was probably full of hunters. Carlyle came in alone and like I said, he got his beer then went over to that corner booth and sat by himself.

"About ten minutes later, Charlie Flanagan—that's the guy who just bumped you a few minutes ago—came in. He ordered his usual boilermaker, a shot of Jack and a Bud, and when I set him up he drank the shot then picked up his beer and went over to Carlyle's booth and sat down."

"Are they friends?"

The bartender snorted. "Not anymore, they aren't, not after what happened." He laughed and shook his head. "No, they weren't really buddies anyway. Grew up here in Rushville and went to school together, played football when they were in high school, but they weren't close friends. At least, not that I ever heard anything about."

A burly fiftyish fellow wearing a faded tan Carhartt jacket and a yellow and green DeKalb cap came in and sat down two stools away from me on the stool Charlie Flanagan had previously occupied. The bartender glanced his way and said, "Evening, Pete."

"Walt," the man replied, nodding at the bartender and shrugging out of his Carhartt. He dropped it on the empty stool on his far side but didn't remove his cap. "My usual," he said.

The bartender moved down to the taps and drew a tall Budweiser. He brought it back and set it in front of Pete, who said thanks and picked it up and took a long pull. I wanted to get Walt the bartender talking again because he'd apparently witnessed the conversation in which Carlyle Wilson had supposedly confessed to killing Frank Reynolds.

"So if they weren't good friends, they were...what?

Drinking buddies?" I asked.

"I guess that's about right," Walt said. He turned to my neighbor. "Charlie Flanagan and Carlyle Wilson—would you call them drinking buddies, Pete?"

Pete shook his head. "I don't think I'd even call them that," he said. "Especially after Carlyle got engaged to Allie Marshall. Everybody knows that *really* didn't set well with Charlie. He'd had his eye on Allie for quite some time, ever since Jolene left him and Allie divorced Bob. Seeing Carlyle steal his prize right out from his under nose…well, that was bound to leave Charlie pretty p-o'ed."

"Except Allie never wanted anything to do with Charlie anyway," Walt said. "It's not like he had any real claim on her."

"That wouldn't matter to Charlie. We both know that."

"Well, you're right about that."

You had to love these small towns where everybody knew everybody else—their personalities, their histories, their everyday comings and goings. I wanted to steer the conversation back to Carlyle Wilson and what had happened when Charlie Flanagan joined him in his booth the night after Wilson found Frank Reynolds' body, but we'd sidetracked into a discussion of their love lives. For want of a better strategy, I decided to play dumb.

"OK," I said, "I'm getting confused here. Too many names. Carlyle Wilson is engaged to Allie Marshall, who used to be married to a guy named Bob, and Charlie Flanagan had his eye on her, and he and Carlyle weren't really friends, but they'd sit down and have a drink together? And Carlyle is now charged with accidentally killing a lawyer while he was out deer hunting? Have I got all that right?" I hoped I sounded befuddled and just trying to sort out the facts.

"That's right," Walt the bartender said. "Allie was married to Bob Marshall, who farms out west of here, but they got divorced a few years ago, about the same time Charlie got divorced from his wife, Jolene, actually. Carlyle has never been married but he and Allie started dating, I guess you'd call it, and they got engaged a few months ago."

"And that rubbed Charlie wrong?"

Walt and Pete both laughed. "Yes, and rubbing Charlie wrong is not something you want to do," Walt said.

"Yeah, I got that impression," I said. "But I'm still not clear on why Carlyle Wilson was charged with killing the lawyer." I was beginning to feel like I was pushing my luck, maybe asking too many questions, but Walt and Pete still seemed eager to talk.

"Well, we haven't got to that part yet," Walt said.

"What part is that?" I asked.

"Charlie Flanagan is the reason, I guess you could say, that Carlyle Wilson got charged."

"How so?"

"Carlyle confessed to Charlie. Or at least that's what Charlie says, anyway."

CHAPTER 27

There it was.

I already knew this, of course, that Carlyle Wilson's arrest and manslaughter charge were based on Charlie Flanagan claiming to have heard him confess. But now I had some local context I could use to better evaluate that fact. It was obvious that both Walt and Pete were skeptical of Flanagan's claim, and that they were more inclined to give Wilson the benefit of the doubt.

"Wilson confessed to Flanagan?" I asked.

"That's what Charlie claims."

"But why would Wilson do that, if the lawyer was already dead when he found him?"

"Well, that's the big question, isn't it? And in fact, Wilson claims he never confessed to Charlie. He says all he told Charlie about was finding the body, reporting it and taking the sheriff back out there."

"So...what? You think Charlie Flanagan made up the bit about Wilson confessing?"

Walt arched his eyebrows and gave an exaggerated shrug, a gesture that implied I'd nailed it but he didn't want to say so aloud.

Pete wasn't quite so reticent. He snorted and said, "If you knew the two of them, you'd almost have to think that's what happened. Carlyle says he never told Charlie he killed that guy, and that's what most of us believe. But Charlie swears he did, and he's planning to testify to that in court."

I nodded toward the bartender. "That's the pressure you

were talking about," I said.

"Yep. When Carlyle was arrested, I almost expected Charlie to back down and say he'd made up the bit about the confession, that it was all just a joke. I didn't really expect him to stick to that story. But he did, and now he's gonna have to swear to it in court. It's almost like he painted himself into a corner and doesn't know how to get out."

"Claiming to have heard a confession and seeing another man arrested for it is one hell of a practical joke," I said. "Would he really do something like that?"

"With Charlie Flanagan, you can never really tell what he's capable of," Walt said. "He's been one of this town's bad boys since he was a little kid. Always in trouble at school, always getting into fights, that kind of thing. Whenever anything bad happened in this town, vandalism or whatever, you could almost bet Charlie Flanagan had a hand in it."

"Sounds like a nice guy," I said. "So what does he do now? Job-wise, I mean?" I knew the answer to this also, but I was curious to get Pete and Walt's take on it.

Pete fielded my question. "He's a guard at the men's prison down to Mt. Sterling, about 20 miles south of here."

"He's a prison guard?" I tried to sound incredulous, like I found the irony hard to believe.

"Yeah, and I wouldn't want to be one of the prisoners on his cellblock." Walt again.

"Me neither," Pete said.

I shook my head. "You think this has anything to do with Wilson being engaged to Allie Marshall?" I knew I was stretching things here, but what the hell, in for a penny, in for a pound.

"That's what a lot of us think," Walt said. "If Charlie can get Carlyle out of the picture—sent to prison for killing that lawyer—then he'd have a clean shot at getting something going with Allie. Or at least, that's what he's hoping."

"Wouldn't that be kind of a stretch, though?" I asked. "Didn't you say Allie didn't want anything to do with him? If he gets her fiancé sent to prison, that's not exactly gonna endear him to her."

"No, it wouldn't. But Charlie probably isn't thinking that far ahead. See, he's one of those guys who, when he sets his sights on something, he goes after it with everything he's got. Tramples anything that gets in his way. And right now, that would be Carlyle Wilson."

"Wow," I said. "What a mess. But about this confession he supposedly heard. What did he do...report it to the sheriff?"

"That's right. He stopped in the sheriff's office early Monday morning. Said Wilson had confessed on Saturday evening and he, Charlie, had wrestled with it all day Sunday then decided he'd better tell what he knew."

"And the sheriff believed him?"

"I don't think the sheriff had much choice. After they removed the lawyer's body from the woods they scoured the area pretty thoroughly, even brought in a team of technicians from Springfield. But they really didn't turn up anything other than the tree stand the lawyer was sitting in when he was shot."

"So the confession was the only reason Wilson was arrested...just on the basis of Flanagan's say-so?"

"Well, remember Charlie's a prison guard, so he works in law enforcement...sort of, anyway, and that might give him a little more credibility," Walt said. "Plus, there *were* one or two other bits and pieces of evidence. Circumstantial, I guess you'd call it. But along with the confession it was enough to get Carlyle arrested and charged."

I glanced at the clock behind the bar. It read 8:35, and like most bar clocks, it was ten minutes fast, the better to hurry people out the door when closing time rolled around. I noticed the place was beginning to fill up, both the stools at the bar and the tables and booths. That told me it would probably be a good idea to wrap up this conversation and take my leave, if I was still hoping to maintain a low profile. But I wanted to hear more about the evidence Walt had mentioned.

"What circumstantial evidence?" I asked. "I thought you said the crime scene techs didn't find anything."

"They didn't, at least not right there where the lawyer was

shot," Walt said, and I inwardly sighed with relief. "But Carlyle's gun had been fired. He said he'd shot at a deer earlier that morning and was trying to track it when he found the lawyer. The fact that his gun had been fired but he didn't have a deer to show for it was enough to convince them, I guess, that he must have been the one who shot the lawyer."

"That still seems like a stretch," I said.

"Well, like we said earlier, if you knew Carlyle, you'd say he almost certainly didn't do this. But it's one of those deals where the facts seem to say otherwise, especially if you believe he confessed to Charlie Flanagan."

"Do most folks believe that?"

"Hard to say. I'd guess opinions are about fifty-fifty here in town, or maybe sixty-forty in favor of Carlyle. But Charlie Flanagan has his own share of friends, even if most of them are troublemakers like him, to a greater or lesser degree. They'll stick by him, even if a lot of the rest of us think he made up the whole story."

"That's right," Pete chimed in. "One thing's for sure. It's big news right now and everyone is talking about it."

"Yep, that's for sure," Walt said, then moved away to fill some customers' orders.

"It still sounds like a case of he said, he said, or maybe he said, he denied," I said to Pete. "I mean, it's basically just Charlie Flanagan's word against Carlyle Wilson's, right?"

"Plus the fact that Carlyle's gun had been fired."

"Does Carlyle have a good lawyer defending him?"

Pete laughed. "He has a lawyer, a guy named Prescott, but I don't know how good he is. He's from Macomb, about 30 miles from here. I guess he's won his share of cases, but he's lost some too. Whether he can get Carlyle off…well, we'll find that out in another few weeks."

"Sheesh," I said. "Talk about being in the wrong place at the wrong time."

"You got that right."

OUR CONVERSATION PRETTY MUCH dwindled to a halt after

that, with Pete and me finishing our beers while Walt tended to other customers. I placed my mug on the bar and stood up to leave. I nodded to Pete, "Nice talking with you."

He nodded in reply and said, "Nice talking with you also. I didn't get your name."

"Rob Vance," I said. I'd already shared my name with Walt and I knew that in a town this size I couldn't hope to keep my identity a complete secret anyhow. I figured word would soon get around about my hunt at Hidden Hollow and that I was there to write a story for my magazine about the hunt. While I still hoped to keep a fairly low profile and not attract undue attention—at least not in any way related to Charlie Flanagan— I also figured the story assignment should keep me fairly well covered.

"Pete Sawyer," he said, sticking out a calloused hand. I shook with him and, to his credit, he didn't try to pulverize my hand with his grip, although I was pretty sure he could have done so.

"Good to meet you," I said, and he nodded. "You too," he said.

Walt the bartender returned and I paid my tab, adding a good tip. He thanked me and told me to stop in again. I nodded and pulled on my jacket, then threaded my way through the tables and pushed through the door out into the cold night air.

Light, feathery snow had begun to fall and there was already about a half inch of accumulation on the sidewalk and street and the vehicles parked at the curb. I'd left my gloves on the passenger seat of the Equinox—duh—so I used my bare hand to brush the snow from the edges of the driver's side doorframe. I climbed in, dried my wet hand on my jeans, and cranked the ignition.

I sat for a moment, then fished the burner I'd been using with James Collins out of my jacket pocket and turned it on. While it was booting up I gazed out the window at the door of the Rushville Tap. A couple came out, laughing, and turned to their right to walk down the street to their vehicle. The man had his arm around the woman's waist and she leaned her head on his shoulder, and I felt a pang of envy.

I also suddenly remembered the vanilla scent of Daryl Nelson's shampoo when I'd kissed her goodnight in the parking lot at Skip's the week before.

The burner made the little chiming sound that signified I had a text message. I thumbed the icon and the message displayed. It read: "CW: 423 West Randolph. CF: 668 Highland Road."

James Collins had come through. I now knew where both Carlyle Wilson and Charlie Flanagan lived.

CHAPTER 28

The navigation system on the phone made it easy to find both places.

Carlyle Wilson's house was the closer of the two, just a few blocks away from the town square. Following the directions voiced by the robotic-sounding lady on the phone, I found it in less than five minutes.

It was a smallish frame two-story house, white with dark trim and a small screened front porch with a row of bushes in front. A detached two-car garage sat behind it and to one side. The garage door was closed so I couldn't tell if there was a vehicle inside. There wasn't one parked in the driveway leading back to the garage.

The house was completely dark, which was what you'd expect if you knew its owner and sole inhabitant was currently in a jail cell.

I circled the block and drove past the house a second time but learned nothing further. It was still dark (no surprise) and I couldn't think of any reason to keep checking it out. I punched up Charlie Flanagan's address and read it into the phone, and Robot Lady—I refuse to call her anything else—began telling me how to get there.

Highland Road was a couple miles outside of town, off Highway 24. I followed the directions and came to a roadside mailbox with the numbers 668 and the name Flanagan in metallic letters on the side. It stood at the corner of a gravel lane that led up a slope to a house sitting atop a hill about a quarter mile from the road. With the darkness and falling snow I couldn't see the house all that clearly, but I could see it was a large two-story and there was at least one light on.

That didn't necessarily mean Charlie Flanagan was inside; maybe he was one of those people who always left a light on because he didn't like coming home to a dark house. Then again, the light could mean he was already home for the night and sitting in his den wearing a velvet smoking jacket, sipping brandy and reading Dostoevsky's *Crime and Punishment*.

I highly doubted that scenario.

I drove on past and continued down Highland Road to the next lane, a little more than a half-mile farther on. I continued on to the next lane and it too was about a half-mile farther. I pulled in, reversed, and headed back toward Flanagan's place. I paused for a moment at the end of his lane and powered down the window for a little better look.

Up on the hill near the house, a dog barked, sounding like something fairly large. Definitely not a yappy ankle-biter, anyway, which wouldn't have fit Charlie Flanagan's tough-guy image. I guessed maybe a Rottweiler or German shepherd or pit bull and hoped it wouldn't come charging down the lane to investigate. But I waited a minute and saw no sign of the dog, suggesting it was either chained or confined in a kennel near the house.

I powered up the window and headed back to town.

THE SNOW WAS STILL FALLING when I came to the town square. The pavilion in the park twinkled with the lights I'd seen workmen stringing that afternoon. Lighted Christmas wreaths adorned the streetlight posts around the square as well, and the snow gave everything a cozy, Norman Rockwell kind of look. Or maybe Thomas Kincaid.

There were still quite a few cars parked outside the Rushville Tap and in front of the other bars on the square. Most of the other businesses were dark. I glanced at the clock on the Equinox's radio display and saw it was 9:10. I pulled into an empty parking space and sat for a moment, watching snowflakes melt on the windshield as I pondered my next move and thought about what I'd learned over the course of the evening.

My thoughts were pretty random. Charlie Flanagan lived outside of town in a large house on a hill and apparently he had a big dog. His nearest neighbors were about a half-mile away. He was a known troublemaker, going all the way back to his childhood. A lot of townspeople doubted he'd actually heard Carlyle Wilson confess to killing Frank Reynolds, but there were also some who believed him.

Carlyle Wilson lived in town and there'd been no one at his house this evening while he sat in jail. I wondered if Allie Marshall had a key to the house and guessed that, as his fiancée, she probably did. I also wondered if she lived with him and would be returning to the house after she finished up her duties for the evening at Hidden Hollow. The townspeople, or at least the two I'd talked to, thought Wilson was basically a good guy and unlikely to have killed Frank Reynolds or to have confessed to doing so. He'd been arrested primarily on Charlie Flanagan's say-so.

Charlie Flanagan had had his eye on Allie Marshall before she got engaged to Carlyle Wilson. Pete Sawyer and Walt the bartender thought Charlie might have made up the confession story to get Carlyle out of the way so he, Charlie, could make a move on Allie, not realizing she wouldn't want anything to do with him if he was instrumental in getting her fiancé sent to prison.

That last part troubled me a bit. Could Charlie Flanagan really be that dumb and think that if Carlyle was sent up, that would simply clear the path to Allie's door?

Walt the bartender seemed to think that yes, Charlie was indeed that dumb. Walt had said something to the effect that once Charlie set his sights on something, he trampled anything that got in his way. That observation fit hand-in-glove with my general impression of Charlie Flanagan as a bullying thug, further confirmed by Pete and Walt's comments about not wanting to be a prisoner under his guard.

I had a sudden disquieting thought. I wondered if Charlie

Flanagan was hoping that in addition to removing Carlyle Wilson as the obstacle to his pursuit of Allie Marshall, he was also hoping that Wilson would be convicted and then incarcerated at the Mt. Sterling prison. That would give Flanagan the opportunity to further torment Wilson, something Flanagan would probably enjoy.

I had no idea if such a scenario would actually play out along those lines; if Wilson would in fact be sent to nearby Mt. Sterling, rather than some other Illinois prison, if he were convicted. But life was too full of cruel ironies for me to entirely dismiss the idea.

By now there was little question in my mind that Charlie Flanagan had borne false witness against Carlyle Wilson and fabricated the story of Wilson's confession. I wasn't alone in my thinking on this, but whether a jury would see it that way was still a real roll of the dice.

Getting rid of Charlie Flanagan before he testified would render the alleged confession moot, I was pretty sure, and that in turn would probably result in the manslaughter charge against Wilson being dropped. The only real question in my mind—and it was the same question I'd been struggling with since first learning of this situation—was whether Flanagan's lie was enough to justify killing him.

Another unsettling thought occurred to me. Rule Number 2 stipulated no collateral damage. Up until now I'd been thinking of Carlyle Wilson as the only possible collateral damage, in that he was being set up to take the fall for something I had done. But now I wondered if I was dodging the realization that Charlie Flanagan might also be considered collateral damage…was I thinking of killing him primarily to get Wilson off the hook, or just to prevent my having to come clean?

I certainly wanted to see Wilson exonerated. But I couldn't deny I was also hoping to bring some closure to the matter of Frank Reynolds' death once and for all and in such a way that authorities would have no choice but to rule it an accidental shooting with no other viable suspects. i.e., leaving Wilson *and* me in the clear.

Once again I found myself wishing for something more, some additional deciding factor, some further bit of incriminating evidence of wrongdoing by Flanagan.

As I sat there parked on the Rushville town square watching the snow fall, backlit by the Christmas lights on that Friday night, I couldn't know that in less than twenty-four hours my wish would be granted and on the following afternoon I'd see Charlie Flanagan do something that would seal his fate once and for all.

CHAPTER 29

The snow had stopped falling by the time I got back to Hidden Hollow. I parked in the same place I had earlier, then walked across to the kennel building. The door was unlocked so I entered and snapped on the light.

I was pleased to note that the kennel building was heated, another amenity worth mentioning in my article. Preacher was curled up on her dog bed but stood up when she saw me. She gave one quick bark and stood by the gate to her kennel run, wagging her tail.

Two other dogs, the German shorthair and the black Lab I'd heard about at dinner, occupied two of the runs, one on either side of Preacher's, with an empty run between each—the shorthair was in run number two and the Lab was in run six.

Good planning on Allie Marshall's part, I thought. Although the Lab and the shorthair both appeared friendly, strange dogs in unfamiliar surroundings don't always hit it off, especially if any or all of them are strongly territorial. By keeping empty runs between the kennel's three occupants Allie had minimized the chance of any conflict.

I unlatched the gate to Preacher's run and stepped inside. I knelt down and ruffled her ears and she sighed and laid her bristly head on my shoulder. I sweet-talked to her for a couple minutes and reminded her that we'd be hunting in the morning. Then I stood—my middle-aged knees couldn't tolerate kneeling on concrete for very long—and stepped back out of Preacher's run. I latched her gate, snapped off the light, and returned to the lodge.

As I stepped up onto the porch I saw someone standing off to my left, leaning against the porch railing. There was enough light coming through the lodge's windows for me to recognize Allie Marshall. She was wearing a heavy canvas barn coat, and a longneck beer bottle stood on the railing next to her. Before I could speak, she said, "Is Preacher settled in for the night?"

I realized she must have watched me park and walk across to the kennel. "Yes, she's fine," I said. "That's a nice facility you have for guests' dogs."

"Thanks. The kennels for our dogs are on the other side of the barn," she said, answering a question I'd been wondering about. She laughed and added, "Their accommodations aren't quite as posh."

"Oh, I'll bet they're fine," I said, then decided to push the envelope. "Do you mind if I join you with one of those?" I gestured toward her beer.

"If you'd like," she said. "Although there's a pretty lively pool tournament going on inside if you want to get in on it." I wasn't sure if she was trying to get rid of me or just playing the helpful hostess.

"'Fraid I'm not much of a pool player," I said. "I'd only embarrass myself, to say nothing of losing some money if there's any betting going on."

She laughed. "I don't think they're playing for money, but you never know…things could get crazy. But sure, join me if you'd like."

"Can I bring you another one?"

"Thanks, but I need to head back to town when I finish this."

"OK," I said. I pushed through the door and headed across the lounge toward the tall cooler behind the bar. One of the pool players—I think it was Aaron—hailed me and asked if I wanted to play but I shook my head and begged off.

I snagged a Winter Lager from the cooler, popped the cap and returned to the porch. Allie had lifted one hip to rest on the porch railing and was swinging that leg. I took a similar position opposite her and raised my bottle.

"So, what did you think of Rushville?" she asked.

"Nice little place," I said. "Pretty town square, with the Christmas decorations and the snow. Kinda quaint, actually."

"Quaint," Allie said. She shook her head. "I guess you could call it that, although those of us who've lived here all our lives might choose some other words to describe it." I wasn't sure if I heard a trace of bitterness in her voice. Maybe just resignation.

I could have asked her to elaborate, but knowing she'd be leaving as soon as she finished her beer, I decided to force the pace. "I stopped in at the Rushville Tap," I said.

Her leg stopped swinging and I saw her stiffen and straighten up a bit. "Oh?" she said.

I'd obviously touched a nerve. I nodded and said, "Yeah. Had a conversation with the bartender, a guy named Walt, and another fellow named Pete Sawyer."

"What did they say? I mean, what did you talk about?" She was definitely on high alert.

"Well..." I glanced away, not wanting to embarrass her. I looked back at her and lowered my voice. "Your name came up."

"Oh, Christ," she said. "I mean...I'm sorry." She shook her head again. "Let me guess. The trial?"

"Yes."

"Of course. It's the talk of the town. What did they tell you?"

"They told me about your fiancé...Carlyle? They said he'd been charged with killing a deer hunter a couple weeks ago and that the trial is scheduled to begin in a few more weeks."

"Actually, probably not until sometime after the holidays," Allie said. "These things take forever."

"And he's in jail in the meantime?"

"Yes. The judge denied him bail. I guess he thought Carlyle was a flight risk, or something. Which is ridiculous. Carlyle has lived here all his life and he's not the type to run away from his problems. Plus...I know he wouldn't leave me."

"They said he was arrested because another guy claimed he

confessed to him."

"Charlie Flanagan. Carlyle didn't confess to him and a lot of us know he didn't. If you knew anything about Charlie, or Charlie and Carlyle both, you'd know Charlie's lying about Carlyle confessing. Charlie Flanagan has been causing trouble all his life and this is just the latest example. He enjoys making trouble for people."

"They mentioned he's a prison guard."

"Right. At Mt. Sterling, about 20 miles from here. It's the perfect job for him; it gives him a chance to bully other people and get away with it."

There it was again.

I pushed the envelope a little further. "Pete and Walt kinda hinted there might be some jealousy involved. That Charlie might be hoping to get Carlyle out of the way because he's...uh...interested in you."

She laughed, but not happily. "That's nuts and Charlie should know it. We all went to school together...Carlyle and Charlie were in Amy's class, and I was one year behind them. I went out with Charlie twice, I think it was, and that was enough to convince me he was bad news."

"But he's been carrying a torch for you ever since?" I was trying to sound like I was just trying to pick my way through the puzzle pieces; I hoped my attempt was convincing.

"Oh, I wouldn't say that. Charlie married another one of my classmates, Jolene Mitchell, and they were together for a few years until she decided she couldn't put up with him, either, and they got divorced. Meanwhile, I got married myself and then divorced a few years later." She stopped suddenly and even in the faint light I could see she looked embarrassed. "Sorry," she said. "I didn't mean to get into all this ancient personal history."

"No problem," I said. "And no need for apology. I asked the question. I shouldn't have pried."

"Oh, that's all right. I mean, I can understand why you might be curious, after Pete and Walt filled you in on all the town gossip."

"Well, they did say this was pretty much the big news right now. If your fiancé is in jail on a manslaughter charge, there's bound to be talk." As soon as I said this I realized she hadn't mentioned that Carlyle had been charged with manslaughter and I gave myself a mental kick in the butt for mentioning it, but she didn't question my knowledge of this. Or maybe she just assumed I'd learned it from Pete and Walt.

"You got that right," she said. "Right now it's like everybody's favorite subject...at least at the Rushville Tap and the other bars."

"You said a lot of people don't believe Carlyle confessed to Charlie."

"No, I said a lot us *know* Carlyle didn't confess to Charlie. See, you have to understand, Carlyle is a really nice guy, and I'm not just saying that because he's my fiancé. He's a straight shooter...sorry, that was a bad choice of words. He's the most honest person I know, and ironically, that's what got him into all this trouble. He found this dead guy out in the woods and reported it, even took the sheriff back out there to show him the location. Then like two days later, he's arrested because Charlie Flanagan says he confessed to him. Which is, pardon my French, total bullshit."

There was no mistaking the bitterness in her voice now. She was certain her fiancé was the victim of a monstrous injustice, one perpetrated by Charlie Flanagan. From everything I'd learned, I was inclined to agree. But I also couldn't ignore the fact that I, too, had played a key role in bringing about Carlyle Wilson's wrongful arrest.

"Truth is, I met Charlie Flanagan tonight myself," I said, not wanting to risk her finding this out later from some other source and thinking I'd been playing her.

"Oh? There at the Tap?"

"Right. He was already there when I went in."

She snorted. "Of course he was. And what was your impression?"

I shook my head. "Nothing positive. He finished his beer a few minutes after I got there and he gave me a pretty good shoulder bump on his way out. Told me to watch it."

"That sounds like him. What did you do?"

"I let it pass. I wasn't going to pick a fight with a stranger in a strange town, and I'm a little too old for barroom brawls anyway." I hoped this answer sounded like common sense and not craven cowardice. "The bartender, Walt, told me to ignore it; said Charlie has been feeling a lot of pressure lately. That's what led to our conversation about the trial and your fiancé."

"You were smart to let it pass. Charlie likes to pick on people that are...um...smaller than him," she said, and I realized she was probably trying to let me off the hook, either for being considerably older than Charlie or for not picking up the gauntlet he'd thrown down. Maybe both.

"Well, I can't deny it didn't set well with me, but I decided it wasn't worth making an issue over."

"That was smart."

"And like I said, that's what led to the conversation about your fiancé. Walt and Pete don't believe he killed that deer hunter, either."

"Well, they're right. I wish more people felt that way. Actually, plenty of people *do* feel that way, but that doesn't change the fact that Carlyle is in jail and he's going on trial."

"Does he have a good lawyer?" I asked, remembering what Pete Sawyer had said.

"His lawyer is a guy named Prescott and yes, he seems to be pretty sharp. But I guess we won't really know how good he is until the trial. In the meantime..." she sighed, "in the meantime, we're just trying to think positive."

"I guess that's all you can do."

"That, and hope Charlie Flanagan gets hit by a truck."

Or something, I thought.

CHAPTER 30

The next morning, to borrow Dave Larson's line from the night before, I couldn't have hit water if I'd capsized a canoe. At least not at first.

I spent a restless night following my visit to the Rushville Tap, my Charlie Flanagan encounter and my conversation afterward with Allie Marshall on the porch of the lodge. Ordinarily I don't have any trouble sleeping in a strange bed, but this time my brain was in overdrive, wrestling with various scenarios and trying to formulate a game plan for getting rid of Flanagan and thereby—I hoped—see the manslaughter charge against Carlyle Wilson dropped.

I wasn't any closer to a solution when I finally said to hell with it at 5:30 a.m. and got out of bed. I stumbled into the bathroom and into the shower—OK, I stopped long enough to piss first—and stood under the shower spray for a good ten minutes, trying to let the warm water clear my head. It didn't have much effect.

I toweled off, decided to forego shaving, and pulled on jeans, moccasins and a sweatshirt, and headed downstairs. When I'd rinsed out my coffee cup at the sink behind the bar last evening, I'd noticed a coffee maker on the counter next to the sink. That coffee maker was my immediate objective. I knew I was going to need a serious caffeine jolt to jump-start the day and get through the morning.

Not surprisingly, none of my fellow bird hunters were up and around yet. The lounge and bar were dark except for a couple of low-intensity nightlights that enabled me to navigate over to the panel of light switches on the wall behind the bar. After a couple of tries I found the switch for the light above the bar and the sink, and I left that one on, the rest of the room dark.

I found a plastic tub of Colombian coffee and a package of paper coffee filters in the cupboard above the sink. I got the coffee maker started—luckily it was a model similar to the one I have at home and didn't require a graduate degree in engineering or computer science to program or operate—then I pulled a clean mug bearing the Hidden Hollow logo from the cupboard.

The coffee maker was one of those with an "interrupt" feature that allows you to pull the carafe out and pour a cup before the brewing cycle has completed. When there was about an inch of coffee in the bottom of the carafe I pulled it off the warming plate and poured myself a cup. I added a spoonful of powdered French vanilla non-dairy creamer (talk about an oxymoron!), stirred it and carried the cup to the bar. I climbed up on a stool and sat there in the semi-dark room, sipping coffee and trying to focus my thoughts on the day ahead and not let myself keep getting sidetracked by the Charlie Flanagan dilemma.

I was scheduled to hunt with Mitch Halvorsen and I knew he would be doing his best to show me a good time. I had booked a 12-bird package, which would consist of eight quail and four chukar partridge. These would be released prior to the hunt in cover that would closely approximate that found during an actual hunt...or at least, so I hoped.

I didn't want to stroll through feed plots along closely mowed paths littered with previous clients' fired shotgun shells. The best hunting preserves are those that provide a realistic hunting experience, not a fish-in-the-barrel type shoot. Hunters and their dogs should have to work for their game, just as they would on a hunt for wild birds in natural cover.

If Hidden Hollow lived up to its claims, that's the kind of hunt I would experience, and I would have no problem writing a feature for the magazine recommending the preserve to readers.

Last night after dinner Amy Halvorsen had told us breakfast was at 8:00 and we would head out to the bird fields at 9:00. I glanced at the clock on the wall behind the bar and saw it was 6:10. I had nearly two hours until breakfast. I sighed and took another sip of coffee.

It was going to be a long morning.

BREAKFAST WAS ANOTHER sumptuous affair, with an egg, cheese and sausage casserole, hash browns and fresh-baked biscuits...and yes, a boat full of sausage gravy to drown the latter. I tried to show some restraint, not all that successfully. The food was just damn good.

Amy Halvorsen handled the serving, with Allie nowhere in evidence. I assumed she was outside preparing for the hunt she'd guide. I remembered she was taking out Dave and Mike Larson this morning.

Conversation among the other clients primarily revolved around the morning hunt, with plenty of good-natured ribbing among the Parks brothers about who'd get the first bird, who'd shoot the most birds, whether Aaron could avoid being confused by Steven's commands to Baron, and so on. Typical brother stuff, in other words.

I sat at an adjoining table with the Larsons. Despite all the cups of coffee I'd consumed, I still felt like I was running on autopilot after my mostly sleepless night. Thankfully Dave and Mike were of a less raucous nature than the Parks brothers and the conversation demands were minimal. They did most of the talking and I managed to get by with mostly monosyllabic replies, hoping I wasn't sounding antisocial.

At one point Dave asked me if I'd found the local color I'd been looking for the night before and I gave him a highly condensed account of my visit to the Rushville Tap, characterizing it as a friendly place and omitting any mention of Charlie Flanagan and the conversation I'd had with Walt and Pete.

That seemed to satisfy him and I allowed my mind to wander, still puzzling over how I was going to handle Flanagan.

I'd driven over to Hidden Hollow with the idea—half-baked, at best—that I would locate him, get a better feel for whether he'd fabricated Carlyle Wilson's confession, and if so, eliminate him. All within the course of a long weekend.

I'd come equipped with a suitable cover story and plenty of firepower, but I realized now that my plan was going to require some modification. I'd identified Flanagan and confirmed that he probably *had* made up the story about Carlyle Wilson confessing to him but killing him while I was still here—my cover story notwithstanding—would be risky. Too many people might find it more than a little suspicious that Charlie Flanagan had died shortly before he was to testify in a criminal trial *and* at the same time an out-of-town sportsman had had a run-in with him (brief though it was) in a local bar.

Whether anyone would really associate our encounter with his subsequent demise was a stretch, admittedly. But it was a chance I didn't want to take. Nor did I want to do anything that might cast suspicion on, say, Allie Marshall. Charlie Flanagan turning up dead just before he was scheduled to testify against her fiancé *would* raise all kinds of questions, no doubt about it, and I didn't want any of that suspicion to blow back on her.

Amy Halvorsen appeared at our table with coffee pot in hand and asked if any of us needed a refill. Dave and Mike declined and I did also, realizing I'd probably already drunk enough coffee that morning to necessitate stopping my hunt every 10 or 15 minutes to take a leak. Thank goodness my guide was going to be Mitch Halvorsen and not Allie Marshall or I might have seriously embarrassed myself.

"In that case," Amy said, "you might want to head back to your rooms and get your gear on. We got about three inches of snow last night and the temp is just a little above freezing so wear insulated waterproof boots if you have them. Your guides will be ready to take you out in about 15 minutes."

WE ALL ASSEMBLED in the parking lot in front of the lodge some 15 minutes later. I'd opted to start the morning with the 20-gauge Remington Premier, figuring it was more than enough gun for quail and chukar on a preserve hunt.

I would soon prove myself wrong and embarrass myself thoroughly in the process.

I stood there in the group with the cased Premier and my fellow hunters did the same with their various firearms. Mitch Halvorsen greeted us and then gave us a quick rundown on safety procedures to be observed in the field. It was similar to speeches I'd heard at many other preserves over the years, and it further confirmed my positive impression of Mitch Halvorsen as a conscientious proprietor and hunt guide.

"I know that with the exception of Rob, you all heard this same speech yesterday before we went out, but a little reminder never hurts," he said. I glanced around and to everyone's credit, they all appeared to be paying attention. "You're all hunting over your own dogs and I'm sure no one wants to see their dog injured, so I'll remind you not to shoot at any bird on the ground, even if it's a cripple.

"Also, don't shoot at any bird that is below the line of the horizon. Try to make sure you see some sky, or at least the horizon line, below any bird you shoot at. That's not always easy to do in some of our thicker cover, but low shots are the cause of accidents, and we don't want any. If you're not sure, pass up the shot. You're going to see plenty of birds today so if you have to pass one up, you'll get another chance soon enough.

"Make sure you know where your partners are at all times…you're all wearing some orange so that should make it easier to keep track of each other. And of course, try to remember where your guide is also, as they're expensive to replace." This got a few laughs.

"Keep your guns unloaded and cased until we get to the field. Once we get started, keep the muzzle of your gun pointed up at all times when you're not taking a shot. A low muzzle is dangerous if you'd happen to trip or stumble, so again, keep your muzzles pointed up if you're not shooting.

"We'll hunt until about 11:30, then we'll load up and return to the lodge for lunch. In the meantime, if you experience any trouble, let your guide know immediately. You all appear to be in pretty good shape but don't hesitate to let us know if you start feeling uncomfortable for any reason. No one has to be a hero and you shouldn't try to tough it out if you're not feeling well.

"I'll be going out with Rob this morning. Dave and Mike, you'll be going out with Allie; and you Parkses will be going out with Matt. They're waiting for us over by the kennels, so if there aren't any questions, let's head over that way and you can load up your dogs."

We all turned toward the kennels where two large ATVs and a Chevy Suburban sat waiting. I guessed the Parks brothers would be riding to their bird field in the Suburban and the Larsons and myself would be on the ATVs, both of which had a large dog crate strapped onto the back. Allie and a tall fellow I hadn't met, presumably the guide named Matt, were waiting for us by the rigs.

We'd only taken a couple steps in their direction when I realized I'd left my camera bag in my room. If I was going to write a feature about my hunt at Hidden Hollow I'd need photos to illustrate it, which meant I'd have to shoot some over the course of the morning. I called ahead to Mitch, who was leading the group.

"Hey, Mitch," I said, "sorry to hold things up, but I need to go back to my room for a minute. Forgot my camera."

He turned and said, "No problem. Just grab your camera and come on over when you're ready. I'll get these guys on their way and then we can be off."

The group continued on to the kennel as I turned back to the lodge. It was no big deal, I realized, and Mitch had handled my forgetfulness politely, another mark of a good host. But I chided myself anyway, feeling like my brain was still stuck in low gear.

Not an auspicious start to the morning.

CHAPTER 31

It only got worse once we started hunting.

The other two groups had already departed by the time I got over to the kennel with my shotgun and my camera bag. Mitch Halvorsen was standing next to the remaining ATV, a large Yamaha four-seater side-by-side. He smiled as I approached.

"Just put your gear on the back seat and then load up your dog and we can get going," he said. I did as instructed and turned toward the kennel.

Preacher was waiting at the gate of her run, whining and doing a little dance with her forepaws. Before breakfast I'd thrown on a coat and boots and walked over to see her. I'd sweet-talked her for a few minutes and promised we'd be going out for birds soon. She'd assured me she was ready.

I unlatched the gate and she stepped out and paced beside me over to the ATV. Mitch was standing at the back of the rig with the gate open to the large dog crate strapped on the equipment rack. "Will she be OK riding back here?" he asked.

"Yeah, she should be fine," I said. I tapped the doorway of the crate and said, "Hop up!" Preacher complied, sailing in and settling immediately. Most folks use the command "Kennel!" or "Kennel up!" when they want their dog to enter something, but I'm more conversational. When you live with a dog 24/7, she quickly becomes attuned to your language and your tone and it's not necessary to bark commands like a drill sergeant.

I latched the crate door and walked around to the passenger side of the ATV. I climbed in as Mitch was doing the same on the other side. He cranked the ignition and we headed down the lane that ran past the barn. Tire tracks in the fresh snow showed where the other two hunting parties had preceded us.

As we came around to the backside of the barn I got my first look at the kennels housing the preserve's dogs. Most of them were barking, no doubt hoping for a chance to be taken along on the hunt. I saw two black Labs, a Brittany, a German shorthair and two English pointers, then we were past the kennels and heading on down the lane.

"That's an interesting mix of dog power you have there," I said, trying to speak loudly enough to be heard over the roar of the ATV's engine.

"We run a little bit of everything," Mitch replied. "Sometimes clients have a preference and I let them choose. Guys hunting quail want to see them pointed, of course, so we run the pointers or the Brit and the shorthair. For pheasants, we use the Labs quite a bit because…" he hesitated, then continued, "you don't always get a clean kill on pheasants and you need a dog that's a surefire retriever to run down the cripples."

"The pointers and the Brit don't retrieve?"

"Oh, they do, but they're not as gung-ho about it as the Labs," he said. "Sometimes we run a mixed brace, a Lab with one or both of the pointers. The Lab stays in close while the pointers work the cover and find the birds. Then we'll send the Lab in to flush the birds and handle most of the retrieves."

"That's a slick operation," I said. "I've hunted on a few quail plantations in the South where they did the same thing, only their pickup dogs were usually Boykins or English cockers."

Mitch laughed. "Funny you should say that," he said. "Amy has been after me for some time now to get an English cocker. I haven't given in yet, but I expect it might happen."

"I don't think you'd be sorry," I said. "I hunted over one in Georgia a few years ago, a little black and white dog named Ralph. There were several other writers on that hunt and by the end of our time there, everybody had hunted with him and we all had Ralph stories to tell. He was kind of a cocky little guy and just a hoot to hunt with."

"I like dogs like that," Mitch said. "Dogs with personality. They make it more fun."

"Yes, they do. And Ralph definitely had personality, no doubt about it."

"What about that big wirehair of yours? I think Amy said her name is Preacher?"

"That's right. She's named for Clint Eastwood's character in *Pale Rider*."

"Amy mentioned that. That's one of my favorite old movies." I winced at the word "old"—I seemed to keep attracting these unwelcome reminders—but then I realized that the movie had probably first been released around the time Mitch had been born and he'd most likely only seen it on cable or DVD...in fact, I remembered Amy mentioning that they'd watched the DVD quite a few times. Well, it was to their credit that they were Eastwood fans anyway, considering they were of a much younger generation.

"We don't see many wirehairs in this area so I'm looking forward to seeing her work," Mitch said.

I laughed. "Well, I hope she doesn't do anything to embarrass us too badly," I said.

I shouldn't have worried. Preacher was more than up to the task at hand. Me, not so much.

WE FOLLOWED THE LANE along a tree line until it forked at a break in the trees, where we turned to the right. The tracks of the other vehicles continued on to the left but there was a single set of tracks going off to the right as well, and I realized those would have been made earlier that morning when Mitch or one of his guides had come out to release the birds we would be hunting.

We traveled another quarter mile or so and then Mitch stopped the ATV. "We'll start here," he said. We were on the edge of a picked cornfield bordered by shelterbelts and stands of briars and multiflora—classic Midwestern quail habitat, in other words. My worries about hunting in an unnatural, too-groomed setting were allayed.

"Looks good," I said. I climbed out of the ATV and walked around to the back to release Preacher from the crate. She jumped down, took a few steps and squatted to pee. That seemed like a good idea to me as well and I stepped away from the rig to take care of matters.

"Too much coffee this morning," I said over my shoulder, and Mitch laughed.

"That can happen," he said.

I zipped up and returned to the ATV to uncase the Remington. I considered taking my camera also but decided to make the first pass without it so I could concentrate on watching Preacher work. After we downed a few birds, I could throttle back a bit and focus on photo ops. I wanted shots of Preacher working the cover and pointing, of course, but also some of Mitch and a few of myself. I'd need Mitch's help to stage and shoot some of the latter.

"You can go ahead and load up," Mitch said. "We'll swing down here to the right along the tree line."

I dropped two Federal low-brass shells with 7-1/2 shot into the breech of the Remington and closed the action. "Hunt 'em up!" I told Preacher and she moved away from us at a lope, quartering out into the corn stubble and then turning back toward the tree line. We followed her down the edge, walking side by side.

"She's got a nice easy gait," Mitch said. "Is that her usual range?" Preacher was about 50 yards in front of us.

"She'll move out farther in open cover, like big CRP fields," I said. "But yeah, when we're working mixed cover like this, she tends to stay within about 50 to 75 yards."

"That's a nice comfortable range. Most guys don't want their dogs out there on the horizon, at least not here in the Midwest."

"I gave up chasing those horizon-busters years ago," I said, and Mitch laughed.

"I take it you haven't always had wirehairs, then?"

"No, my first three dogs were setters," I said. "A couple of them came from field trial stock, so they were bred to run in front of a horse. Trying to keep up with them always gave me a good workout. But my arthritic old knees just aren't up to that anymore." Good Lord, here I was using the O word on myself now.

Mitch laughed again. "That's why you switched to wirehairs?"

"That was one of the big reasons, yes. I wanted something a little closer working and easier handling. Plus, I hunted over a couple of wirehairs belonging to friends and I liked their looks. Before Preacher I had another one named Bristol."

As we'd been talking, Preacher had been working the cover strip next to the corn stubble. Now she slowed, stopped, then moved forward another few feet. She stiffened into a point before a large clump of multiflora at the base of a huge oak tree, her head outstretched, her docked tail erect and quivering slightly.

"There we go," I said, and Mitch and I picked up our pace.

"You go on in and take the shot," Mitch advised. "If you don't mind, I'll just hang back and watch."

"That's fine," I said, mentally kicking myself now for not bringing the camera. I could have asked Mitch to shoot a couple of photos of me flushing the bird or birds in front of Preacher and, I hoped, dropping at least one for her to retrieve.

A few seconds later, I was glad the camera was still in its case on the back seat of the ATV.

I moved up behind Preacher and reminded myself, as I'd done thousands of times before, not to try to spot the birds on the ground in front of her. Looking at the birds on the ground almost guarantees you won't be able to get your eyes back up high enough and quickly enough to make the shot when the birds flush. It's better, as any shooting coach will tell you, to keep your gaze out at about horizon-level and let the birds rise into your sight picture.

That little trick didn't work for me this time, however. As I came abreast of Preacher's flank two quail flushed from beneath the multiflora. Both swung to my left toward the cornfield and I swung with them, pulling the trigger just as the

Remington's muzzle swept past the lead bird. Or so I thought.

Both birds kept flying.

I tried to correct my swing and center on the trailing bird, which was now flying almost straight away. I pulled the trigger a second time and watched as both birds flew on untouched across the corn stubble to land in the tree line on the opposite side of the field, maybe 100 yards away.

"Damn," I said, glancing back at Mitch, who was standing a few yards away with a sympathetic smile on his face. At least I thought it was meant to be sympathetic.

"Not sure what happened there," I said apologetically. "Thought I was on those birds."

"Not your fault," Mitch said. "Federal just forgot to load the shot in those two shells."

I smiled weakly at the lame joke. "Yeah, that must be it," I said. But I was reviewing both shots in my mind, wondering what the hell had gone wrong.

"We'll just continue on down this edge," Mitch said. "We can work all the way around this field and try to pick up those two bobs on the other side."

"OK," I said. Preacher had relaxed from her point and stood looking at me reproachfully. I gave her a little wave and said, "Go on, find us another one." She trotted away and began questing through the cover.

Mitch and I followed, walking side by side like before. Neither of us spoke and I wondered if he was considering the possibility that I might be all words and no birds—an outdoor writer who talked (well, wrote) a good game but couldn't hit squat when he went afield.

I knew better, my poor performance notwithstanding. I just hoped I could prove it.

CHAPTER 32

We were almost at the far end of the field, opposite where we'd parked the ATV, when Preacher locked up again. This time she was pointing at a large brush pile, a tangle of downed limbs and branches surrounded by briars and tall grass. If I hadn't known better—that the brush pile most likely harbored another bird or birds, released earlier that morning—I'd have guessed, based on the cover, she might have been pointing a rabbit.

That's considered a cardinal sin among bird dog purists, but wirehairs were developed as a versatile breed expected to handle both feathers and fur in their native Germany. I don't take the versatility thing that far—I never shoot rabbits when I'm hunting with Preacher—but neither do I make a big issue of it with her if she points one.

Why not? Because I don't know, and no human knows, what a gamebird or a rabbit smells like to a dog. For all we know, they may have similar scents. I once posed a question in one of my magazine editorials, asking readers to write in and share what non-gamebird species their dogs had pointed.

The results were varied—everything from the expected meadowlarks and field sparrows (referred to by gun dog trainers as "stink birds") to more exotic creatures like mice, groundhogs and box turtles. But the most unusual answer of all came from a guy who described in detail how, during an early spring outing, he and a buddy had seen their two setters lock up tight on a newborn Hereford calf nestled in a multiflora thicket.

So, given the vagaries of scent, I don't fault Preacher if she occasionally points a rabbit. But as I moved up on her point this time, I was reasonably certain I'd be flushing a bird, and I hoped I could make a good shot and redeem myself in Mitch Halvorsen's eyes…and Preacher's, to boot.

Well, I was right about it being a bird, anyway.

A single chukar partridge flushed from the brush pile and, like the two quail a few minutes earlier, headed out across the corn stubble. I told myself not to rush the shot and I mounted the gun carefully, tracked the bird and fired.

The chukar flew on, crossing the field and landing on the fence line not far from where the two quail had pitched down. Another miss.

"Sheesh!" I said, shaking my head. I broke the Remington, caught the fired shell and pocketed it. I dropped in a fresh shell and closed the action. I looked over at Mitch and said, "What am I doing wrong?"

"Well, that time you lifted your head just as you fired," he said. He smiled and added, "I think you were a little too eager to see the bird fall." To his credit, he'd withheld his comment until I'd asked, not offering unsolicited advice or critique.

"OK, thanks," I said, and I meant it. I'm not opposed to constructive criticism, and the error in my shooting form he'd just pointed out—lifting my head off the stock—would indeed explain my miss. I vowed to keep my head down the next time.

I also sympathized with Mitch's situation. He wanted to show me a good hunt and so far I wasn't holding up my part of the bargain. The birds were presented well in natural cover, the dog was pointing them solidly, and the shooter was letting the team down. I definitely needed to up my game.

I glanced over at Preacher, who appeared less forgiving than Mitch. She was favoring me with the look that says, "What the hell is your problem?" Anyone who's spent much time hunting with bird dogs knows that expression, a combination of disgust and disappointment. Veteran gun dogs *know* when you should be able to make a shot, and they don't hesitate to show their displeasure when you whiff. Preacher was letting me have it with both barrels.

I sighed and said, "OK, let's try for another one." Preacher swung down the edge and Mitch and I followed, just as a burst of shooting sounded from another part of the preserve. Either the Larsons or the Parkses were getting some action and I hoped they were having better luck than I was. I said as much to Mitch.

"Oh, you'll start connecting here directly," he said, then repeated something he'd mentioned during his safety talk at the lodge. "You're going to see plenty of birds this morning so you'll have a lot more chances."

"I'm going to need them," I said, attempting a laugh. I tried to relax and concentrate on what my dog was doing. I hoped I wasn't heading into a major slump—the occasional curse, usually inexplicable, of all shooters. In this case, however, there *was* an explanation—a near-sleepless night caused by my preoccupation with Charlie Flanagan.

We'd reached the end of the cornfield and Preacher swung away to our left, quartering at right angles to the direction we were walking. "OK to head that direction?" I asked.

"Yep, it's fine," Mitch said. "We have this area completely to ourselves so we'll let her pick the course."

We followed Preacher for another fifty yards or so and I noticed her casts narrowing. She was moving with her muzzle held high, trying to pinpoint the scent, and her tail became a blur. "Getting birdy," I said, and Mitch nodded.

Preacher made another half cast and then wheeled back toward us. She froze in a half circle, head turned so she appeared almost to be pointing over her shoulder. One hind leg was cocked off the ground in mid-stride and, my miserable shooting notwithstanding, I wished now I'd brought my camera to get a photo of her.

"She's got that bird nailed cold," Mitch said.

"Right," I said, moving up on her point with my shotgun at port arms. When I was within a couple yards another chukar flushed, coming almost directly at me. It veered just as it passed my head so close I could feel the wind on my face from its wingbeats. I instinctively ducked, then spun around as the bird headed straight out across the corn stubble.

I straightened up and recovered my balance, mounted the gun and remembered to keep my cheek tight on the stock. I gave it another second, then I fired and, miraculously, the bird dropped.

"Now you're cookin'!" Mitch said. "You just needed a little more of a challenge!"

"Challenge, hell!" I said. "That was self-defense!" I knew I was grinning. "That bird nearly flew up my nose."

Mitch laughed. "Yeah, we breed 'em aggressive!" he said.

Preacher located the chukar in the corn stubble, picked it up and was on her way back to us as I broke the Remington again and replaced the fired shell. I closed the action and bent to take the bird from her, but as always, she made a short victory lap around us before stopping in front of me to deliver. I'm not a stickler for the field trial etiquette that requires a dog to sit at heel before presenting a retrieved bird, and apparently Mitch wasn't either.

"That's a mighty good dog you've got there," he said. "I wouldn't mind having her in my string."

"Thanks." I took the bird from Preacher and smoothed its feathers. "She's probably a better dog than I deserve, considering the way I've been shooting."

"Aw, you've got your groove back," Mitch said, and with a bird in hand, I hoped he was right.

"These chukars are beautiful birds," I said, admiring the plumage of the one I held. Primarily dove gray with black and white bars on the flanks and a striking black outline around an ivory-colored face, chukars have red bills and eye-rims and bright orange-red legs. The birds aren't native to North America—they were introduced from southern Europe and Asia—but they are now well established throughout the mountain West, and they are popular quarry on shooting preserves as well.

They are also wonderful table fare.

"Yes, they are," Mitch agreed. I started to slip the bird into the game bag of my vest and Mitch said, "I'll carry your birds if you'd like."

"That's OK," I said. "I doubt I'll shoot enough for the weight to be a problem."

He laughed and said, "Well, you never know!"

We continued on around the edge of the cornfield and it wasn't long before Preacher struck another point.

The remainder of the morning went much better. I missed a couple more shots but dropped most of the birds Preacher pointed—enough to get myself back into her good graces, anyway—and even managed to score a double on another brace of bobwhites. When Mitch told me it was time to head back to the lodge for lunch, I was feeling reasonably good about how things had played out.

A final tally of the birds I'd taken—I had eventually acquiesced and let Mitch share the carrying duties—showed six quail and three chukar. So I'd shot nine of the twelve birds released for my hunt, a respectable number.

We'd returned to the ATV a couple times over the course of the morning to move to adjoining areas, and after our first pass I had carried my camera as well as my shotgun. I had photos of Preacher on point and making retrieves, Mitch walking the cover, and even a few of myself swinging and firing on flushing birds. Mitch had proven to be a quick study in the operation of my camera, a Nikon Coolpix P520 that I've used for quite a few years—not super-sophisticated as cameras go but user-friendly and adequate for the job at hand—and he was happy to help me get the photos I needed.

We'd heard shooting throughout the morning but had never seen the other two hunting parties, and I considered that another plus worth mentioning in my article. There's a certain amount of unavoidable artificiality to any shooting preserve operation, but not being crowded by other hunters helps reduce that feeling. It was to Mitch's credit that he'd planned our hunt so that we'd avoided bumping into the other groups.

"This was a good morning, even if my shooting was pretty dismal there at the start," I said as we settled into the seats of the ATV for the trip back to the lodge. "You've got great cover and strong-flying birds. This is the kind of place we like to feature in the magazine."

"Thanks," Mitch said. "I really appreciate that. We try to make it as realistic as possible."

"Well, you're doing a good job. I don't think any of our readers would be disappointed if they came here for a hunt."

"That's good to hear. And as far as your shooting earlier..." he laughed, "believe me, I've seen a lot worse."

"Yeah, I suppose," I said.

Mitch cranked the ignition and we started back up the lane toward the lodge.

I wondered what Amy would be serving for lunch.

CHAPTER 33

Lunch was every bit as good as the previous two meals I'd eaten at the lodge—BLT wraps and white chili made with pheasant meat. Once again I had to struggle to show some restraint.

Mitch and I were the last to arrive at the lodge after the morning's hunt. We stopped first at the kennel building, where Jasper the Lab and Baron the shorthair, already back from their hunts, barked a welcome. Mitch headed on over to the lodge while I got Preacher squared away in her run, feeding her and giving her fresh water. I knew that after eating she'd most likely snooze the afternoon away.

As for my own afternoon itinerary, a nap definitely sounded inviting but I needed to shoot some photos of the lodge, both inside and out, for my article. After that, I planned to head back into Rushville to do a little more poking around and see if I could turn up anything more that might help me figure out what to do about Charlie Flanagan, and how to do it.

I carried my cased shotgun and camera bag over to the lodge. As I mounted the steps to the porch I saw a hand-lettered sign taped to the front door that read: *Please leave your boots on the carpet inside.* I stepped through the door and saw a row of wet and muddy boots on a strip of all-weather carpet beside the doorway. I followed suit and removed my boots.

In stocking feet I crossed the lounge and went upstairs to my room. I dropped my gun and camera on the second bed and took off my cap, vest, and the insulated hoody I'd worn underneath. I shucked off my brush pants and pulled on the jeans I'd worn earlier. I stepped into my moccasins and headed back downstairs.

The Larsons and the Parkses were already eating when I got there, and they hailed me as I came in and took the same seat I'd occupied at breakfast. I helped myself to a wrap from the platter on our table and a bowl of the chili from the crockpot next to the platter. A matching crockpot sat on the table occupied by the Parkses. Dave Larson grinned at me and asked, "So, how'd it go?"

"A little rocky at the start, but I eventually figured out where to point the gun," I said. "Wound up with six quail and three chukar and I got some good photos of my dog, so all in all, it was a good morning. How'd you fellows do?"

"We had a good morning also," Dave said. "We got seven pheasants, and Mike was responsible for six and a half of those. But no complaints on my part…Jasper had a ball, and it was just a fine morning to be out."

"It was that," I agreed.

Amy Halvorsen came in from the kitchen with another platter of BLT wraps and asked who wanted seconds. I was tempted but opted for a second bowl of the pheasant chili instead. The Parks brothers and Mike Larson all took another wrap but Dave declined.

"You're going out again this afternoon, right?" I said.

"Mike is," Dave said. "I was going to, but I'm thinking a nap might be in order instead. My old knees could stand a break, anyway."

"I hear that," I said. "I'm gonna shoot a few more pics around the lodge and make some notes for my article while everything's fresh in my mind." I didn't mention that I was planning to make another run into town.

It got quiet for a few minutes while everyone concentrated on their food. Then Amy returned from the kitchen again, this time bearing a pumpkin pie in one hand and an apple pie in the other. She set them on an empty table and said, "OK, we have pumpkin and apple pie, so let me know your preference." She laughed and added, "Of course, you can have a slice of each if you'd like."

The Parks brothers laughed in return and I guessed they might take her up on the latter offer. Dave Larson groaned and said, "It's a good thing we're leaving tomorrow. If we stayed much longer I wouldn't be able to waddle into my house when we get home."

"Yeah, no kidding," I said.

THE RUSHVILLE TOWN SQUARE was a busy place on a Saturday afternoon with strolling shoppers on the sidewalks and no available parking places on the street. I circled the square a couple times before I finally caught a break when a car backed out of a parking space in front of the Subway sandwich shop. I pulled into the vacated spot and sat for a moment, trying to decide what to do.

I considered paying another visit to the Rushville Tap but I didn't really want a beer so early in the afternoon, the old "it's five o'clock somewhere" rationale notwithstanding. Plus, I was still feeling the effects of Amy's lunch and wasn't sure I had the capacity for twelve more ounces of anything just yet.

That feeling of fullness helped me reach a decision. After lunch I'd spent about 45 minutes shooting the photos I needed of the lodge, but a little more exercise wouldn't hurt. I turned off the engine and climbed out of the Equinox. I didn't bother locking the door, figuring my vehicle was safe enough in a small town during daylight hours. Call me trusting.

During my circuits of the square I'd spotted an antique shop on one corner and for want of any other goal I decided to go in and browse a bit. That probably wasn't going to help me come up with a plan for dealing with Charlie Flanagan but it gave me a reason to walk around the square, at least, and once in a while I've found an interesting piece of sporting dog memorabilia—an old print or a nice statuette—in such places. My home is decorated with those pieces.

I never made it into the antique shop.

I'd walked about halfway around the square when a white F150 pickup passed me. As it did so, I glanced at the driver and saw it was Charlie Flanagan. Though I'd only seen him for a few minutes the night before and he was now wearing a camouflage bill cap, I recognized him by his profile and his mustache and his scowl.

Standing in the open bed of the pickup was a good-looking yellow Labrador, shifting his weight to keep his balance.

I immediately bristled. A dog riding loose in the open bed of a pickup is an injury waiting to happen. Even if the dog doesn't attempt to jump out if it sees something it wants to chase or investigate—say, a cat, a squirrel, another dog—any unexpected movement by the vehicle like a sharp turn could send the dog flying out of the bed and into the path of oncoming traffic.

There was little danger of that happening at the moment as the pickup was moving slowly around the square while Flanagan jockeyed for a parking space. Still, knowing that Flanagan lived out of town off the highway meant the dog had ridden some distance at higher speeds. Whether from ignorance or carelessness, or more likely both, Flanagan was apparently not too concerned about the dog's safety.

I took a deep breath and kept watching. The pickup kept moving until it was a half block away, then I saw its brake lights flash. Just ahead of the truck, another car was backing out of a parking space. Flanagan waited for it to leave and then pulled into the space. Without thinking I quickened my pace, wanting to close the distance between us.

I was maybe thirty yards away when Flanagan climbed out of the cab. He stepped up onto the sidewalk and started walking toward me. As he did so, I looked past him and saw the yellow Lab brace his forepaws on the side rail of the pickup bed, then jump out and onto the pavement. He started after Flanagan and I could see by his legginess and lanky build that he was a young dog, not yet filled out with a Lab's typical sturdiness. He was probably no more than a year old.

Flanagan apparently heard the dog coming. He turned and, as the dog drew alongside him, he drew back his right leg and delivered a vicious kick to the dog's hindquarters, knocking the

Lab's back legs out from under him.

The Lab yelped and scrambled to his feet. Flanagan bellowed, "God *damn* it, Dusty! Get back in that truck!" The Lab wheeled and made for the truck at a limping half run. Flanagan watched as the dog jumped at the side, hooked his forepaws over the rail and managed to pull himself back into the bed.

Flanagan turned back toward me, shaking his head. He muttered, "Son of a bitch" to himself but paid no attention to me. He walked another few paces and turned to enter a barber shop.

I stood frozen on the sidewalk, replaying in my mind what I'd just witnessed and thinking only one thought.

Charlie Flanagan, you miserable motherfucker, you're a dead man.

CHAPTER 34

Like thousands of other Baby Boomers, I grew up reading the stories of Albert Payson Terhune.

Terhune was a newspaperman and also a prolific writer of popular fiction in the early 20th century, and his widespread popularity continued for at least another two or three decades after his death in 1942. He wrote mysteries, adventure stories— he called them "yarns"—and domestic dramas, but he is best remembered for the many stories he wrote about his Sunnybank collies—Lad, Bruce, Wolf, Gray Dawn, and others. A cult following of his admirers—myself among them—exists to this day.

In some ways, Terhune was a man ahead of his time. Long before the current crop of celebrity dog trainers and multi-degreed animal behaviorists, Terhune studied and wrote knowledgably and accurately of canine intelligence. He espoused the importance of the early socialization of puppies, and he advocated a regimen of strict obedience for his dogs, but one based on firmness, patience, consistency and rewards rather than harsh physical discipline. A favorite saying of his, repeated throughout his writings, was this: "*A human can show his inferiority to his dog in better ways than by kicking him.*"

Obviously, Charlie Flanagan was not a student of Terhune's school of dog ownership.

I was enraged by what I'd just seen Flanagan do, to the point that my first instinct was to follow him into the barber shop and inflict the same savage ass-kicking on him, consequences and probable subsequent mayhem be damned.

But I gave it a moment and forced myself to relax...or attempted to, anyway.

I started walking toward Flanagan's truck. As I did so, I passed the barber shop and glanced in the front window. Along with two or three other men, Flanagan was seated in one of the regular chairs at the front of the shop, awaiting his turn for a haircut. Apparently he strictly adhered to a high-and-tight sense of style and was going to get his already-short hair cut even shorter.

When I got to Flanagan's truck I stepped off the sidewalk and moved alongside the bed. The yellow Lab was lying there licking his haunch but lifted his head and regarded me warily.

"Hey, buddy," I said. "You doin' OK?"

I saw the wariness leave the Lab's eyes and his tail began thumping the truck bed. He started to get to his feet but I leaned forward and stretched out a hand and said, "Take it easy. You don't need to get up." He settled back down and I ruffled his ears. The tempo of his tail thumping increased.

This was a fine dog, one far better than Charlie Flanagan deserved to own...in fact, after what I'd just witnessed, I was convinced he shouldn't own an animal of any kind. His bullying obviously wasn't limited to other humans.

I gave the Lab a final pat and straightened up. "Take it easy, fella," I repeated by way of farewell. He returned to licking the haunch that had caught the brunt of Flanagan's kick and I moved away from the truck, seething.

As a breed, Labradors have a fairly high incidence of hip dysplasia and any trauma to their hindquarters can exacerbate this condition. I hoped Flanagan's kick hadn't done any permanent damage.

Unlike what I was planning to inflict on Flanagan himself.

I CUT DIAGONALLY ACROSS the square to return to my vehicle, passing the decorated pavilion on the way. I had a plan in mind but I knew I had to move quickly. Because of the other customers ahead of him, I guessed Flanagan would be in the barber shop for at least a half hour or 45 minutes. Not a lot of time, but enough—maybe—for me to accomplish what I needed to do.

If I could find a way to get inside, I was going to toss Flanagan's house.

I doubted that he would be so accommodating as to have left a door unlocked. But I also thought there was a fair chance that he might have a key hidden somewhere. If I could find it— and again, I knew I didn't have much time to spend searching— I was going to let myself in and see if anything inside his house might suggest a course of action…specifically, a way to kill him without incriminating myself or anyone else.

I started the engine and sat for a moment, still trying to calm myself. I couldn't afford to get reckless and make any careless moves. Driving out to Flanagan's house in broad daylight and going inside was risky enough; I needed to do everything I could to not add to that risk.

As I sat there, a curious thought crossed my mind. Less than 24 hours earlier I'd sat in a similar spot here on the Rushville square and wished for some deciding factor, something that would convince me once and for all that Charlie Flanagan's death was necessary.

My wish had been granted. But I was damned sorry that an animal had to suffer to make it happen…an animal whose only real sin was his apparent desire to remain close to his owner.

Dusty—I was pretty sure that was what I'd heard Charlie call him—was, like almost all Labradors, friendly and apparently very loyal. My mind wandered for a moment and I recalled that it was a yellow Labrador named Luath who, motivated by his intense desire to rejoin his master, had led his companions, a Siamese cat and an old bull terrier, on a dangerous cross country trek through the Canadian wilderness in Sheila Burnford's beloved classic, *The Incredible Journey*.

That sort of loyalty deserved a better owner than Charlie Flanagan.

I shook my head, shifted into reverse and backed out of the parking space. I drove halfway around the square, turned at the next intersection and headed out to the highway.

CHAPTER 35

There were tracks in the snow of the lane that went up the hill to Flanagan's house, presumably made by Flanagan himself when he'd driven down the lane to go into town. As I turned in off Highland Road, I tried to center the Equinox in those tracks so Flanagan wouldn't notice a second set when he returned. I didn't know how observant he ordinarily was, but a clearly visible second set of tracks was bound to attract attention and leave him wondering who'd paid him a visit while he was gone.

I got to the top of the hill and looked around before getting out of my vehicle. Flanagan's house, a white, frame two-story with a covered front porch facing the road below, sat to my left. To my right was a large metal equipment shed that appeared to double as a garage. Just beyond the shed was a dog kennel with its gate hanging open. A row of tall windbreak pines stood behind the shed and dog kennel, a space of maybe 30 feet separating the trees from the buildings.

I turned off the ignition and pulled on a pair of cotton gloves, the brown jersey kind you can buy for a buck or so at any gas station or convenience store. I hadn't thought to bring a pair of latex gloves, but these would suffice to prevent leaving fingerprints. They also had the advantage of being brand new, so they were a tight fit, not yet stretched out to hinder dexterity.

I climbed out of my vehicle. The area between the house and the equipment shed was crisscrossed with tracks, both human and vehicular, so I didn't worry about adding mine to the mix. Most of the snow was packed down hard anyway, so any tracks I left would be minimal.

Before approaching the house I paused and looked around in all directions. The land was rolling and wooded and although Flanagan's house sat atop a hill, no other houses were visible in the distance, at least not from where I stood. I remembered from my drive-by the night before that his nearest neighbor was a half mile on down the road, meaning that Flanagan was fairly isolated out here.

That was good. I wasn't likely to be spotted by a nosy neighbor who might tell Flanagan about my unscheduled visit.

I walked over to the front porch of the house and mounted the steps. As I did so, I glanced at my wristwatch. About 20 minutes had passed since I'd seen Flanagan kick his Lab on the town square. That didn't leave me with much time to toss his place, especially if Flanagan came directly home after his haircut.

I was guessing—OK, hoping—he wouldn't, but I couldn't be sure. I figured he'd probably take care of a few additional errands while he was in town, maybe stop in at the Rushville Tap or one of the other bars for a beer or two. It was Saturday afternoon and he might be in the mood to socialize a bit with some of his buddies.

Then again, maybe not. He'd been anything but social the night before and what I had just seen him to do to his dog suggested he was still in a bad mood.

To put it mildly.

Two all-weather chairs stood on the front porch, along with a table made out of a cable spool. Two European-style skull mounts, one an eight-pointer and the other a ten, hung on either side of the front door.

I tried the latch of the aluminum storm door. It was locked. Shit.

But I should have known. I realized that like a lot of folks, Charlie Flanagan probably came and went through his back door most of the time…especially in winter, when snowy or muddy boots were likely. He probably kept the front doors locked from the inside and seldom opened them unless he was planning to sit on his front porch—something he wouldn't be doing at this time of year.

I stepped down off the porch and walked around to the back of the house. Sure enough, the walkway outside the back door was shoveled clear, a pretty good indication this was the door Flanagan primarily used. A snow shovel leaned against the front of a small wooden garden shed a few feet away.

I tried the latch on this storm door and it opened. Progress.

The inner door, a heavy wooden number, was locked, however. No surprise, and this is where things would get interesting.

I'm not an expert at picking locks...hell, I'm not even an amateur. I wasn't going to be able to let myself into Flanagan's house unless I found a hidden key or broke a window. The second option was out for obvious reasons...I didn't want Flanagan to know anyone else had been there.

I looked around to see if I could spot where Flanagan might have hidden a key.

I doubted he'd leave one in such an obvious place as under the rubber doormat I was standing on, but I stepped off the mat and checked anyway. Nope.

That left the garden shed. Its double doors were closed and latched with a hasp, but it wasn't locked. I stepped over to it and moved the snow shovel aside. I unlatched the hasp, opened the doors and peered into the gloomy interior.

The windowless shed held the usual assortment of garden tools—a spade, a leaf rake and a garden rake, a maul and a few other pieces—plus some resin lawn chairs. A coil of garden hose hung on the wall to my left, along with a pruning saw and a pair of long-handled branch loppers. A roll of four-foot fence wire stood in one back corner, and a stack of lumber scraps was piled in another.

Two shelves ran the length of the wall to my right. A sizable collection of hand tools was scattered along the lower shelf, and the higher shelf held stacked flowerpots, the old orange ones made of terra cotta. The flowerpots surprised me a bit; I wouldn't have figured Charlie Flanagan for a green thumb. Then again, they might have belonged to his mother and he'd just never gotten around to disposing of them.

I glanced at my watch. More than a half hour had elapsed since I'd seen Flanagan kick Dusty. I had to move more quickly.

I started with the row of flowerpots. They were stacked in threes and fours. I tipped back each stack, brushed my fingers beneath them, found nothing. I also looked behind each stack hoping to find a key hanging on a nail. Again, nothing.

I finished the row and stood back, perplexed. A couple of coffee cans sat at the far end of the lower shelf, past the assortment of hand tools. I stepped further into the shed to check out the contents of the cans.

They contained miscellaneous bits of hardware—curtain brackets, nails, screws, washers, the usual collection of odds and ends. I thought about dumping them out to see if there might be a key lurking in the jumble somewhere but decided against it, figuring Flanagan probably wouldn't want to bother rummaging through the stuff when he needed the key.

I turned back toward doors of the shed, momentarily at a loss.

The doors to the shed opened outward. I'd pushed them open and left them open to let as much light as possible into the shed. Looking back toward the doors, I let my gaze wander around their frame. I looked at the hinges—two on either side—then stepped closer for a better look.

Son of a bitch.

Charlie Flanagan had driven a single nail into the wooden wall of the shed just above the top hinge for the right-hand door. Hanging from that nail by a split key ring—and almost perfectly camouflaged because its brass color matched that of the hinge it hung against—was a single house key.

I grabbed the key and returned to the back door of the house.

The key slid in easily. I turned it and the door unlocked.

I was in.

CHAPTER 36

Now I *really* had to move quickly.

I glanced at my watch again and noted the time. I'd give myself 15 minutes to find out whatever I could, then leave, regardless. Staying any longer would be cutting it too close.

I was standing in an enclosed and heated back porch, what some folks call a mud room. A washer and dryer stood against the opposite wall nearest the kitchen, and there was also a good-sized deep freeze unit. A row of coat hooks, most of them filled, ran along the wall just inside the door. On the floor beneath the assortment of hanging jackets and insulated hoodies were several pairs of boots and shoes.

It was a mud room like thousands of others in other words, except that in the far corner beside the freezer unit stood an uncased Remington 870 shotgun. On a shelf above the freezer were several boxes of 12-gauge shells.

I wondered if the gun was loaded and guessed it probably was. Flanagan lived by himself in the country, where keeping a loaded firearm handy was by no means an uncommon practice. As a prison guard and a person with a reputation as some kind of badass, Flanagan probably figured he needed to be prepared for any late-night intruders who might come calling.

I'd do well to remember that when I paid him a return visit.

I didn't take time to check the gun—I felt fairly confident of my assumption—but crossed the mud room and stepped up into the kitchen. It was a fairly large room as country kitchens are inclined to be, but sparsely furnished with an aged wooden table and matching chairs, a refrigerator and a gas stove. A small microwave sat on the counter next to a coffee maker.

A good-sized walk-in pantry was just to the right of the doorway, covered with a louvered door. I popped the door and looked inside. The shelves were stocked with a couple of boxes of cereal, a few basic spices and an assortment of canned goods—several varieties of Campbell's soup predominating—and boxes of prepared food like Hamburger Helper and Kraft mac and cheese. Charlie Flanagan was not an epicure, obviously.

Next to the pantry was the refrigerator. A quick look revealed a half gallon of two percent milk, a container of orange juice, and several rows of longneck Budweiser. Condiments filled the shelves on the inside of the door, and Charlie Flanagan was one of those people who kept his bread in the fridge.

I checked my watch. I'd already spent five minutes of my allotted 15. I needed to pick up my pace and see the rest of the house. The real clues to a person's character—his secrets, in other words—are usually found in the bedroom and bathroom.

I crossed the kitchen and stepped into the living room. The furniture was worn; the décor was man plain. A better-than-average whitetail head mount with a 12-point rack hung on one wall and a large HDTV hung on another. A few outdoor magazines and movie DVDs—Flanagan appeared to be a Jason Statham and Dwayne Johnson fan—were scattered on a battered coffee table.

A wooden gun cabinet with a glass door stood in one corner. The glass was etched with a scene of ducks flying over a marsh. The cabinet had slots for six guns, all of which were full. I counted a lever-action Marlin, an AR-15, an old bolt action .22, and three shotguns. Two of the latter were 12-gauge semi-autos, one with a matte black finish and the other in camouflage, most likely used for turkey and/or duck hunting. The remaining gun was a 20-gauge over-under.

The cabinet was locked, but a thief could break the glass and grab everything inside with no trouble whatsoever. Charlie Flanagan obviously wasn't worried about that happening or he would have opted for a heavy duty gun vault like the one I owned.

Nothing else in the living room struck me as out of the ordinary, so I moved on.

I passed the stairs leading to the second floor and continued down a small hallway. A half-bath opened off to the right, opposite a closet under the stairway. I pulled open the closet door and saw some odds and ends of clothing and a couple of file boxes on the floor.

I didn't have time to examine the files and I doubted there would be much of interest there anyway. So far everything I'd seen indicated a single guy living alone, with nothing to suggest Flanagan was engaged in any kind of nefarious activity…aside from his habitual bullying, that is.

I turned to the half-bath. It boasted a stool and a sink with a medicine cabinet above the latter. I opened the cabinet; aside from a box of Band-Aids and a tube of Neosporin ointment it was empty. A half bar of soap lay on one corner of the sink and a hand towel with several smudges hung on a rack on one wall.

Again, nothing.

I moved on down the hallway to a corner room at the back of the house. This appeared to be a combination office and storage room, with a tall metal shelf unit along one wall. The shelves held stacks of old magazines, some medium-sized file boxes and a bunch of loose folders. A gray metal desk, the kind you might buy at a warehouse or office liquidation sale, stood against the opposite wall, with a black office chair pushed into the leg receptable. A black two-drawer file cabinet stood next to the desk.

An Apple computer sat on the desk next to a large, black, Soyo monitor. I clicked the mouse and the screen lit up with a desktop image of a snow-covered mountain range. A dozen icons were arranged in a vertical row on the left side of the screen.

I resisted the urge to try to get into Flanagan's computer files. Even if they weren't password protected, I didn't have the time to peruse the files, looking for God knows what. Sure, I might have discovered he was addicted to online porn, but that wasn't going to give me anything useful in terms of how to plan his execution. Ditto any financial records I might find. I didn't care where he did his banking or whether he paid his bills on time.

Instead, I started opening the drawers of his desk. The center drawer contained the usual assortment of office supplies—several ballpoint pens, pencils, paper clips, a pair of scissors, a roll of scotch tape, a brass letter opener with a handle in the shape of a duck's head.

The top drawer to the right held several notepads and a box of business envelopes. I shut it and opened the second drawer.

It was empty except for a holstered handgun and a box of cartridges.

I looked at the gun for a long moment, then gave into temptation and pulled it out of the drawer.

It was a nine millimeter Glock in a polished, high gloss black leather holster. I didn't know if prison guards carried sidearms—I guessed they probably didn't, as the danger of a prisoner wresting one away would be too great—but Charlie Flanagan had definitely equipped himself with a man-stopper, nonetheless. When or where he carried it was a question worth considering. I'd seen no sign of it on his person when he'd given me the hard shoulder bump the night before, but then I hadn't really been looking for a gun. My bad.

I unsnapped the retaining strap and pulled the Glock from the holster.

It slid out easily. I released the slide and pulled it back far enough to verify there was a shell in the chamber.

Charlie Flanagan obviously believed in being prepared.

I slid the Glock back into the holster, snapped the retaining strap and returned it to the drawer.

I closed the drawer and opened the one below it. This one was filled with old photo envelopes, the kind you used to get from the drugstore when you had film processed and prints made, in the days before digital photography. I picked up the top envelope and checked the date. The envelope was eight years old.

Again, I didn't bother looking at the photos. They were most likely snapshots of family or friends and wouldn't be any help. I tossed the envelope back onto the stack and closed the drawer.

I checked my watch. My 15 minutes were up but I still wanted to take a quick look upstairs. I returned to the living room and mounted the stairs two at a time, realizing that if Charlie Flanagan came home now I'd be well and truly caught. I needed to wrap it up and get the hell out and away from this place.

There were three bedrooms upstairs, plus a full bath. I ducked into the bathroom first. Tub and shower stall, sink with some Axe brand men's toiletries scattered on the side. I popped open the medicine cabinet and saw some nail clippers, a Gillette Techmatic razor, a couple of bottles of Advil and Tylenol, but no prescription meds.

Interesting.

I closed the cabinet and moved on to the bedrooms.

I came to the master bedroom first. Flanagan's bed was unmade and there were some clothes tossed on an easy chair in one corner. A tall dresser of dark wood stood against one wall. I pulled out the drawers and saw nothing but socks, underwear, t-shirts and sweatshirts. To Flanagan's credit—not that I was inclined to give him any—these were all folded neatly.

I opened his bedroom closet and saw two guard uniforms hanging in plastic bags from a dry cleaners. Several flannel shirts, a few sport shirts and pairs of blue jeans hung beside the uniforms, and toward the back of the closet I could see a gray suit, probably seldom worn.

I closed the closet door and stepped out of the bedroom and back into the hallway.

That's when I heard a dog bark.

CHAPTER 37

Fuck.

The dog barked again, and it sounded close…right outside the house, in fact. My first inclination was to move to a window and check to see if Flanagan had returned. I was guessing that the dog I heard was Dusty, the yellow Lab, barking from the back of Flanagan's pickup.

But I resisted the urge to look out a window. I hadn't turned on any lights inside the house—it was a sunny afternoon and there was enough ambient light inside for me to see well enough to conduct my cursory search—and that meant that anyone outside looking in would be unlikely to see me…that is, unless I appeared at a window. I didn't want to make that mistake.

I needed to find out if Flanagan had returned. I hadn't heard his truck pull into the driveway but the house was closed up and the dog's bark was a sharper sound, more likely to penetrate.

I quickly descended the stairs. Looking across the living room through the open blinds but staying well back from the window, I could see my own vehicle in the driveway but nothing else. To see more of the driveway—and whether Flanagan had pulled in behind me—I needed a wider angle of vision, not possible from where I stood.

I turned and headed for the kitchen. As I did so, the dog barked again, sounding a little farther away. What the hell?

I crossed the kitchen to the back door. I hesitated a second, then opened the door and stepped outside.

The dog barked again. From where I stood just outside the back door, I could look directly across to Dusty's kennel at the end of the equipment shed. The dog was standing next to the kennel, facing me.

It wasn't Dusty the yellow Lab. This was a much larger animal, almost the size of a Great Dane. At first glance I thought it *was* a Great Dane—it had the Dane's huge head and deep, square muzzle—but then I noticed several characteristics that told me otherwise. Its color and markings, for starters.

It was a deep, golden tan color, much darker than the light fawn that is one of the several acceptable colors recognized by the Great Dane standard. It also had a large white patch on its chest, a white muzzle and a blaze down its foreface, along with four white paws. Its ears were smaller than a Great Dane's, either cropped or uncropped…they resembled those of a greyhound, folded lengthwise and canted back. It might have been, I guessed, a Great Dane-greyhound cross.

It stood next to the kennel staring directly at me. It appeared neither aggressive nor fearful, but simply alert and watchful. "Hey, fella," I said, and its ears pricked up momentarily.

Then it turned away and trotted down alongside the kennel, its long tail swinging low. It trotted on around behind the equipment shed and was gone.

I let out a long breath and stepped forward to look around the corner of the house to the driveway. My vehicle was right where I'd left it and nothing else was in sight.

I crossed to the garden shed and hung the house key on the nail above the hinge. I closed and latched the shed doors, returned the snow shovel to where it had been leaning previously, and walked quickly out to the Equinox.

I started the engine and made a tight turn on the packed snow in front of the equipment shed. Once again I centered the SUV in Flanagan's tracks—and mine—and drove down the driveway. I was reasonably confident Flanagan wouldn't be able to tell that anyone had been here in his absence.

I got to the end of the lane and pulled out onto Highland Road. I'd gone no more than a mile when I saw a white pickup approaching from the direction of town.

It was Flanagan in his F150. As we passed each other he

glanced my way but again gave no sign of recognizing me. He was still wearing a scowl and I wondered if that was his perpetual expression, a sort of "don't fuck with me" look that he probably hoped people found intimidating.

As he barreled past me I glanced in the rearview mirror. Dusty the Labrador was standing in the bed of the pickup. I made a quick note of Flanagan's license number, reversed in the mirror but still readable—GDX 189—and repeated it several times to commit it to memory. Something told me it might be useful.

I BYPASSED THE TOWN SQUARE and drove back to Hidden Hollow. I was still somewhat unnerved by the close call I'd just had, and I knew most of it—hell, all of it—was my own fault.

The fury I'd felt after seeing Flanagan kick his dog had made me reckless, dangerously so. I realized now that driving out to his place in broad daylight and breaking in—even though technically there wasn't any real breaking involved—was nothing short of foolhardy…idiotic, even. Not to mention illegal. Sure, I'd gotten away with it, but that was due entirely to the barking of a stray dog.

If the dog hadn't happened along when it did and barked, presumably because it hadn't recognized my vehicle in Flanagan's driveway, I'd almost certainly have been caught by Flanagan when he returned home. That couldn't have ended happily.

I had the dog to thank for my getaway. I wondered if it belonged to a neighbor and assumed it probably did. It wasn't wearing a collar but a lot of country dogs didn't, their owners believing that a collar increased the risk of a dog getting hung up in a fence or caught in some brush.

Regardless of where it had come from or to whom it belonged, its barking had warned me to get the hell out of Flanagan's house and I'd done so in just enough time to avoid being caught.

I tried to shake off my unease, telling myself a miss was as good as a mile.

Right?

CHAPTER 38

It was a quarter to four when I got back to Hidden Hollow and neither of the other hunting parties had returned to the lodge from their afternoon hunt. That was fine with me because I needed a little time to decompress without feeling obligated to be social. I also wanted to jot down a few notes while the details of my quick toss of Flanagan's house were fresh in my mind.

After parking in front of the lodge, however, I did walk across to the kennel to check on Preacher. I fussed with her for a couple minutes, told her I'd be back in about an hour to feed her, then returned to the lodge.

The first thing I noticed was that Amy had apparently made good on her vow to have Mitch put up Christmas decorations. The porch railing was now hung with pine boughs and a large wreath adorned with a bright red bow and pheasant tail feathers hung on the front door.

I stepped inside. A fully decorated tree now stood near the fireplace and when I moved over for a closer look, I could see that most of the ornaments were species of wildlife—deer, gamebirds, ducks, as well as various miniaturized pieces of sporting equipment such as tiny shotguns, a little orange vest that looked like it might have fit an original G.I. Joe action figure, and so on. A beautiful garland of pheasant feathers was draped around the tree as well.

I went upstairs to my room and opened the battered old silvery-gray Samsonite briefcase that I always carry when I travel. I realize such a relic immediately brands me as a bona fide geezer now that everyone these days carries backpacks, but

I don't care—the briefcase is sturdier than any backpack known to man, and it also has a lot of sentimental value.

It was a Christmas present from a former girlfriend (since deceased) and the combination of its lock are the digits of her birthday. It has a dull metallic finish that suggests to some people it's actually a handgun case, and when asked I've occasionally joked that it contains a pair of matched .44 magnums. A few of those folks weren't sure I was kidding.

I withdrew a pen from one of its zippered pockets and a legal pad and sat down on the bed. I began by sketching a floor plan of Flanagan's house, both the ground floor and the upstairs. Although I hadn't had a chance to check the remaining two bedrooms, I'd seen the master bedroom and that was going to have to suffice. Given that Flanagan lived alone, I guessed the other two bedrooms were used for storage—glancing in from the hallway, I'd seen some boxes piled in the closer of the two—so not getting a better look at either one probably wasn't critical.

I labeled the rooms, then flipped the page and started making notes, jotting down in list format what I felt were the important details, each on a separate line.

Large equipment shed/garage to right of driveway, house to left.
Kennel at far end of shed.
Key in garden shed by back door.
Shotgun (loaded?) in mud room, shells on shelf above.
Large pantry in kitchen. Louvered door.
Longneck Buds in fridge.
Gun cabinet (full) in living room.
Nice 12-pointer on the wall.
Glock 9 in middle desk drawer, downstairs office.
Computer on desk.

I paused to reread what I'd written. I added *empty downstairs bathroom* and *small closet beneath stairs, boxes on floor* to the list, then paused again. For the moment I couldn't think of anything else to add about the downstairs that seemed significant. I moved on to the upstairs.

Shower stall and tub in large bathroom.

Men's toiletries.

Advil and Tylenol in cabinet; no prescription meds.

Two guard uniforms in master bedroom closet, jeans and sport clothes, one suit.

Unmade bed. (Don't know why I bothered noting this.)

Two additional bedrooms—storage?

I reviewed my list again. It was all pretty basic stuff, about what you'd expect to find in a house inhabited by a single guy. Well, except perhaps for all the firearms I'd seen. But even those weren't unusual for someone who obviously hunted a great deal. The holstered Glock in the desk drawer was a self-defense weapon, not a hunting firearm, but again, it wasn't really anything out of the ordinary, given Flanagan's profession and the fact that he lived alone in the country.

I reread the list, from beginning to end. I closed my eyes, trying to picture the house, the surrounding grounds, everything I'd seen, inside and out. I remembered the windrow of pine trees behind the equipment shed, the stacked flower pots and the assortment of tools on the shelves in the garden shed, the snow shovel leaning against the shed door, the coats and jackets hanging on the mud room wall just inside the back door and the jumble of boots and shoes on the floor beneath the jackets. None of these seemed especially noteworthy.

I thought again of the Remington 870 leaning against the mud room wall in the corner by the freezer. If Flanagan kept it loaded—and now I kicked myself mentally for not checking—I wondered if I could somehow stage a scenario that would suggest Flanagan had accidentally shot himself. Doing so would almost certainly require me to overpower him initially, and I wasn't confident I could do that.

Unless I could first weaken him in some way.

I looked at my notes again. I paused just before the end of the list. *No prescription meds.*

And just like that, I had it. I'd have to fine-tune the details, but I knew how I was going to take care of Charlie Flanagan.

With a little help from a friend, I was confident I could even gain Flanagan's cooperation for what I had in mind.

CHAPTER 39

Saturday night was steak night at Hidden Hollow.

About an hour before dinner, while we clients were gathered in the lounge enjoying some libation and swapping stories about the day's hunts, Amy had made the rounds and asked us how we wanted our steaks prepared. Medium rare was the most popular choice, with only a couple of guys asking that theirs be well done. Predictably, those requests generated some sarcastic rejoinders.

"Anybody who would order a steak well done would probably also eat yogurt," said Steve Parks upon hearing his brother Aaron's request.

"And what's wrong with yogurt?" Aaron asked.

"Nothing, if you like food with the texture of snot," Steve said. Wayne Parks said, "Gross!" and the rest of us groaned.

Dave Larson shook his head, laughing. He'd also ordered his steak well done. "How was your afternoon?" he asked me. "Did you get the photos you needed?"

"I think so," I said. I wanted to steer the conversation away from what I'd done that afternoon. "I'll shoot a few more in the morning and that should have me pretty well covered. Are you fellows hunting again in the morning?"

"No, we're heading back to Chicago right after breakfast. It's about a five-hour drive and we don't want to get home too late. What about you?"

"I'm scheduled to go out again in the morning but I think I'm gonna cut it a little short," I said. "Maybe hunt for an hour or an hour and a half and then load up and head home. It's about a five-hour drive back to Des Moines also, and like you said, I don't want to get home too late."

I didn't add that I was feeling impatient to get away from Hidden Hollow and Rushville for at least a couple reasons. Originally I had thought I would take care of Charlie Flanagan while I was here for my hunt at Hidden Hollow, but now I realized there was no way to do so without potentially incriminating myself.

I was a stranger in town whose name was known to a fair number of folks. Walt the bartender and at least a few of the Rushville Tap patrons had seen Charlie Flanagan give me a hard shoulder bump on his way out of the bar. To prevent even the possibility of anyone thinking I might have decided to retaliate—that is, if Flanagan suddenly and inexplicably turned up dead—I needed to establish that I'd left town. So killing him while I was still known to be here wasn't an option.

I also wanted to put some distance between this place and myself to help clarify my thinking. I needed a little time to sift through the details of everything I'd learned. Doing so would help me nail down the specifics of a plan for Charlie Flanagan's demise. I already had a pretty good idea of what I was going to do, but I figured the drive back to Des Moines would give me plenty of time to mull things over, weigh the various possibilities and, I hoped, come up with a strategy that was reasonably foolproof.

Of course "foolproof" was a relative term. There were always going to be some unknowns or unanticipated factors that could throw a major wrench into the works. It was up to me to try to minimize those factors based on what I'd discovered about Flanagan—his habits, his lifestyle, his personality—and I knew this would occupy much of my thinking during the trip home.

I was eager to get started, partly because I knew I was going to have to return to Rushville to conclude the Flanagan business once and for all. The sooner I got back to Des Moines to pick up what I needed—at this point I was missing a key ingredient—the sooner I could head back to Rushville to finish what had begun a couple weeks earlier with the death of Frank Reynolds.

This was going to require some long hours and a lot of road time and it would put nearly another 500 miles on my SUV's odometer, but I couldn't see any way around that. Rule Number 2 stipulated no collateral damage, so this wasn't something I could sidestep.

THE STEAKS WERE GRILLED TO PERFECTION over mesquite coals, and if there's anything better for dinner than beef cooked over mesquite, I've yet to discover it. Cardiologists might have a problem with that observation but then, to paraphrase Steve Parks, they probably also eat yogurt. Or at least recommend their patients do so.

After dinner I let myself get talked into taking part in the 8-ball tournament in the lounge. Dave Larson and I—the old guys—paired up to take on his son Mike and Wayne Parks, with Steve and Aaron Parks set to play the winners. Ordinarily I'd have tried to beg off like I had the night before, but I didn't want to appear anti-social on my last night at Hidden Hollow.

Nor did I want to make another trip into Rushville and risk running into Charlie Flanagan again. We'd already crossed paths several times, and his shoulder bump the previous night notwithstanding, so far he seemed fairly oblivious to my presence. I didn't want to do anything to change that.

Mike and Wayne gave us the break, deferring to us on the basis of our "advanced age," as Mike put it. Dave insisted I do the honors and when I cracked the rack, the 10-ball obligingly dropped into a corner pocket. I missed my next shot at the 12 and left Mike with a gimme on the 4, which he quickly sunk. He followed up with the 6 then missed on the 5. Dave missed a shot at the 13, after which Wayne proceeded to run the table, finishing with the 8 in a side pocket.

"I think we've been hustled," Dave said, and I laughed.

"At least it was reasonably quick and merciful," I replied. We racked our cues and headed over to the bar, leaving Mike and Wayne crowing about sending the geezers home to bed early as Steve and Arron stepped up to take our place.

Dave and I uncapped beers and had just settled on tall stools when Amy came in to announce the guide assignments for the morning. Mitch was guiding the Parks brothers and I would be going out with Allie.

I was happy to hear this. I hadn't requested Allie but if she was going to be guiding me, I planned to make the most of the opportunity. If I had the chance to renew our conversation from the night before, I might pick up a few more details about Charlie Flanagan that could prove useful.

When you were planning to kill someone, you never knew what little tidbit might come in handy.

CHAPTER 40

The groove I'd finally found on Saturday morning was fortunately still with me when Allie, Preacher and I took to the field on Sunday. Unlike the previous day, I didn't start off with any embarrassing misses. I flushed a brace of quail over Preacher's first point and dropped them both, causing Allie to whoop like a cowgirl.

"Nice shooting!" she said, and I smiled and thanked her. What guy doesn't like being complimented by an attractive woman after he's just made a good showing? And there was no denying Allie's attractiveness that morning. In her trim-fitting brush pants and orange game vest over a heavy green-and-gold plaid flannel shirt, and with her long dark hair in a ponytail pulled through the back of her orange Hidden Hollow cap, she did indeed make a mighty fetching bird-hunting guide. Pardon the atrocious pun.

Earlier the Larsons, the Parks brothers and I had enjoyed a breakfast of waffles (our choice of pecan, blueberry or plain; I opted for pecan), country fried ham and scrambled eggs. In deference to Sunday, breakfast began a half hour later, and this time Mitch and Allie joined us. Matt, the other guide, apparently had the morning off.

Following breakfast we'd all said goodbye to Dave and Mike Larson before they loaded up Jasper the Lab and headed home to Chicago. As I shook hands with Dave he said, "I'll be looking for your article on this place. In the meantime, we should both practice our pool."

"Indeed we should," I replied. "Have a safe trip."

"Thanks, we will. You do the same."

"Will do."

After the Larsons departed, Allie and I loaded Preacher onto the back of one of the ATVs and headed out to the field. Allie took us to a different area than the one Preacher and I had hunted with Mitch the day before but the cover was similar— fields of corn stubble and sorghum strips bordered by brushy tree lines.

"I'm probably gonna want to cut this a little short this morning," I told Allie as we climbed out of the ATV and I uncased my gun. "I've got a five-hour drive back to Des Moines and I'd like to get home fairly early. I always need a little time to decompress before turning on the company computer on Monday morning."

"I understand, and that's fine," she said. "We can wrap things up whenever you'd like."

I released Preacher from the crate on the back of the ATV and dropped two shells into the breech of the Remington. We started out with Preacher quartering about 50 yards ahead.

"She's a good-looking dog," Allie commented, and in another moment or two Preacher locked up. "There we go!" Allie said and we quickened our pace.

I moved in and killed the first bird going straight away, then swung to my right and dropped the second. After complimenting me, Allie said, "If you keep shooting like that, we'll be done before ten o'clock!"

I laughed. "Well, I don't want it to end *too* soon," I said, thinking, *not before I have the chance to pump you for more information about Charlie Flanagan.*

"Oh, I'm sure we can make things last awhile longer," she said. "We try not to make things *too* easy for our clients."

"That's good to hear," I said, again reflecting that the mark of a topnotch preserve was a realistic presentation of birds in a natural setting, ensuring that the hunters had to work for their game.

We moved on down the tree line and Preacher was soon on point again. I flushed another brace of quail and dropped the first one, but the second bird managed to put a tree between us just as I swung on it and fired. My shot clipped off a couple of low-hanging branches and Allie laughed. "That tree needed a little pruning anyway," she said.

"I thought so too," I replied, grinning.

THE REST OF THE HUNT PLAYED OUT along similar lines. I shot two chukars and four more quail, and as Preacher retrieved the last bird I glanced at my watch. It was a quarter to eleven and I was ready to call it a morning. I said as much to Allie, and she agreed we could head back to the lodge.

The only drawback to quitting early was that I hadn't managed to steer the conversation around to Charlie Flanagan. Unlike some guides who feel the need to keep up a constant line of patter, Allie wasn't the chatty type in the field. That's something I ordinarily appreciate as I'm not fond of a lot of needless babble, preferring to keep things relatively quiet so I can concentrate on my dog and the hunt. But in this case I'd have welcomed a little more talk.

When we got back to the ATV and Preacher was settled in her crate, I decided to force the issue. Apropos of nothing, I said, "When I went back into town yesterday afternoon I saw Charlie Flanagan again."

"Really?" Allie said. "Where...at the Rushville Tap?"

"No, this was on the square," I said. "At least, I'm pretty sure it was him. He was driving a white Ford pickup with a yellow Lab in the back. He passed me and I got a pretty good look at him as he went by."

"Yes, that would have been him," she said. "He has a yellow Lab that always rides in the back."

I didn't mention that I'd watched Flanagan park his truck and then kick the Lab's hind legs out from under him when the dog had jumped out of the bed and attempted to follow him. Nor, of course, did I tell Allie that I'd immediately driven out to Flanagan's house and given it a quick toss. Instead, I said, "He was wearing a scowl when he drove past...is that his usual expression?"

She snorted. "Probably. Charlie always wants to make sure people appreciate what a badass he is—or thinks he is, anyway."

"I remember you saying something like that a couple nights ago when we talked on the porch."

"Right. He's used to bullying people and getting away with it. Didn't you say he bumped into you in the bar?"

I winced inwardly. "Yes, he did. It kinda caught me by surprise. But before I could do anything about it, he'd gone out the door."

"He does stuff like that a lot, just to see if he can get a rise out of people."

"Well, like I said, it caught me surprise. But why'd you ask if I saw him in the Rushville Tap again…does he spend a lot of time there?"

She laughed. "He's there every night, and a lot of Saturday afternoons. He'd be there on Sunday also if they were open, but they aren't. I told you, didn't I, that that's where he claimed Carlyle confessed to him?"

I couldn't remember if she'd told me this but I knew it anyway, first from the newspaper clipping James Collins had sent me about Wilson's arrest, then from the conversation I'd had with Pete Sawyer and Walt the bartender. "Yes, you did," I said, playing along.

She shook her head angrily, her dark ponytail swinging. "Such bullshit," she said. She seemed about to add something, but she hesitated. Then she smiled sheepishly and said, "Sorry. I shouldn't use that kind of language with a client."

"No problem," I said. "I don't blame you for feeling the way you do."

When we returned to the lodge I put Preacher back in her kennel run and fed her a light meal, not enough to induce car sickness on the drive home. Allie took my birds and headed off to the barn to clean them, telling me that along with those I'd shot yesterday, she would have these packaged and tagged for transportation when I left. She asked if I'd brought a cooler and said that if I hadn't, they could provide one.

"There's one on the backseat of my SUV," I said. "I'll go get it and bring it over."

"No need," she said. "Just leave it on the porch and I'll get it when I'm done."

I did as instructed then went inside and up to my room. I had just pulled off my vest and was getting ready to undress and hit the shower when someone knocked at my door. I opened it to see Amy standing in the hallway.

"Hi," she said. "How was the hunt?"

"Excellent. Very good morning, in fact. Your sister is one heckuva guide."

Amy laughed. "Thanks. I'll be sure and tell her you said that. In the meantime, are you staying for lunch?"

I glanced at my watch. It was 11:15 and although I wanted to hit the road, I decided one more meal at Hidden Hollow might be worth the short delay.

"Twist my arm," I said.

PREACHER AND I WERE ON OUR WAY BACK to Des Moines by a few minutes past one. Mitch and the Parks brothers had returned while I was loading my gear into the SUV and we'd all clomped inside to sit down to Amy's lunch of stuffed pork chops, creamed corn, green salad and fresh dinner rolls. I passed on the peach cobbler she offered for dessert, trying to show a little restraint but knowing I would probably be fighting to stay awake on the drive home anyway.

After lunch the Parkses went upstairs to pack up for their trip home. I settled my bill, thanked Amy, Mitch and Allie—she'd come in and joined us about midway through lunch—and handed each of them an envelope containing a generous tip. I complimented them on their operation and said that I was planning to run my story on Hidden Hollow in one of next year's summer issues.

"That's about the best placement I can offer in terms of getting you some exposure in time for guys looking to book their fall hunts," I said.

"That's terrific," Mitch said. "We'll be looking for it. I'll also be contacting your publisher about placing an ad."

"Good deal. That's a win-win for all of us," I said.

We shook hands all around and Amy said, "Thank you so much, and please do come see us again!"

"I might very well do that," I said.

If everything played out the way I was planning, I'd be returning to Rushville again in just another few days. But— assuming my luck held—no one at Hidden Hollow, or in the town itself, for that matter, would know of my follow-up visit.

No one, that is, except Charlie Flanagan. And when I was finished he wouldn't be in any condition to tell anybody about it.

If my luck held.

CHAPTER 41

Staying awake on the long drive back to Des Moines proved to be less challenging than I expected.

Despite the belt-busting lunch with which Amy had sent us off—I couldn't help wondering how much weight I'd gained in the past two and a half days—I didn't find myself struggling against the stupor that often follows a heavy meal. Instead, my mind was busily working on the details of the plan to resolve the Charlie Flanagan matter, and that exercise kept me alert.

I had the basic plan pretty well nailed down, but I kept running through it, weighing it against everything I'd learned and probing for possible oversights or slip-ups. I also replayed the conversations I'd had with Allie and with Walt the bartender and Pete Sawyer, trying to plug in all of the details so as to confirm, once and for all, that eliminating Flanagan was the correct course…the only course, really, if Carlyle Wilson was to be exonerated.

Finally, I tried to remind myself that I needed to keep a cool head. Yes, I was rankled by Flanagan's unprovoked shoulder bump in the Rushville Tap, but I could dismiss that—well, almost—as nothing more than the action of a stupid thug. But seeing him kick his Lab on Saturday afternoon had infuriated me, and I couldn't afford to let that anger cloud my thinking.

Lesley Gore launched into "Judy's Turn to Cry" on the SUV's CD player and I felt myself smiling. It might not be Charlie Flanagan's turn to cry but it was definitely his turn for some comeuppance. If my plan held together, his bullying days were now numbered in the low single digits.

I MADE MY USUAL STOP AT THE CASEY's in New London, Iowa for gas and a bathroom break. After filling up I pulled the Equinox over to the parking area at the side of the building and let Preacher out to pee. While she was doing so, I logged onto the burner I'd been using with James Collins.

I sent him a quick text: *Heading home. Will return to R'ville next week to conclude business.*

Ordinarily I don't provide progress reports to my clients but this was something of a unique situation, in that it went beyond the job for which James Collins had originally hired me. He had proven trustworthy so far, coming through with a lot of useful information at my request, and I figured he would appreciate an update. Keeping him apprised was, I felt, a professional courtesy.

After sending the text I logged off the burner and picked up my personal cell, the one I use with friends. I scrolled through my contact list and punched in the number for a woman named Rachel James.

She answered on the third ring. "Hey you," she said, our standard greeting to each other.

"Hey you," I replied. "Sorry to bother you on a Sunday, but I was wondering if we could get together this evening for a few minutes. I need a favor."

"Sure," she said. "What time?"

"Whatever works for you. I'm driving back from Illinois right now but I should be home by six or a little after."

"How about seven-thirty?"

"That'll work."

"Want me to come over to your place?"

"That would probably be best," I said. Rachel is married and her husband Al is also a friend, but the business we'd be transacting—Rachel knew this was business when I said I needed a favor—was best handled between just the two of us.

"OK, I'll see you then," she said.

"See you then," I said, and ended the call.

I was confident Rachel James could supply me with the

missing ingredient I still needed to complete my plan for handling Charlie Flanagan.

JAMES COLLINS READ THE TEXT sent to him by the man he called Tom. He smiled and deleted the text, then scrolled through his list of contacts. He found the number he wanted and punched it in.

His call was answered on the first ring.

"No worries," he said to the other person. "You can chill. Everything is still on track."

PART 3: IN FOR A PENNY

"Never, never be afraid to do what's right, especially if the well-being of a person or animal is at stake. Society's punishments are small compared to the wounds we inflict on our soul when we look the other way."

-Martin Luther King, Jr.

CHAPTER 42

"I need him pliable, not poleaxed," I said.

"Cooperative, not comatose?"

"Right. Tractable, not trashed."

"Malleable, not moribund."

I laughed. "OK, you win," I said. I'd never been able to beat Rachel James in our alliteration games. "But yeah, that's what I need."

We were sitting at my kitchen table. She was drinking a Miller 64—I keep some in my fridge for her—and I was drinking a Winter Lager. Of necessity, I'd given her a quick rundown on Charlie Flanagan, including the bit about him kicking his dog on the town square.

She smiled and said, "Got it. For what you want, I think alprazolam will work."

"That is…?"

"Generic Xanax. Fairly easy to come by. It should mellow him out and make him docile, which is what you want. The trick, of course, is figuring the right dosage. How big did you say he was?"

"About six-two, probably 220 or 225 pounds. And remember, I didn't find any prescription drugs at his place. Only the usual painkillers, Advil and Tylenol."

"That's probably to your advantage. If he's not used to taking anything stronger, the alprazolam should hit him harder."

"That's what I figured."

Rachel smiled again. It's hard not to be reminded of Sofia

Vergara when Rachel smiles. Or, for that matter, even when she's not smiling. Her mouth isn't quite as wide as the actress's, and her boobs aren't quite as big…but almost. She lacks Ms. Vergara's Latin accent—Rachel was born in Kansas, not Colombia—but she has the same long, wavy brown hair and the same tawny eyes.

And, as I've already mentioned, she's married. She and her husband Al are both good friends of mine, and they have been for quite a few years. We live in the same neighborhood, just a few blocks apart, and they are the only people besides myself with keys to my house. Yes, I trust them that much.

Rachel is my source for pharmaceuticals. I'm not going to divulge her day job, but I will tell you that it has nothing to do with what I was purchasing from her. And just as I would never think of asking A.C. where he gets the handguns I occasionally buy from him, neither will I ever ask Rachel where she acquires the drugs I occasionally require for my work.

"I'm thinking about 50 milligrams—say, two 25-mil tablets—in each bottle of beer will probably be enough," she said. "Especially if he's already had several beers. The alcohol will strengthen the effects of the drug. It should make him groggy and slow his reflexes. But again, this is guesswork. I can't guarantee anything."

"I wouldn't expect you to," I said. "And yes, I'm pretty sure he'll already have had several drinks…boilermakers, in fact." I was remembering what I'd seen and what Walt the bartender had told me. Also what Allie Marshall had said about Flanagan being at the Rushville Tap every evening.

"Well, that should be enough to do it, then," Rachel said. "How many bottles of beer are you planning to spike?"

"Probably four," I said, trying to remember how many rows of Budweiser I'd seen in Flanagan's refrigerator. "I need to make sure I have all the front bottles covered so he'll grab one of the right ones."

"Do six," Rachel advised. "You don't want to chance him grabbing one of the undoctored ones."

"You're right; I don't."

RACHEL TOLD ME SHE'D HAVE what I needed by Wednesday afternoon, and that she would stop by and drop it off on her way home from work. I thanked her and asked for one more favor.

"I'm going to be leaving town again on Friday afternoon at around three o'clock," I said. "Do you think you could swing by that evening and feed Preacher at about five-thirty or six, then come back and let her out again at ten? I know that's asking a lot, but…"

"No problem," Rachel said. "But what about Saturday morning?"

"If everything goes as planned, I should be back by Saturday morning." I hesitated, then added, "It'll be kind of an all-night road trip, over to Illinois and back. I'll buy you lunch one day next week at Tumea's for taking care of Preacher."

She smiled. "Safe travels," was all she said.

THE NEXT SEVERAL DAYS passed quickly. I spent much of the time on magazine-related work. I downloaded all the photos I'd shot at Hidden Hollow onto my computer and transcribed the rough notes I'd made about my hunt. I didn't write the story—there was plenty of time for that, since it wouldn't run until sometime the following year. Plus, I had other more immediate editing work requiring my attention for the spring puppy issue.

I tried to focus on that work and not let myself dwell on my return trip to Rushville. Now that I had the plan set in my mind I didn't want to start second-guessing myself…that could lead to hesitation or uncertainties, which could be fatal.

There was also the danger of overthinking things and trying to embellish the plan unnecessarily. Once again, I kept reminding myself of the rule of KISS.

On Tuesday I called Daryl Nelson and suggested that, weather permitting, we should shoot for the promised pheasant dinner sometime the following week. She agreed and I hung up the phone, smiling.

And, just as she'd promised, Rachel James stopped by my house on Wednesday afternoon to drop off the alprazolam. She laughed as she handed me the small ziplock bag containing 12 white pills.

"Here you go," she said. "The priapic prick's prescription."

I couldn't help laughing myself. "Stop that," I said.

I didn't attempt a comeback.

CHAPTER 43

I left Des Moines at 3:15 on Friday afternoon. Allowing for one stop for gas at New London—the Casey's there was getting quite a bit of my business lately—I figured to be in Rushville by 8:30 that evening. The weather was clear, cold but sunny, and I didn't anticipate any delays. Of course, it would be dark by the time I got to Rushville, and that was to my advantage.

With the exception of Rachel James, I hadn't told anyone I was making this trip. I was gambling that no one from work would try contacting me on Friday afternoon—they usually didn't—and even if someone did, the likelihood of them having an insurmountable problem was pretty slim. In other words, I could feel reasonably safe about waiting until Monday to respond to any messages.

I was planning to get to Rushville, do what needed to be done, and return to Des Moines before anyone except Rachel knew I was gone.

I spent most of the drive time running through my plan, looking for any possible slip-ups, omissions or places where something could go wrong. I was fairly confident I had all the bases covered but there was always the potential unknown that could derail things in a major way.

Most troubling was the fact that so much of what I had planned depended on chance combined with some precise timing. I was counting on what Allie Marshall had told me about Flanagan spending every evening at the Rushville Tap.

If he didn't do so tonight, my plan was blown.

As I HAD DONE ONE WEEK EARLIER, I came into Rushville on Highway 67, passing the high school where Flanagan and Carlyle Wilson had played football. I turned left onto Highway 24 and headed toward the town square.

I stopped two blocks short of the square and turned onto a dark side street. I pulled over and parked in front of a row of houses. Several other vehicles were parked on the street so I figured mine wouldn't attract attraction. I was counting on the darkness to keep anyone from noticing my Iowa license plates.

I climbed out of the Equinox and locked the doors. I was wearing a black winter jacket and a dark gray bill cap. I wanted a quick look at the square—I was hoping to spot Flanagan's white F150—but I was going to take that look on foot. I couldn't take a chance on someone seeing, and possibly remembering, my vehicle with its Iowa plates.

It was Friday evening so I could expect some strolling shoppers and people coming and going from the bars and restaurants, but I thought it unlikely I'd run into anyone who might recognize me—say, someone from Hidden Hollow. I was also counting on blending in among the shoppers.

I reached the square and headed toward the Rushville Tap, a block distant. The wreaths on the streetlights and the lighted pavilion in the park reminded me again of a Norman Rockwell scene. As I'd anticipated, a fair number of people were on the sidewalks and I took care to match my pace to theirs, neither hurrying nor dawdling. A few folks nodded at me in passing and I did the same, but no one I saw showed any sign of actually recognizing me. All to the good.

I spotted Flanagan's pickup when I was still a half block from the Rushville Tap.

It was angle parked just a few spaces down from the bar, looming large and white among the smaller vehicles parked on either side. I continued strolling toward the bar, taking care not to break stride and pause as I passed the truck. But a quick sideways glance at the license plate—GDX 189—confirmed it was Flanagan's.

Game on.

CHAPTER 44

Now I needed to get back to my vehicle as quickly as possible but I couldn't afford to attract attention by moving at anything faster than a normal pace.

After checking Flanagan's license plate I continued walking to the next corner, which left me at the far side of the square, diagonally opposite the corner where I'd entered. Rather than completing the entire circuit, it would be quicker to cut back through the center of the park, passing the pavilion.

Several other people were walking through the park, so this seemed like a safe move, unlikely to look suspicious.

I crossed the pavement and entered the park. A couple of elementary school-age kids, bundled up against the cold with puffy jackets and stocking caps, were chasing each other around the lighted pavilion, yelling and laughing. I glanced at them and smiled as I passed, just a benevolent old geezer out for his evening constitutional. At least, that's the vibe I hoped I was projecting.

I crossed the park to the opposite corner and continued on away from the square. Once I'd put a half block behind me, I quickened my pace. Now I was just someone hurrying to get home out of the cold.

Except, of course, I wasn't heading for home.

CHARLIE FLANAGAN DRAINED HIS BEER and set the mug down next to the empty shot glass on the bar. Walt the bartender glanced his way and asked, "Another one, Charlie?"

Flanagan hesitated. Then he shrugged and said, "Sure,

why not?"

IT TOOK ME 10 MINUTES to drive to Flanagan's house on Highland Road.

I had no idea, of course, how long Flanagan had been in the Rushville Tap, or more importantly, how much longer he'd stay. Those were just a couple of the variables over which I had no control. But I'd cleared the first hurdle. For the moment, at least, I knew where he was.

I turned off the highway and pulled up the lane toward Flanagan's house. When I got to the top of the hill I swung to my right, easing the Equinox off the driveway and into the grass. I pulled around behind the equipment shed into the space between the shed and the row of windbreak pines. I continued on and stopped after about 10 yards. I put the vehicle in park, turned off the ignition and climbed out. I donned the same brown cotton gloves I'd worn during my last visit, got the items I needed from the backseat and closed the door.

From his kennel at the far end of the shed, Dusty the Labrador began barking. I considered walking down to the kennel and trying to quiet him but decided not to take the time. I hoped he wasn't one of those dogs that, once started barking, couldn't stop. I'd have to take that chance.

I hurried across the driveway toward the back door of the house, carrying the six-pack cooler of long-neck Budweiser bottles, the ones I'd spiked earlier that afternoon with the alprazolam Rachel James had supplied. The beauty of beer bottles with twist-off caps is that the caps can also be twisted back on.

I set the cooler on the rubber mat outside the back door and turned to the garden shed. I unlatched the shed doors, opened them and grabbed the key from its nail above the hinge. I unlocked the back door of the house, pushed it open, then returned the key to its hiding place and latched the shed doors.

I wouldn't need the key again, and when I left Flanagan's place later that night, I'd be doing so in a hurry.

CHARLIE FLANAGAN FINISHED his third boilermaker and stood up from the barstool he'd been occupying. "Calling it a night?" Walt the bartender asked.

"I think so. Gotta work tomorrow. Caught the weekend shift."

"OK, I'll cash you out."

"Thanks."

FLANAGAN HAD OBLIGINGLY left a small light on above the kitchen sink.

The first action I took when I stepped through the mud room into the kitchen was to remove the Colt Python from where I'd been carrying it, tucked into the waistband of my jeans. I laid the gun on the kitchen table, then turned to the refrigerator.

I removed the first six bottles of Budweiser from the shelf in the fridge and replaced them with the six I'd brought with me. I put Flanagan's six in the cooler, opened the louvered pantry door, and set the cooler on the floor in a back corner.

Then I crossed the kitchen to the short hallway that led back to Flanagan's office. Navigating by penlight—it was too dark in this part of the house to see without one, and I didn't want to risk turning on any other lights—I found his desk.

I hesitated for a moment, hoping the holstered Glock was still in the center drawer where I'd seen it a week ago. I pulled open the drawer.

The gun was there.

I pulled it out and returned to the kitchen.

CHARLIE FLANAGAN GLANCED at his watch as he left the Rushville Tap. 9:15. Too early, really, to go home on a Friday night. He considered heading over to the American Legion for a final nightcap, his comment to Walt about working on Saturday notwithstanding.

He started down the sidewalk toward his truck.

NOW IT WAS JUST A MATTER OF WAITING until Flanagan got

home. I pulled the Glock from its holster and checked to make sure there was still a cartridge in the breech. Then I laid the gun on the table next to the Colt.

I pulled out a chair and sat down at the table, figuring I might as well be comfortable while I waited. When I heard Flanagan pull up in his truck, I would step into the pantry with both guns and close the louvered door. Not the most original hiding place, but it should suffice.

KISS.

CHARLIE FLANAGAN CLIMBED into his truck and started the ignition. He backed out of the parking space and thought again about stopping at the Legion for one last drink.

"Fuck it," he said. He had beer at home that he could drink and it wouldn't cost him anything.

He drove around the square and headed out to the highway.

I SAT THERE AT THE KITCHEN TABLE, waiting and listening to the silence. I realized that at some point Dusty the Labrador had stopped barking.

CHAPTER 45

Waiting for Charlie Flanagan to come home gave me plenty of time to think about what was going to happen.

I wasn't having second thoughts or misgivings. Rather, I focused on Flanagan's probable course of action when he returned and entered his house. I was counting on him having at least one beer before he turned in for the night. This was, in fact, the biggest gamble.

If he didn't—if he came home already drunk, or semi-so— there was a strong possibility he'd head straight for bed. But the fact that he kept his refrigerator so well stocked with beer suggested he'd probably opt for a nightcap. Two or three cases full of empty bottles out in the mud room suggested likewise.

If he *didn't* crack a beer when he got home, I was going to have to improvise. My best bet would probably be to wait until he was asleep and then put my plan, with some modification, into effect. But I hoped this wasn't the way it played out.

As I'd told Rachel James, I needed Flanagan cooperative. Or at least, I needed to be able to briefly manipulate him.

Thinking of what I was going to make him do gave rise to an ironic realization. This whole business had begun with a bogus suicide, that of Mandi Collins.

If things went according to plan, it would end the same way.

CHARLIE FLANAGAN SLOWED to make the turn off the highway and into his lane. He gunned the pickup slightly to make it up the hill. He swung the truck into the empty bay at the near end of the open equipment shed. He turned off the ignition and climbed out.

From his kennel at the far end of the shed, Dusty the Labrador let out a sharp, attention-seeking bark.

"Quiet!" Flanagan said gruffly as he turned and headed toward the back door of the house.

I HEARD FLANAGAN'S TRUCK as he gunned it up the hill. I heard Dusty's bark and Flanagan's command to be quiet.

I stood up. "Here we go," I said softly. I pushed the chair I'd been sitting in back beneath the table and picked up the Colt and the Glock. I stepped into the pantry and closed the door behind me.

CHARLIE FLANAGAN FUMBLED his house key only slightly when he unlocked his back door. He stepped into the mud room and bent over to untie his boot laces. He toed off his boots, kicked them to the side and pulled off his jacket. He hung it on one of the pegs beside the door and stepped into the kitchen. He tossed his keys onto the kitchen table and turned toward the refrigerator.

I HEARD FLANAGAN UNLOCK his back door and step into the mud room. After a few seconds I heard a couple of soft thuds and guessed that was him kicking off his boots. In another few seconds, through the slanted louvered slats of the pantry door I saw him step into the kitchen in his stocking feet and drop his keys on the kitchen table. I held my breath as he turned toward the refrigerator.

FLANAGAN REACHED FOR THE HANDLE on the refrigerator door, then hesitated. He dropped his hand, shook his head and turned away.

He crossed the kitchen and turned down the short hallway next to the staircase.

I LET MY BREATH OUT in a hiss. I managed to keep from

uttering a quiet "Fuck!" but only just barely.

Then I heard a sound that, if not exactly music to my ears, was at least somewhat reassuring. Maybe even a cause for optimism…an indication that things still might work out as planned.

Living by himself, Flanagan apparently didn't bother shutting the door when he used the bathroom.

CHARLIE FLANAGAN ZIPPED UP, flushed and returned to the kitchen. He headed straight to the refrigerator, opened the door and grabbed one of the bottles of Budweiser from the shelf. He twisted off the cap and tossed it into the wastebasket next to the sink.

He held the bottle to his lips and took a long pull. Then he turned and walked out to the living room. He settled himself on the sofa and picked up the TV remote. He clicked it on and started channel surfing.

FROM MY POSITION BEHIND the louvered pantry door I could see through the kitchen and out into the living room. When Flanagan sat down on the sofa—actually, it was more of a sprawl—I still had a fair visual on him. The living room was dark but he immediately turned on the TV and that provided enough light for me to see him pretty well.

I could hear different snatches of dialogue as he surfed through the channels. He finally settled on one and I recognized the voices of Mel Gibson and Danny Glover in one of the early *Lethal Weapon* movies.

Why was I not surprised.

CHARLIE FLANAGAN TOOK ANOTHER PULL at his beer, finishing it. He set the bottle on the coffee table and thought about going out to the kitchen for another one. He was starting to feel sleepy but the movie was getting good and although it was an oldie and he'd seen it several times before, he didn't want to miss the climactic martial arts fight between Mel and Gary Busey.

He decided one more beer would put a nice cap on the evening.

IT LOOKED LIKE IT REQUIRED quite a bit of effort for Flanagan to haul himself up off the sofa. But he got himself upright without stumbling and as he came back out to the kitchen, I instinctively stepped back from the pantry door.

I hoped he hadn't had a sudden attack of the munchies and was coming to the pantry to look for something to snack on. If that was the case, I could resolve things immediately with either of the two handguns when he opened the pantry door, but that would make it tough—probably impossible—to implement the rest of my plan.

I got lucky. Flanagan wasn't hungry. He went straight to the refrigerator and pulled out another bottle of Bud. As before, he twisted off the cap and tossed it at the wastebasket.

This time he missed.

CHARLIE FLANAGAN WAITED UNTIL he'd settled himself on the sofa again before starting on his last beer for the night. He took a couple of drinks then set the bottle on the table. He could feel himself fighting to stay awake and he wasn't sure he was going to make it to the end of the movie, no matter how much he wanted to hear Mel ask Gary, "Care for a shot at the title?"

His eyes closed and his chin dropped to his chest.

I EASED OPEN THE PANTRY DOOR and stood still for a moment, watching Charlie Flanagan. Rachel James had told me that the alprazolam would probably hit him hard and that alcohol would hasten and heighten the effect. It appeared she had nailed it.

I left the Glock on a shelf in the pantry and stepped into the living room carrying the Colt Python at my side.

"Hey, Charlie," I said, and Flanagan opened his eyes.

CHAPTER 46

"What the fuck!"

Flanagan may have been nodding off under the dual effects of alcohol and alprazolam, but he still had a belligerent edge. I'd have to be careful.

"Turn the TV off," I said.

"Who the fuck are you?"

"I'm the guy calling the shots." I pointed the Colt at his chest. "Turn the TV off."

Flanagan hesitated. Then, somewhat surprisingly, he picked up the remote and did as I'd told him.

I half expected him to throw the remote at me or try something else desperate. But instead, he dropped the remote on the coffee table next to his beer bottle. "Who are you?" he asked again, minus "the fuck" this time.

"We met a week ago," I said. "You bumped into me on your way out of the Rushville Tap."

I could see him trying to remember. He also looked like he was struggling to stay awake. Finally he said, "The magazine guy."

"That's right. The magazine guy."

"What the fuck do you want?"

"I want you to stand up and walk out to the kitchen."

"I'm not walking anywhere."

"Then I'll shoot you right where you sit."

I saw him weighing the possibilities. I remembered what Rachel had said about the drug slowing his reflexes and I hoped she was right.

"I don't know what the fuck this is all about," he said, stalling. "You're pissed off just because I bumped you in the bar?"

"No," I said. "This has nothing to do with that." I waggled the Colt at him. "Get up."

He lowered his head and looked to one side. Then he planted both fists on the cushions and pushed himself upright. As he stood fully erect, he had to catch himself to keep from listing to one side.

"Easy does it," I said. I waggled the Colt again. "Step around the table and walk out to the kitchen." As I said this, I took a couple steps to the side to give him room to pass.

He shuffled forward. "I still don't know what this is all about," he said. He walked past me and as he did so I leaned back and snagged his beer bottle with my free hand. I followed him out into the kitchen.

"Sit down," I said. He pulled out the chair I'd been sitting in earlier and sat.

I set the beer bottle down in front of him and quickly stepped back. "Have a drink," I said.

"I don't want any more," he said, and the last part came out slurred, something like "wa-aay-more."

"Suit yourself," I said.

His head was drooping but he snapped it up and suddenly asked, "Why you wearing gloves?"

"My hands were cold," I said. His head drooped again. He was definitely nodding off and I needed to move quickly.

"Charlie!" I said, and he lifted his head, blinking. "Pick up that pen," I said, pointing to a ballpoint on the table next to a small notepad.

"What?"

"Pick up that pen. I want you to write something."

"Fuck you. Not gonna write anything." Nodding off but still belligerent.

"Then I guess we're done here," I said, cocking the Colt and pointing at his face. "No point in wasting any more time."

My bluff worked. He picked up the pen with his right hand

and said, "OK, OK." He was struggling to form the words. "Wha' am I s'posed to write?"

"Just two words," I said. "I want you to write 'I'm sorry.'"

"I'm sorry?"

"That's right."

Flanagan pulled the notepad toward him and wrote the words. He dropped the pen and said, "What am I sorry for?"

"For lying about Carlyle Wilson confessing to you," I said.

"Wasn't lying," Flanagan said. His chin dropped again. The drug was overpowering him. In another minute he'd be falling out of the chair.

I stepped quickly to the pantry and grabbed the Glock. I placed it on the table in front of Flanagan. His eyes were closed and his breathing was just short of a snore.

"Charlie!" I said again, but this time he didn't open his eyes.

I lifted his right hand from the table and he didn't resist. Even through my gloves I could feel the coldness.

I hesitated. I'd told Rachel James I needed Flanagan tractable, but this was way beyond tractable. This was helpless.

I wavered.

I'd spent the last couple weeks convincing myself that Flanagan deserved the fate I was about to deliver. I'd gathered, to the best of my ability, the evidence to support that decision. An innocent man's life hung in the balance. This was no time to balk. And yet...

A dog barked outside.

I flashed again on the scene I'd witnessed last Saturday afternoon, when Flanagan had kicked his Lab on the town square. A dog whose only sin was attempting to remain close to his master, and for that attempt Flanagan had sworn viciously and kicked his legs out from under him.

I reached down and carefully fitted Flanagan's right hand around the grip of the Glock.

CHAPTER 47

Here's what I'd like to tell you.

I'd like to tell you that at the last second, in a burst of adrenaline and an attack of conscience, Charlie Flanagan lifted the gun of his own accord and used it to commit the suicide I'd gone to such lengths to stage.

I'd like to tell you that.

But I'd be lying.

I WON'T LIE TO YOU about what happened, but I will spare you the grisly details.

Before leaving Charlie Flanagan's kitchen, I pulled the four remaining alprazolam-spiked bottles of Budweiser out of his refrigerator and replaced them with four of the bottles I'd removed earlier. I added the four spiked bottles to the two unspiked bottles still in the cooler.

Carrying the cooler, I exited through the back door and pulled it shut behind me, making sure it was locked. I crossed the driveway to the dog kennel next to the equipment shed. The big yellow Lab was standing at the gate, whining softly and wagging his tail.

I unlatched the gate, which wasn't locked. I'd brought along a pair of bolt-cutters but they were still in the Equinox and I was happy to see I wouldn't need to take time to retrieve them.

"C'mon, Dusty," I said. "We're going for a little ride." With my free hand I caught my fingers in his collar and headed around the equipment shed to where I'd parked the Equinox. He paced alongside me willingly.

Snow was beginning to fall as I opened the passenger side door and told the Lab to climb in. For a dog who'd apparently spent most of his life in a kennel or riding in the open bed of a pickup truck, he was surprisingly cooperative. Then again, Labs haven't held their position as the most popular dog breed in the country for nearly three decades by being incorrigible knuckleheads.

He settled himself on the old towels I'd spread on the passenger seat, sighing as he curled his 70-pound bulk into a fairly compact ball. I'd considered bringing a crate and confining him in the cargo space under the hatch—where Preacher usually rode on her thick dog pillow—but decided against it. I had no idea if Dusty had ever been crated and if he hadn't, the close confinement might have caused him to panic, biting at the crate and whining with anxiety. I didn't want to have to deal with that, or listen to it, for the five-hour drive to Des Moines.

I just hoped Preacher would forgive me for letting another dog ride in her vehicle…and in the front seat, no less.

I placed the cooler on the floor behind the front seat occupied by Dusty. I pulled the Colt Python out of my waistband, unloaded it and returned it to the pistol case I'd carried it in from Des Moines. I walked around to the driver's side, climbed in and took off my gloves.

I started the Equinox. The headlight beams caught something large standing maybe ten yards ahead of us, just behind Dusty's now-empty dog kennel. Its eyes glowed amber-green in the headlights, and though it was somewhat obscured by the falling snow, I recognized the same dog I'd seen the previous Saturday afternoon—the huge tan and white dog whose barks had caused me to quit searching Flanagan's house and make a hasty exit…and not a moment too soon, as it had turned out.

I wondered if it was this dog, rather than Dusty, I'd heard bark a few minutes ago. I stared hard at the dog for a few seconds and it seemed to lock eyes with me. Then it turned and vanished behind the windbreak of pine trees. As it did so, a curious word slipped into my mind. *Benediction.*

I shook my head. "Friend of yours?" I asked Dusty. He looked up at me and thumped the seat with his tail but gave no indication he'd been aware of the other dog's presence.

I backed out from behind the equipment shed and eased onto the gravel driveway.

The snow was coming down harder now and I realized it was an unexpected blessing—it would surely obliterate any tracks my vehicle had made in the gravel of the driveway when I'd pulled in earlier, as well as covering any tracks in the grass behind the equipment shed.

Once again, I was reminded of my former co-worker's pearl of wisdom: Every once in a while, you get dumbass lucky.

WHEN WE REACHED THE END of the driveway I paused for a moment, looking both directions and hoping to see no flashing lights heading our way. I was reasonably certain the single gunshot from the Glock inside the closed house wouldn't be heard by Flanagan's neighbors a half-mile away, but I also knew that—my co-worker's saying notwithstanding—I'd already stretched my luck about as far as I could reasonably expect it to hold. It was now well and truly time to get the hell out of Dodge—well, Rushville—once and for all.

I pulled out onto Highland Road and headed back toward Highway 24. The snow was coming down even harder now, which slowed our pace a bit, but it also forced me to concentrate totally on my driving. And that was a good thing—it kept my mind focused on the road rather than the image of Charlie Flanagan sprawled back in his kitchen chair with...

Sorry. I promised I'd spare you those details.

CHAPTER 48

I spent a good part of the five-hour, late-night drive back to Des Moines replaying and analyzing everything that had happened in the past few weeks.

Just as I often tend to rethink—OK, overthink— conversations I've just had, weighing both my words and those of the other person, I always engage in a review of my actions, from beginning to end, when I've completed an assignment. I especially look for slip-ups, things I could (and should) have done differently. While I'm not big on self-flagellation, I do try to note and learn from any mistakes I've made so as to avoid repeating them.

In this case, my single biggest mistake early on was assuming that Frank Reynolds' death would be classified as an accident. The kill itself was clean and while I knew his body would eventually be found, I hadn't factored in the possibility that the person who found Reynolds and reported the find to authorities would very soon be charged with his death.

I couldn't have known that Carlyle Wilson would be hunting in the same area as Frank Reynolds that morning and I'd assumed Reynolds' shooting would ultimately be ruled a hunting accident, that he'd been killed by a stray slug, and nothing more. In this I'd miscalculated, big time, and that miscalculation had very nearly seen an innocent man tried— and possibly convicted and imprisoned—for a crime he hadn't committed.

Of course, I also couldn't have foreseen Charlie Flanagan coming forward with a trumped-up confession allegedly made by Carlyle Wilson. I had no knowledge whatsoever of their history, no knowledge of Charlie Flanagan's reputation as a local badass, nor any of the other details involving the two of them and Allie Marshall.

In the latter case, at least, I'd gotten supremely lucky. That Allie was Amy Halvorsen's sister and I'd been able to fill in a bunch of the blanks—especially, whether Charlie Flanagan deserved the death I was planning to bring his way—during my stay at Hidden Hollow had been a rare stroke of good fortune. Good for me, that is; not so good for Flanagan.

I knew I couldn't count on that kind of luck very often...maybe never again.

I also knew that Rule Number 2—no collateral damage—had come dangerously close to being violated this time. I was confident that with Charlie Flanagan now out of the way and his suicide note suggesting he had fabricated Carlyle Wilson's confession, Wilson would soon be released and the charges against him dropped.

But I also knew there would be some questions hanging out there that would never be answered, at least not to everyone's complete satisfaction. Charlie Flanagan's immediate cause of death would be obvious, but those who knew him best might find it difficult to believe he'd committed suicide.

The ME would undoubtedly find traces of the alprazolam in his blood, and those same people might wonder about that, as well. I told myself they'd surmise he'd acquired and used the drug to numb himself before pulling the trigger. That was halfway plausible, anyway, and no one could prove otherwise.

The empty dog kennel would also raise the question of what had happened to his Labrador.

Again, I told myself that people might speculate that prior to killing himself he'd given the dog away to a hunting buddy (although in such a small community, any buddy of Flanagan's would probably be known to just about everyone) or even that the dog had run away on its own, perhaps escaping through an unlatched kennel gate. At any rate, the dog was gone and its whereabouts would remain unknown.

And finally, these latest developments—Charlie Flanagan's supposed suicide and Carlyle Wilson's subsequent release—would reopen the question of who had really killed Frank Reynolds. I was once again gambling, just as I had at the outset, that it would ultimately be ruled an accident. I felt slightly more certain of this the second time around, as there were no other likely suspects, and there never would be.

Bottom line, while I felt like I could now file this in the "All's well that ends well" category, some fast and semi-dangerous footwork had been required to make it happen. I'd been forced to cut things a lot closer than I like.

I wondered if I was getting too old for this stuff.

GRAY DAWN WAS JUST BREAKING when I pulled into my driveway. Considering the kind of life he'd had up to this point, Dusty had been a surprisingly good passenger, staying curled up on the old towels on the passenger seat and sleeping most of the way. He'd roused a time or two but I'd ruffled his ears again and spoken to him quietly and he'd quickly settled back down.

I let him out of the SUV and into the back yard. I heard Preacher's bark from inside the house. I quickly unlocked the door and she rushed out. Spotting the big yellow dog in her back yard—he was at that moment lifting his leg against the maple tree, and after a five-hour trip, who could blame him—she hurried over, hackles raised.

Dusty finished and dropped his leg. He stood still, ears pricked and tail waving slowly. Preacher approached stiffly and they sniffed noses. "Take it easy," I cautioned both of them, but I could see they were already relaxing. Fights between a male and female are rare in the canine world—humans should take note—and Preacher was soon dropping into what's known among dog people as a "play bow"—a sort of semi-crouch with the forelegs extended and the rear end raised. It is, as you'd guess from the name, an invitation to play.

Apparently my bristle-faced housemate found this big handsome Lab to her liking.

I LEFT THE DOGS IN THE BACKYARD and went inside to start a pot of coffee. The last 14 hours, 10 of which had been spent on the road, were beginning to take their toll. I needed a shower and some sleep.

But I had a few other matters to attend to first. I was going to have to give Dusty a bath and I groaned at the thought. Living in an outdoor kennel, he'd acquired a heavy doggy odor—I'd been smelling it for the past five hours and the Equinox now needed a thorough airing. But just as you don't give someone a gift with the price tag still attached, I didn't want to present the dog to his new owner without cleaning him up first.

I also had a couple of phone calls to make, but those would have to wait until a more reasonable hour.

CHAPTER 49

I called James Collins first.

It was a couple minutes past ten when I dialed his number from the burner I'd been using to correspond with him and, surprisingly, he answered on the second ring. Apparently he was not a late sleeper.

"Hey, Tom," he said.

"Done," I replied.

"Done?"

"Yes. The confession should now be moot." I knew he'd connect the dots.

"That's great. Well...I mean, I'm glad it's been resolved."

"I am too. I'd appreciate it if you'd continue to monitor things for a few more days, though, just to confirm that Wilson has been released."

"I can do that. I'll let you know."

"Thanks."

"One more thing. Is there any...uh...additional charge? I mean, you had a lot of extra travel and expense and so on."

I had to hand it to him; he was one conscientious client. By now most people would be wanting to wash their hands of the whole matter and put it behind them, to say nothing of not wanting to incur any more cost.

"No," I replied. "You've covered your part of it with the additional background info you supplied. The rest of the cost...well, I'll just eat it." As I said this, I again realized that James Collins still had no idea who I really was—he still only knew me as a guy he called Tom—or what I actually did for a living. I couldn't tell him I was going to expense my travel because I'd be writing a feature for my magazine on the preserve where I'd hunted, and that in return, the preserve was buying some ad space with us, a win-win.

"You're sure about that?" he asked.

"Yes."

"Well, all right then. But hey, something else I wanted to mention, kinda related to what you just said about supplying additional information. You may not be interested, but it occurred to me that I might, uh, be able to help you again sometime." He laughed a little nervously. "I mean, in case you ever need something or somebody...researched, or whatever. I really do appreciate what you've done here in bringing some closure to the whole matter with my sister, and maybe I could return the favor."

Hmmm. It was an interesting proposition. My first knee-jerk inclination was to turn him down and adhere to the "no further contact" clause of our unwritten contract. But again, he had a good point. There was no question that he and his friends could accomplish more with their laptops than I could ever hope to when it came to, as he'd called it, research. I *might* be able to use his help again sometime.

"Thanks," I said. "I'll keep that in mind."

MY SECOND CALL, THIS TIME made from the old landline phone in my office, was to Mike Stevenson, and he too answered on the second ring.

"What the hell do you want?" he said with mock irritation. He'd recognized my number on his caller ID and this was, in fact, our standard greeting to each other. I was happy to hear it because it suggested he was in better spirits than he had been the last time we'd talked.

I laughed. "As a matter of fact, I was just calling to see if you had a little free time this afternoon. I'd like to swing by for a few minutes after lunch if you're going to be home."

"Sure, come on by. What's this all about?"

"Oh, just something I want to run by you," I said. "Are

Janice and the kids going to be there?"

"As far as I know," he said. "What's going on?"

"A little surprise," I said. "I'll see you about 1:30."

I hung up before he could ask more questions. I left the office and headed out to the kitchen, passing through the living room where Preacher and Dusty were sprawled at opposite ends of the sofa.

The big yellow Lab now smelled like dog shampoo instead of a dirty kennel. Convincing him to step into my bathtub with its sliding glass shower doors had taken some doing, but he'd eventually acquiesced. Luckily my shower head is one of those detachable numbers with a long flexible hose, which made bathing him a little easier.

I'd also replaced the dirty orange nylon collar he'd been wearing with a new one I'd picked up a couple days earlier. It too was nylon but in a RealTree camouflage pattern, as befitted a waterfowl dog.

I paused next to the sofa. Both dogs raised their heads to look at me. I spoke to the Lab.

"You and I are gonna take another ride this afternoon," I said. "You're entering something like the witness protection program, but I think you're going to like it. One thing I know for certain is that no one will ever kick you again."

My plan was to tell Mike that the Lab was an abuse case that had come to me through a rescue organization that had contacted my magazine. Sure, that last part was a lie, and I don't make a habit of doing that with my friends, but I obviously couldn't tell Mike the real way in which I'd acquired the dog. The less he knew of the Lab's origins, the better for all involved.

"One more thing," I said, as I reached down to ruffle one of the dog's russet ears. "You now have a new identity. From now on, your name is Rusty, not Dusty." In response to hearing his name, the Lab thumped the sofa cushions with his tail.

I figured the name switch would be an easy transition.

CHAPTER 50

The pheasant dinner was a smashing success.

We were enjoying one of those mild spells that occasionally occur in Iowa in mid-December, when the temps rise into the 50s, the sun shines and the snow melts. Inspired by the warm-up, I'd pulled the Weber kettle grill out of the garage and onto the deck and grilled the bird over indirect heat (charcoal, not gas; I'm a purist, and why are you not surprised) and basted with the same marinade in which I'd soaked it overnight.

I won't tell you the ingredients of the marinade—it's a formula I've perfected over quite a few years—but I will tell you that dinner guests have offered me money to do so.

Other than the marinade, I believe in keeping things fairly simple when I serve game. Foil-wrapped baked potatoes (also done on the grill) and lightly steamed fresh broccoli rounded out my part of the menu. Daryl Nelson had brought a tossed salad of her own making and two chilled bottles of Kendall Jackson chardonnay. While I'm usually not much of a wine drinker, I can't deny the KJ was the perfect accompaniment to the pheasant.

Which Daryl loved. She said exactly the right things, commenting on how moist the meat was, how it didn't have a strong gamy flavor, and so on. And fortunately, she didn't crack a tooth or a filling on an errant piece of shot that I'd missed when cleaning the bird.

That had happened with another dinner date several years earlier. The woman in question was dubious about trying pheasant to begin with and cracking a filling—actually an expensive crown—had brought a very abrupt end to our evening and an equally abrupt end to our budding romance.

But now dinner was over; the table had been cleared and the dishwasher loaded. We were sitting at opposite ends of the sofa with Daryl's legs stretched out and her feet in my lap; I was giving her an after-dinner foot rub while we watched the DVD of one of my favorite holiday movies, *Grumpy Old Men*, with Jack Lemmon, Walter Matthau and Ann-Margret. OK, so it's not exactly *It's a Wonderful Life* (which I happen to despise) but it's a darned funny movie and its climactic scene occurs at Christmastime, so that qualifies it as a holiday film in my book.

Preacher was sprawled on the throw rug in front of the sofa—and yes, we'd shared a few bites of the pheasant with her. We'd just watched the scene in which Ann-Margret convinces Jack Lemmon it's time for bed. I decided to spring my surprise. I paused the DVD and said, "I want to ask you something."

"OK," Daryl replied, smiling but looking a bit mystified.

"I kinda rolled the dice and took a chance on something. I managed to score two tickets to the Billy Joel concert at the Target Center in Minneapolis on the night of the 18th. That's next Saturday…I was wondering if you'd like to drive up with me for the concert. We could have dinner, see the concert, spend the night, have brunch on Sunday and then head back home."

I didn't tell her how I'd really acquired the tickets, that James Collins had sent them to my P.O. box with a note thanking me for "tying up the loose ends" in Rushville and confirming that Carlyle Wilson had been released and the charges against him dropped. But what I said about rolling the dice was true enough, in that so much of my plan for resolving the Charlie Flanagan matter had depended on luck.

God only knew how Collins got the tickets on such short notice or what he must have paid for them. But hey, I don't look gift horses in the mouth, and haven't I been saying he was a stand-up guy?

Daryl laughed. "That's quite an itinerary!" she said. "But it sounds like fun." She grinned impishly. "Are they good seats?"

"Yes, very good seats. Twelve rows back, slightly off center."

"Wow. OK. But where will we stay?"

"Probably one of the hotels in downtown Minneapolis near the Target Center. I haven't made the reservation yet because I…uh, wasn't sure if you'd accept or…um, what you'd prefer."

She laughed again. "What do you mean, prefer?"

"Well…you know. Share a room or…if you'd like, we could get a couple of singles." Good Lord, here I was in my early 60s and I was stammering like a guilty 10-year-old.

She pulled her feet from my lap so she could draw up her knees and lean toward me. She grasped my shoulders and pulled me forward for a kiss.

"Don't be silly," she said. "We'll share a room."

THREE DAYS BEFORE CHRISTMAS Carlyle Wilson opened his mailbox and withdrew the usual assortment of junk mail, a Schuyler County Co-op utilities bill, two Christmas cards from relatives and a business-sized white security envelope.

He tossed the junk and opened the Christmas cards first. One was from a cousin in Arkansas, the other from an aunt in Pennsylvania. He ignored the utilities bill for the moment and opened the business envelope. Inside was a sheet of plain white printer paper folded in thirds. He opened it and read a single typewritten line: "For your trouble. Sorry about the wrongful imprisonment. Merry Christmas."

There was also a cashier's check, drawn on a well-known nationwide bank, made out to him for $10,000. The signature on the check was an illegible scrawl, impossible to decipher.

"What the…" he said aloud, immediately reaching for his phone to call Allie. As he did so he glanced again at the plain white envelope on the table. Whoever had addressed it—the writing was neat block printing—had used his, Carlyle's, own address for the return address as well.

He speed-dialed Allie and picked up the envelope for a closer look. He could make out the postmark of the city from which it had been mailed.

Minneapolis.

He burst out laughing.

EPILOGUE

James Collins answered his phone on the second ring at 7:15 on the morning of December 23.

He recognized the caller's number and said, "Hey, cuz. What's up?"

"Hey, Jimmy," Allie Marshall replied. "Sorry to be calling so early but I wanted to catch you before work." She laughed. "You're gonna love this."

"No problem; I was up. What am I gonna love?"

"You know that old joke, the difference between a classic fairy tale and a redneck fairy tale?"

"Never heard that one. Tell me."

"A classic fairy tale begins, 'Once upon a time'; a redneck fairy tale begins"—she mimicked a Southern drawl—"'Y'all ain't gonna believe this shit!' Well, that saying applies here."

James Collins laughed. "What are you talking about?"

"Your hit man sent Carlyle a check for $10,000."

"What?!"

"Yep, Carlyle got it yesterday. The envelope had a Minneapolis postmark. So he must have used those Billy Joel tickets you sent him and mailed the check while he was up there."

"Oh, man. That's crazy! But let me guess...he sent the check anonymously."

"Well, almost. It's a cashier's check and you can't read the signature. There was also a typed note apologizing for Carlyle being in jail. There's no signature on the note."

"That's crazy!" James Collins said again.

"I told you you wouldn't believe it."

"Let me think about this for a second. Ten thousand is what I paid him to kill Frank Reynolds. The last time we talked, I asked him if he wanted me to share the cost for the follow-up on Charlie Flanagan but he said no, he'd eat the cost. So basically, if he sent Carlyle a check for ten thousand, he refunded what I paid him…we got both hits for free."

"That's right."

"You're right; I don't believe this shit."

"I know; I couldn't believe it, either, when Carlyle called me last night to tell me."

"That's crazy," Collins said for the third time. "How's he doing, by the way?"

"Carlyle? Oh, he's doing OK. He started back to work last week at Pella and he said everyone was very nice about his absence; said they were glad the charges had been dropped and that they knew all along he couldn't have done such a thing."

James Collins laughed again. "Wouldn't they be surprised if they knew what he did do…deliver an Academy Award performance by getting himself arrested for killing a guy by confessing to a crime he didn't commit."

"Right. He says sitting in that jail cell for all those weeks was the toughest thing he's ever done, but it was worth it to avenge Mandi's death and my rape."

Collins snorted. "Big football stud Charlie Flanagan had it coming after what he did to you in high school…I'm glad things fell into place like they did."

Allie laughed. "I still can't believe how it all worked out," she said. "Almost like it was…what's the word I want? Pre-ordained?"

"I don't know if I'd go that far. But yeah, we got super lucky when Vance decided to kill Reynolds while he was deer hunting. If he'd killed him in Chicago we never would have had the chance to rope Charlie in."

"Right. And if we hadn't known about the deer hunt beforehand, there's no way Carlyle could have gone out there to find the body," Allie said. "Which, by the way, he said was pretty tough to do. There's a lot of woods on that farm where Reynolds hunted, and Carlyle said it took him nearly three hours to find him."

"I can believe it." They'd already gone over a lot of this during a couple of previous calls but they were enjoying the rehash. It wasn't every day you got to put one over on a contract killer.

They were silent for a moment, then Allie said, "In some ways, Vance was pretty smart about things, but in others, he was pretty dumb. I mean, he never suspected anything the entire time he was at Hidden Hollow, that I knew why he was really there."

Collins interrupted. "Props to you for *your* performance, cuz."

"Thanks. I did my best to convince him that Charlie was a bully and had framed Carlyle, and some of the people in town evidently told him the same thing. But even if he never knew that *I* knew what he was really there for, it was still pretty clever the way he made Charlie's death look like a suicide. And with Charlie's own gun, no less."

"Right. There's no question that he's good at what he does."

"No question. But I still think it's pretty funny that he didn't know that we knew why he was at Hidden Hollow."

"Well, that's another place we got lucky. When I sent him the clip about Carlyle being arrested in Rushville, he went online to find out what he could about the town and apparently he found Hidden Hollow on his own...I didn't have to guide him to it by dropping hints. When you called and told me he'd talked to Amy and scheduled a hunt, I knew he'd be heading over to take care of Charlie Flanagan. But he still doesn't know that I know who he really is. Early on he told me to call him Tom and that's what I've been doing."

"Oh, one other thing," Allie added. "He also took Charlie's dog...at least, that's what we think happened."

"Really?"

"Yes. Charlie had a nice yellow Lab and it was missing

from its kennel. No one knows what happened to it so I'm guessing Vance took it. Unless it just ran away. That's what everyone else thinks happened."

"Interesting. Maybe he took the dog as a bonus for himself."

"Yeah, maybe."

Another moment of silence, then Allie said, "So…now we have this check for $10,000. Do you want us to send it to you, or…?"

"No, you don't need to do that. That's what I paid Vance anyway so I wasn't expecting to get it back. Why don't you and Carlyle keep it…consider it an early wedding present."

"That's some wedding present!" Allie sounded incredulous. "Are you sure about that?"

"I'm sure. Believe me, it was worth $10,000 to get some justice for Mandi. And for you."

"Wow. I mean…well, OK, then. I'm sure Carlyle will be thrilled and I know we can put it to good use."

"I'm sure you can. Maybe take that Hawaii trip you've always wanted to take. That would make a great honeymoon for you two."

"I'll suggest that to Carlyle. Oh, and before I forget, Vance is going to write a story about Hidden Hollow for that magazine he's the editor of. So Mitch and Amy are getting a bonus out of this also—the publicity should help their business."

"That's great. Have you told Amy about any of this?"

"No. Some secrets even sisters don't share."

Another laugh. "Probably safer that way," Collins said.

"That's what I thought. Anyhow, I'd better let you go. I just wanted to let you know about the check."

"Thanks, I appreciate it. And FYI, when I talked to Vance a few days ago I offered to help him again in the future…I said I might be able to do some backgrounding for him if he needed information on a new target."

"Really? Are you sure that's safe? I mean, isn't that kinda playing with fire, keeping in touch with the guy?"

"Oh, maybe. But I doubt he'll take me up on it anyway."

"Well, just be careful."

James Collins laughed. "Always. And hey, you and Carlyle have a merry Christmas, Allie. And please tell Amy and Mitch the same."

"Thanks, I will. Merry Christmas to you too, Jimmy."

James Collins hung up the phone, smiling and shaking his head. So Vance had sent $10,000 to Carlyle to make up for his supposed wrongful imprisonment, and now Allie could have the Hawaiian honeymoon she'd always dreamed of.

Imagine that.

Sometimes folks just got dumbass lucky.

ACKNOWLEDGMENTS

Let me begin with a disclaimer: This is a work of fiction.

Yes, the same statement appears in small type on the copyright page, but it bears repeating here. This is a work of fiction; it's neither autobiography nor instruction manual. To paraphrase (badly) Mark Twain's "Notice" at the beginning of *Huckleberry Finn,* persons attempting to find anything but fiction or entertainment in this narrative will be shot. (Kidding!)

OK, with that out of the way, it's time to thank some folks who provided valuable assistance on my maiden voyage into novel writing.

I'll start with my three cousins, Randy, Doug and Ryan Clark. The four of us grew up sharing many happy days afield and they each contributed to this effort. Randy shared his considerable expertise on hunting preserve operations and also served as first reader of the entire manuscript, tactfully pointing out the errors, inconsistencies and typos throughout.

Doug—our family's resident comedian and punster—supplied the much-needed laughs at critical moments along the way, and Ryan patiently answered my too-numerous questions about computers and the mysteries of their operation. Readers would not be mistaken in assuming that the Parks brothers in this story are based on Randy, Doug and Ryan.

Thanks also to Kerry Nielsen, my best friend since third grade, for input on the forensics details in a criminal case and the effects of alprazolam combined with alcohol, and to Thomas G. Ross, attorney at law (retired), for help on matters of evidence in a homicide investigation. Additional thanks to

Abby Gripp, formerly a relationship banker at the Southridge branch of Bankers Trust in Des Moines, Iowa, for explaining certain regulations concerning LLCs and cashier's checks.

Any inaccuracies, errors or exaggerations in the foregoing areas are mine alone.

More thanks to Marcia Thompson, another long-time friend and former colleague, for providing, via email, the joke—parable, actually—that appears in Chapter 25. Additional thanks to friends John Brynda and David A. Moeller, Lieutenant Colonel, US Army (Retired), for their readings, input and encouragement; and still more thanks to Charles Ardai at Hard Case Crime...although my manuscript didn't "make the cut," Charles nevertheless provided positive and helpful comments regarding my writing.

And speaking of writing...special thanks to authors John Connolly and Dave Carty. I'm a huge fan of the former's Charlie Parker series and I greatly appreciate John's permission to quote from *The Wolf in Winter* at the beginning of Part 2. Dave Carty is another former colleague whose writing I've long admired and I'm grateful for his willingness to read this book in draft form and provide a dynamite quote for the cover. Dave's novel, *Leaves on Frozen Ground*, is definitely worth your attention.

In a similar vein, I'm also grateful to Loren Spiotta-DiMare, author of the award-winning *Sergeant Reckless: Hero War Horse*—as heartwarming and inspirational a story as you'll ever find—and many other fine works for children and adults, for her help and encouragement, and especially for directing me to Karen Hodges Miller at Open Door Publications. Karen masterfully guided me through the myriad steps of getting a book into print, in addition to providing many helpful editorial suggestions that greatly improved the final product, and she in turn introduced me to designer Eric Labacz, who came up with a killer (sorry!) design for the book's cover.

Karen also steered me to Lisa Snyder at Silver Hoop Edge; Lisa did a terrific job of setting up my website, something that (a) I couldn't have accomplished on my own in a million years, and (b) is an absolute must for any author hoping to sell books nowadays.

Shifting gears for a moment, an acknowledgment of an entirely different sort to the decision-makers at Sturm, Ruger Firearms, who elected several years ago to drop the company's line of Red Label shotguns. The 12-gauge Red Label carried and cherished by Robert Vance was one of the originals, made before the company decided to "improve" the guns—a classic case of "it wasn't broken but they fixed it anyway," in my opinion. A couple years after the so-called improvement, the line was discontinued entirely, which prompts me to ask the Ruger folks, what the *hell* were you guys thinking?

On a more positive note, I would also like to acknowledge that Macomb, Rushville and Mt. Sterling, Illinois, and New London, Iowa—and, of course, Des Moines—are real places. My descriptions of them are reasonably accurate (allowing for some editorial license) but there is no Rushville Tap or Hidden Hollow hunting preserve, to the best of my knowledge.

On the other hand, Skip's restaurant on Fleur Drive in Des Moines is a real place, and if you ever have the opportunity to dine there, you should do so. Besides the ribeye steak and seared ahi tuna enjoyed by Vance and Daryl Nelson, I can also recommend the pork shank…just be warned that it's big enough for two people to share. If you're a jambalaya fan, I recommend it also, but be sure you have plenty of cold beverage at hand, and maybe a fire extinguisher as well. Truth is, I've never had a bad meal at Skip's.

I'll wind this up with special thanks to some special people…first, a couple of dear friends, Jamie Lamb and Kathleen "Kat" MacMurray. Jamie has been prodding me for many years to write a book, always convinced I could do so—more convinced than I was myself, in fact—so I hope she will be pleased with this effort. Kat shares my love of the stories of Albert Payson Terhune (referenced in Chapter 34) and I hope she too will be pleased.

Next, more special thanks to fellow mystery and crime-fiction fans Ruth Smith and Nichole Staker. Paraphrasing (again, badly) Gene Hackman's statement to Kevin Costner in *Wyatt Earp*, nothing is more important than family. Ruth and Nikki, you're the best...I love you both.

And finally...extra-special thanks to you, gentle reader, for taking a chance on this first-time author. I hope you liked what you've read and will consider paying us another visit because, Good Lord willin' and the crick don't rise...

Robert Vance and Preacher will return.

ABOUT THE AUTHOR

Rick Van Etten is a former college English instructor, corporate communications professional and retired magazine editor whose numerous articles and features have appeared in *Gun Dog, Wing & Shot, Sports Afield, Ducks Unlimited, Game & Fish, Petersen's Hunting, Farm & Ranch Living* and *Reader's Digest*. An Illinois native and lifelong upland bird hunter, Rick now lives in Iowa with a middle-aged Irish setter and an elderly tortoiseshell cat. *The Killer in the Woods* is his first novel. You can find out more information about Rick's books at www.ProudPointPress.com.

Made in the USA
Monee, IL
24 August 2020